The Old Gray Homestead

Frances Parkinson Keyes

Contents

THE OLD GRAY HOMESTEAD

BY

Frances Parkinson Keyes

To the farmers, and their mothers, wives, and daughters, who have been my nearest neighbors and my best friends for the last fifteen years, and who have taught me to love the country and the people in it, this quiet story of a farm is affectionately and gratefully dedicated.

CHAPTER I

For Heaven's sake, Sally, don't say, 'Isn't it hot?' or, 'Did you ever know such weather for April?' or, 'Doesn't it seem as if the mud was just as bad as it used to be before we had the State Road?' again. It *is* hot. I never did see such weather. The mud is *worse* if anything. I've said all this several times, and if you can't think of anything more interesting to talk about, I wish you'd keep still."

Sally Gray pushed back the lock of crinkly brown hair that was always getting in her eyes, puckered her lips a little, and glanced at her brother Austin without replying, but with a slight ripple of concern disturbing her usual calm. She was plain and plump and placid, as sweet and wholesome as clover, and as nerveless as a cow, and she secretly envied her brother's lean, dark handsomeness; but she was conscious of a little pang of regret that the young, eager face beside her was already becoming furrowed with lines of discontent and bitterness, and that the expression of the fine mouth was rapidly growing more and more hard and sullen. Austin had been all the way from Hamstead to White Water that day, stopping on his way back at Wallacetown, to bring Sally, who taught school there, home for over Sunday; his little old horse, never either strong or swift, was tired and hot and muddy, and hung its unkempt head dejectedly, apparently having lost all willingness to drag the dilapidated top-buggy and its two occupants another step. Austin's manner, Sally reflected, was not much more cheerful than that of his horse; while his clothes were certainly as dirty, as shabby, and as out-of-date as the rest of his equipage.

"It's a shame," she thought, "that Austin takes everything so hard. The rest of us don't mind half so much. If he could only have a little bit of encouragement and help--something that would make him really happy! If he could earn some money-

-or find out that, after all, money isn't everything--or fall in love with some nice girl--" She checked herself, blushing and sighing. The blush was occasioned by her own quiet happiness in that direction; but the sigh was because Austin, though he was well known to have been "rather wild," never paid any "nice girl" the slightest attention, and jeered cynically at the mere suggestion that he should do so.

"How lovely the valley is!" she said aloud at last; "I don't believe there's a prettier stretch of road in the whole world than this between Wallacetown and Hamstead, especially in the spring, when the river is so high, and everything is looking so fresh and green."

"Fortunate it is pretty; probably it's the only thing we'll have to look at as long as we live--and certainly it's about all we've seen so far! If there'd been only you and I, Sally, we could have gone off to school, and maybe to college, too, but with eight of us to feed and clothe, it's no wonder that father is dead sunk in debt! Certainly I shan't travel much," he added, laughing bitterly, "when he thinks we can't have even one hired man in the future--and certainly you won't either, if you're fool enough to marry Fred, and go straight from the frying-pan of one poverty-stricken home to the fire of another!"

"Oh, Austin, it's wrong of you to talk so! I'm going to be ever so happy!"

"Wrong! How else do you expect me to talk?--if I talk at all! Doesn't it mean anything to you that the farm's mortgaged to the very last cent, and that it doesn't begin to produce what it ought to because we can't beg, borrow, or steal the money that ought to be put into it? Can you just shut your eyes to the fact that the house--the finest in the county when Grandfather Gray built it--is falling to pieces for want of necessary repairs? And look at our barns and sheds--or don't look at them if you can help it! Doesn't it gall you to dress as you do, because you have to turn over most of what you can earn teaching to the family--of course, you never can earn much, because you haven't had a good enough education yourself to get a first-class position--so that the younger girls can go to school at all, instead of going out as hired help? Can't you feel the injustice of being poor, and dirty, and ignorant, when thousands of other people are just *rotten* with money?"

"I've heard of such people, but I've never met any of them around here," returned his sister quietly. "We're no worse off than lots of people, better off than some. I think we've got a good deal to be thankful for, living where we can see green things growing, and being well, and having a mother like ours. I wish you could come to feel that way. Perhaps you will some day."

"Why don't you marry Fred's cousin, instead of Fred?" asked her brother, changing the subject abruptly. "You could get him just as easy as not--I could see that when he was here last summer. Then you could go to Boston to live, get something out of life yourself, and help your family, too."

"No one in the family but you would want help from me--at that price," returned Sally, still speaking quietly, but betraying by the slight unevenness of her voice that her quiet spirit was at last disturbed more than she cared to show. "Why, Austin, you know how I lo--care for Fred, and that I gave him my word more than two years ago! Besides, I heard you say yourself, before you knew he fancied me, that Hugh Elliott drank--and did all sorts of other dreadful things--he wouldn't be considered respectable in Hamstead."

Austin laughed again. "All right. I won't bring up the subject again. Ten years from now you may be sorry you wouldn't put up with an occasional spree, and sacrifice a silly little love-affair, for the sake of everything else you'd get. But suit yourself. Cook and wash and iron and scrub, lose your color and your figure and your disposition, and bring half-a-dozen children into the world with no better heritage than that, if it's your idea of bliss--and it seems to be!"

"I didn't mean to be cross, Sally," he said, after they had driven along in heavy silence for some minutes. "I've been trying to do a little business for father in White Water to-day, and met with my usual run of luck--none at all. Here comes one of the livery-stable teams ploughing towards us through the mud. Who's in it, do you suppose? Doesn't look familiar, some way."

As the livery-stable in Hamstead boasted only four turn-outs, it was not strange that Austin recognized one of them at sight, and as strangers were few and far between, they were objects of considerable interest.

Sally leaned forward.

"No, she doesn't. She's all in black--and my! isn't she pretty? She seems to be stopping and looking around--why don't you ask her if you could be of any help?"

Austin nodded, and pulled in his reins. "I wonder if I could--" he began, but stopped abruptly, realizing that the lady in the buggy coming towards them had also stopped, and spoken the very same words. Inevitably they all smiled, and the stranger began again.

"I wonder if you could tell me how to get to Mr. Howard Gray's house," she said. "I was told at the hotel to drive along this road as far as a large white house--the first one I came to--and then turn to the right. But I don't see any road."

"There isn't any, at this time of year," said Sally, laughing,--"nothing but mud. You have to wallow through that field, and go up a hill, and down a hill, and along a little farther, and then you come to the house. Just follow us--we're going there. I'm Howard Gray's eldest daughter Sally, and this is my brother Austin."

"Oh! then perhaps you can tell me--before I intrude--if it would be any use--whether you think that possibly--whether under any circumstances --well, if your mother would be good enough to let me come and live at her house a little while?"

By this time Sally and Austin had both realized two things: first, that the person with whom they were talking belonged to quite a different world from their own--the fact was written large in her clothing, in her manner, in the very tones of her voice; and, second, that in spite of her pale face and widow's veil, she was even younger than they were, a girl hardly out of her teens.

"I'm not very well," she went on rapidly, before they could answer, "and my doctor told me to go away to some quiet place in the country until I could get--get rested a little. I spent a summer here with my mother when I was a little girl, and I remembered how lovely it was, and so I came back. But the hotel has run down so that I don't think I can possibly stay there; and yet I can't bear to go away from this beautiful, peaceful river-valley--it's just what I've been longing to find. I happened to overhear some one talking about Mrs. Gray, and saying that she might consider taking me in. So I hired this buggy and started out to find her and ask. Oh, don't you think she would?"

Sally and Austin exchanged glances. "Mother never has taken any boarders, she's always been too busy," began the former; then, seeing the swift look of disappointment on the sad little face, "but she might. It wouldn't do any harm to ask, anyway. We'll drive ahead, and show you how to get there."

The Gray family had been one of local prominence ever since Colonial days, and James Gray, who built the dignified, spacious homestead now occupied by his grandson's family, had been a man of some education and wealth. His son Thomas inherited the house, but only a fourth of the fortune, as he had three sisters. Thomas had but one child, Howard, whose prospects for prosperity seemed excellent; but he grew up a dreamy, irresolute, studious chap, a striking contrast to the sturdy yeoman type from which he had sprung--one of those freaks of heredity that are hard to explain. He went to Dartmouth College, travelled a little, showed a disposition to read--and even to write--verses. As a teacher he probably would have been successful; but his father was determined that he should become a farmer, and Howard had neither the energy nor the disposition to oppose him; he proved a complete failure. He married young, and, it was generally considered, beneath him; for Mary Austin, with a heart of gold and a disposition like sunshine, had little wealth or breeding and less education to commend her; and she was herself too easy-going and contented to prove the prod that Howard sadly needed in his wife. Children came thick and fast; the eldest, James, had now gone South; the second daughter, Ruth, was already married to a struggling storekeeper living in White Water; Sally taught school; but the others were all still at home, and all, except Austin, too young to be self-supporting--Thomas, Molly, Katherine, and Edith. They had all caught their father's facility for correct speech, rare in northern New England; most of them his love of books, his formless and unfulfilled ambitions; more than one the shiftlessness and incompetence that come partly from natural bent and partly from hopelessness; while Sally and Thomas alone possessed the sunny disposition and the ability to see the bright side of everything and the good in everybody which was their mother's legacy to them.

The old house, set well back from the main road and near the river, with elms and maples and clumps of lilac bushes about it, was almost bare of the cheerful white paint that had once adorned it, and the green blinds were faded and broken; the barns never had been painted, and were huddled close to the house, hiding its fine Colonial lines, black, ungainly, and half fallen to pieces; all kinds of farm implements, rusty from age and neglect, were scattered about, and two dogs and several cats lay on the kitchen porch amidst the general litter of milk-pails, half-broken chairs, and rush mats. There was no one in sight as the two muddy buggies pulled up at the little-used front door. Howard Gray and Thomas were milking, both somewhat out-of-sorts because of the non-appearance of Austin, for there were too many cows for them to manage alone--a long row of dirty, lean animals of uncertain age and breed. Molly was helping her mother to "get supper," and the red tablecloth and heavy white china, never removed from the kitchen table except to be washed, were beginning to be heaped with pickles, doughnuts, pie, and cake, and there were potatoes and pork frying on the stove. Katherine was studying, and Edith had gone to hastily "spread up" the beds that had not been made that morning.

On the whole, however, the inside of the house was more tidy than the outside, and the girl in black was aware of the homely comfort and good cheer of the living-room into which she was ushered (since there was no time to open up the cold "parlor") more than she was of its shabbiness.

"Come right in an' set down," said Mrs. Gray cheerfully, leading the way; "awful tryin' weather we're havin', ain't it? An' the mud--my, it's somethin' fierce! The men-folks track it in so, there's no keepin' it swept up, an' there's so many of us here! But there's nothin' like a large family for keepin' things hummin' just the same, now, is there?" Mrs. Gray had had scant time to prepare her mind either for her unexpected visitor or the object of her visit; but her mother-wit was ready, for all that; one glance at the slight, black-robed little figure, and the thin white face, with its tired, dark-ringed eyes, was enough for her. Here was need of help; and therefore help of some sort she must certainly give. "Now, then," she went on quickly, "you look just plum tuckered out; set down an' rest a spell, an' tell me what I can do for you."

"My name is Sylvia Cary--Mrs. Mortimer Cary, I mean." She shivered, paused, and went on. "I live in New York--that is, I always have--I'm never going to any more, if I can help it. My husband died two months ago, my baby--just before that. I've felt so--so--tired ever since, I just had to get away somewhere--away from the noise, and the hurry, and the crowds of people I know. I was in Hamstead once, ten years ago, and I remembered it, and came back. I want most dreadfully to stay--could you possibly make room for me here?"

"Oh, you poor lamb! I'd do anything I could for you--but this ain't the sort of home you've been used to--" began Mrs. Gray; but she was interrupted.

"No, no, of course it isn't! Don't you understand--I can't bear what I've been used to another minute! And I'll honestly try not to be a bit of trouble if you'll only let me stay!"

Mrs. Gray twisted in her chair, fingering her apron. "Well, now, I don't know! You've come so sudden-like--if I'd only had a little notice! There's no place fit for a lady like you; but there are two rooms we never use--the northeast parlor and the parlor-chamber off it. You could have one of them--after I got it cleaned up a mite--an' try it here for a while."

"Couldn't I have them both? I'd like a sitting-room as well as a bedroom."

"Land! You ain't even seen 'em yet! maybe they won't suit you at all! But, come, I'll show 'em to you an' if you want to stay, you shan't go back to that filthy hotel. I'll get the bedroom so's you can sleep in it to-night--just a lick an' a promise; an' to-morrow I'll house-clean 'em both thorough, if 't is the Sabbath--the 'better the day, the better the deed,' I've heard some say, an' I believe that's true, don't you, Mrs. Cary?" She bustled ahead, pulling up the shades, and flinging open the windows in the unused rooms. "My, but the dust is thick! Don't you touch a thing--just see if you think they'll do."

Sylvia Cary glanced quickly about the two great square rooms, with their white wainscoting, and shutters, their large, stopped-up fireplaces, dingy wall-paper, and beautiful, neglected furniture. "Indeed they will!" she exclaimed; "they'll be lovely when we get them fixed. And may I truly stay--right now? I brought my hand-bag with me, you see, hoping that I might, and my trunks are still at the station--wait, I'll give you the checks, and perhaps your son will get them after supper."

She put the bag on a chair, and began to open it, hurriedly, as if unwilling to wait a minute longer before making sure of remaining. Mrs. Gray, who was standing near her, drew back with a gasp of surprise. The bag was lined with heavy purple silk, and elaborately fitted with toilet articles of shining gold. Mrs. Cary plunged her hands in and tossed out an embroidered white satin negligee, a pair of white satin bed-slippers, and a nightgown that was a mere wisp of sheer silk and lace; then drew forth three trunk-checks, and a bundle an inch thick of crisp, new bank-notes, and pulled one out, blushing and hesitating.

"I don't know how to thank you for taking me in to-night," she said; "some day I'll tell you all about myself, and why it means so much to me to have a--a refuge like this; but I'm afraid I can't until--I've got rested a little. Soon we must talk about arrangements and terms and all that--oh, I'm awfully businesslike! But just let me give you this to-night, to show you how grateful I am, and pay for the first two weeks or so."

And she folded the bill into a tiny square, and crushed it into Mrs. Gray's reluctant hand.

Fifteen minutes later, when Howard Gray and Thomas came into the kitchen for their supper, bringing the last full milk-pails with them, they found the pork and potatoes burnt to a frazzle, the girls all talking at once, and Austin bending over his mother, who sat in the big rocker with the tears rolling down her cheeks, and a hundred-dollar bill spread out on her lap.

CHAPTER II

For several weeks the Grays did not see much of Mrs. Cary. She appeared at dinner and supper, eating little and saying less. She rose very late, having a cup of coffee in bed about ten; the afternoons she spent rambling through the fields and along the river-bank, but never going near the highroad on her long walks. She generally read until nearly midnight, and the book-hungry Grays pounced like tigers on the newspapers and magazines with which she heaped her scrap-baskets, and longed for the time to come when she would offer to lend them some of the books piled high all around her rooms.

Some years before, when vacationists demanded less in the way of amusement, Hamstead had flourished in a mild way as a summer-resort; but its brief day of prosperity in this respect had passed, and the advent of a wealthy and mysterious stranger, whose mail was larger than that of all the rest of the population put together, but who never appeared in public, or even spoke, apparently, in private, threw the entire village into a ferment of excitement. Fred Elliott, who, in his role of prospective son-in-law, might be expected to know much that was going on at the Grays', was "pumped" in vain; he was obliged to confess his entire ignorance concerning the history, occupations, and future intentions of the young widow. Mrs. Gray had to "house-clean" her parlor a month earlier than she had intended, because she had so many callers who came hoping to catch a glimpse of Mrs. Cary, and hear all about her, besides; but they did not see her at all, and Mrs. Gray could tell them but little.

"She ain't a mite of trouble," the good woman declared to every one, "an' the simplest, gentlest creature I ever see in my life. The girls are all just crazy over her. No, she ain't told me yet anything about herself, an' I don't like to press her none. Poor lamb, with her heart buried in the grave, at her age! No, I don't know how long she means to stay, neither, but 'twould be a good while, if I had my way."

To Mrs. Elliott, her best friend and Fred's mother, she was slightly more communicative, though she disclosed no vital statistics.

"Edith helped her unpack an' she said she never even imagined anything equal to what come out of them three great trunks; she said it made her just long to be a widow. The dresses was all black, of course, but they had an awful expensive look, some way, just the same. An' underclothes! Edith said there was at least a dozen of everything, an' two dozen of most, lace an' handwork an' silk, from one end of 'em to the other. She has a leather box most as big as a suitcase heaped with jewelry--it was open one morning when I went in with her breakfast, an' I give you my word, Eliza, that just the little glimpse I got of it was worth walkin' miles to see! An' yet she never wears so much as the simplest ring or pin. She has enough flowers for an elegant funeral sent to her three times a week by express, an' throws 'em away before they're half-faded--says she likes the little wild ones that are beginnin' to come up around here better, anyway. Yes, I don't deny she has some real queer notions--for instance, she puts all them flowers in plain green glass vases, an' wouldn't so much as look at the elegant cut-glass ones they keep up to Wallacetown. She don't eat a particle of breakfast, an' she streaks off for a long walk every day, rain or shine, an' wants the old tin tub carried in so's she can have a hot bath every single night, besides takin' what she calls a 'cold sponge' when she gets up in the mornin'--which ain't till nearly noon."

"Well, now, ain't all that strange! An' wouldn't I admire to see all them elegant things! What board did you say she paid?"

"Twenty-five dollars a week for board an' washin' an' mendin'--just think of it, Eliza! I feel like a robber, but she wouldn't hear of a cent less. Howard wants I should save every penny, so's at least one of the younger children can have more of an education than James an' Sally an' Austin an' Ruth. I don't look at it that way--seems to me it ain't fair to give one child more than another. I want to spruce up this place a little, an' lay by to raise the mortgage if we can."

"Which way 've you decided?"

"We've kinder compromised. The house is goin' to be painted outside, an' the kitchen done over. I've had the piano tuned for Molly already--the poor child is plum crazy over music, but it's a long time since I've seen the three dollars that I could hand over to a strange man just for comin' an' makin' a lot of screechin' noises on it all day; an' we're goin' to have a new carry-all to go to meetin' in--the old one is fair fallin' to pieces. The rest of the money we're goin' to lay by, an' if it keeps on comin' in, Thomas can go to the State Agricultural College in, the fall, for a spell, anyway. We've told Sally that she can keep all she earns for her weddin' things, too, as long as Mrs. Cary stays."

"My, she's a reg'lar goose layin' a golden egg for you, ain't she? Well, I must be goin'; I'll be over again as soon as spring-cleanin' eases up a little, but I'm terrible druv just now. Maybe next time I can see her."

"You an' Joe an' Fred all come to dinner on Sunday--then you will."

Mrs. Elliott accepted with alacrity; but alas, for the eager guests! when Sunday came, Mrs. Cary had a severe headache and remained in bed all day.

She was so "simple and gentle," as Mrs. Gray said, that it came as a distinct shock when it was discovered that little as she talked, she observed a great deal. Austin was the first member of the family to find this out. All the others had gone to church, and he was lounging on the porch one Sunday morning, when she came out of the house, supposing that she was quite alone. On finding him there, she hesitated for a minute, and then sat quietly down on the steps, made one or two pleasant, commonplace remarks, and lapsed into silence, her chin resting on her hands, looking out towards the barns. Her expression was non-committal; but Austin's antagonistic spirit was quick to judge it to be critical.

"I suppose you've travelled a good deal, besides living in New York," he said, in the bitter tone that was fast becoming his usual one.

"Yes, to a certain extent. I've been around the world once, and to Europe several times, and I spent part of last winter South."

"How miserable and shabby this poverty-stricken place must look to you!"

She raised her head and leaned back against a post, looking fixedly at him for a minute. He was conscious, for the first time, that the pale face was extremely lovely, that the great dark eyes were not gray, as he had supposed, but a very deep blue, and that the slim throat and neck, left bare by the V-cut dress, were the color of a white rose. A swift current of feeling that he had never known before passed through him like an electric shock, bringing him involuntarily to his feet, in time to hear her say:

"It's shabby, but it isn't miserable. I don't believe any place is that, where there's a family, and enough food to eat and wood to burn--if the family is happy in itself. Besides, with two hours' work, and without spending one cent, you could make it much less shabby than it is; and by saving what you already have, you could stave off spending in the future."

She pointed, as she spoke, to the cluttered yard before them, to the unwashed wagons and rusty tools that had not been put away, to the shed-door half off its hinges, and the unpiled wood tossed carelessly inside the shed. He reddened, as much at the scorn in her gesture as at the words themselves, and answered angrily, as many persons do when they are ashamed:

"That's very true; but when you work just as hard as you can, anyway, you haven't much spirit left over for the frills."

"Excuse me; I didn't realize they were frills. No business man would have his office in an untidy condition, because it wouldn't pay; I shouldn't think it would pay on a farm either. Just as it seems to me--though, of course, I'm not in a position to judge--that if you sold all those tubercular grade cows, and bought a few good cattle, and kept them clean and fed them well, you'd get more milk, pay less for grain, and not have to work so hard looking after more animals than you can really handle well."

As she spoke, she began to unfasten her long, frilled, black sleeves, and rose with a smile so winning that it entirely robbed her speech of sharpness.

"Let's go to work," she said, "and see how much we could do in the way of making things look better before the others get home from church. We'll start here. Hand me that broom and I'll sweep while you stack up the milk-pails--don't stop to reason with me about it--that'll only use up time. If there's any hot water on the kitchen stove and you know where the mop is, I'll wash this porch as well as sweep it; put on some more water to heat if you take all there is."

When the Grays returned from church, their astonished eyes were met with the spectacle of their boarder, her cheeks glowing, her hair half down her back, and her silk dress irretrievably ruined, helping Austin to wash and oil the one wagon which still stood in the yard. She fled at their approach, leaving Austin to retail her conversation and explain her conduct as best he could, and to ponder over both all the afternoon himself.

"She's dead right about the cows," declared Thomas; "but what would be the use of getting good stock and putting it in these barns? It would sicken in no time. We need new buildings, with proper ventilation, and concrete floors, and a silo."

"Why don't you say we need a million dollars, and be done with it? You might just as well," retorted his brother.

"Because we don't--but we need about ten thousand; half of it for buildings, and the rest for stock and utensils and fertilizers, and for what it would cost to clean up our stumpy old pastures, and make them worth something again."

At that moment Mrs. Cary entered the room for dinner, and the discussion of unpossessed resources came to an abrupt end. Her color was still high, and she ate her first hearty meal since her arrival; but her dress and her hair were irreproachably demure again, and she talked even less than usual.

That evening Molly begged off from doing her share with the dishes, and went to play on her newly tuned piano. She loved music dearly, and had genuine talent; but it seemed as if she had never realized half so keenly before how little she knew about it, and how much she needed help and instruction. A particularly unsuccessful struggle with a difficult passage finally proved too much for her courage, and shutting the piano with a bang, she leaned her head on it and burst out crying.

A moment later she sat up with a sudden jerk, realizing that the parlor door had opened and closed, and tried to wipe away the tears before any one saw them; then a hot blush of embarrassment and shame flooded her wet cheeks, as she realized that the intruder was not one of her sisters, but Mrs. Cary.

"What a good touch you have!" she said, sitting down by the piano, and apparently quite unaware of the storm. "I love music dearly, and I thought perhaps you'd let me come and listen to your playing for a little while. The fingering of that 'Serenade' is awfully hard, isn't it? I thought I should never get it, myself--never did, really well, in fact! Do you like your teacher?"

"I never had a lesson in my life," replied Molly, the sobs rising in her throat again; "there are two good ones in Wallacetown, but, you see, we never could af--"

"Well, some teachers do more harm than good," interrupted her visitor, "probably you've escaped a great deal. Play something else, won't you? Do you mind this dim light? I like it so much."

So Molly opened the piano and began again, doing her very best. She chose the simple things she knew by heart, and put all her will-power as well as all her skill into playing them well. It was only when she stopped, confessing that she knew no more, that Mrs. Gary stirred.

"I used to play a good deal myself," she said, speaking very low; "perhaps I could take it up again. Do you think you could help me, Molly?"

"*I*! help *you*! However in the world--"

"By letting *me* be your teacher! I'm getting rested now, and I find I've a lot of superfluous energy at my disposal--your brother had a dose of it this morning! I want something to do--something to keep me busy--something to keep me from thinking. I haven't half as much talent as you, but I've had more chances to learn. Listen! This is the way that 'Serenade' ought to go"--and Mrs. Cary began to play. The dusk turned to moonlight around them, and the Grays sat in the dining-room, hesitating to intrude, and listening with all their ears; and still she sat, talking, explaining, illustrating to Molly, and finally ended by playing, one after another, the old familiar hymns which they all loved.

"It's settled, then--I'll give you your first real lesson to-morrow, and send to New York at once for music. You'll have to do lots of scales and finger-exercises, I warn you! Now come into *my* parlor--there's something else I wanted to talk to you about."

"Do you see that great trunk?" she went on, after she had drawn Molly in after her and lighted the lamp; "I sent for it a week ago, but it only got here yesterday. It's full of all my--all the clothes I had to stop wearing a little while ago."

Molly's heart began to thump with excitement.

"You and Edith are little, like me," whispered Mrs. Cary. "If you would take the dresses and use them, it would be--be such a *favor* to me! Some of them are brand-new! Some of them wouldn't be useful or suitable for you, but there are firms in every big city that buy such things, so you could sell those, if you care to; and, besides the made-up clothes there are several dress-lengths--a piece of pink silk that would be sweet for Sally, and some embroidered linens, and--and so on. I'm going to bed now--I've had so much exercise to-day, and you've given me such a pleasant evening that I shan't have to read myself to sleep to-night, and when I've shut my bedroom door, if you truly would like the trunk, have your brothers come in and carry it off, and promise me never--never to speak about it again."

Monday and Tuesday passed by without further excitement; but Wednesday morning, while Mr. Gray was planting his newly ploughed vegetable-garden, Mrs. Cary sauntered out, and sat down beside the place where he was working, apparently oblivious of the fact that damp ground is supposed to be as detrimental to feminine wearing apparel as it is to feminine constitutions.

"I've been watching you from the window as long as I could stand it," she said, "now I've come to beg. I want a garden, too, a flower-garden. Do you mind if I dig up your front yard?"

He laughed, supposing that she was joking. "Dig all you want to," he said; "I don't believe you'll do much harm."

"Thanks. I'll try not to. Have I your full permission to try my hand and see?"

"You certainly have."

"Is there some boy in the village I could hire to do the first heavy work and the mowing, and pull up the weeds from time to time if they get ahead of me?"

Howard Gray leaned on his hoe. "You don't need to hire a boy," he said gravely; "we'll be only too glad to help you all you need."

"Thank you. But, you see, you've got too much to do already, and I can't add to your burdens, or feel free to ask favors, unless you'll let me do it in a business way."

Mr. Gray turned his hoe over, and began to hack at the ground. "I see how you feel," he began, "but--"

"If Thomas could do it evenings, at whatever the rate is around here by the hour, I should be very glad. If not, please find me a boy."

"She has a way of saying things," explained Howard Gray, who had faltered along in a state of dreary indecision for nearly sixty years, in telling his wife about it afterwards,--"as if they were all settled already. What could I say, but 'Yes, Mrs. Cary'? And then she went on, as cool as a cucumber, 'As long as you've got an extra stall, may I send for one of my horses? The usual board around here is five dollars a week, isn't it?' And what could I say again but 'Yes, Mrs. Cary'? though you may believe I fairly itched to ask, 'Send *where*?' and, 'For the love of Heaven, how *many* horses have you?'"

"I could stand her actin' as if things was all settled," replied his wife; "I like to see folks up an' comin', even if I ain't made that way myself, an' it's a satisfaction to me to see the poor child kinder pickin' up an' takin' notice again; but what beats me is, she acts as if all these things were special favors to *her*! The garden an' the horse is all very well, but what do you think she lit into me to-day for? 'You'll let me stay all summer, won't you, Mrs. Gray?' she said, comin' into the kitchen, where I was ironin' away for dear life, liftin' a pile of sheets off a chair, an' settlin' down, comfortable-like. 'Bless your heart, you can stay forever, as far as I'm concerned,' says I. 'Well, perhaps I will,' says she, leanin' back an' laughin'--she's got a sweet-pretty laugh, hev you noticed, Howard?--'and so you won't think I'm fault-findin' or discontented if I suggest a few little changes I'd like to make around, will you? I know it's awfully bold, in another person's house--an' such a *lovely* house, too, but--'"

"Well?" demanded her husband, as she paused for breath.

"Well, Howard Gray, the first of them little changes is to be a great big pi-azza, to go across the whole front of the house! 'The kitchen porch is so small an' crowded,' says she, 'an' you can't see the river from there; I want a place to sit out evenings. Can't I have the fireplaces in my rooms unbricked,' she went on, 'an' the rooms re-papered an' painted? An', oh,--I've never lived in a house where there wasn't a bathroom before, an' I want to make that big closet with a window off my bedroom into one. We'll have a door cut through it into the hall, too,' says she, 'an' isn't there a closet just like it overhead? If we can get a plumber here--they're such slippery customers--he might as well put in two bathrooms as one, while he's about it, an' you shan't do my great washin's any more without some good set-tubs. An' Mrs. Gray, kerosene lamps do heat up the rooms so in summer,--if there's an electrician anywhere around here--' 'Mrs. Cary,' says I, 'you're an angel right out of Heaven, but we can't accept all this from you. It means two thousand dollars, straight.' 'About what I should pay in two months for my living expenses anywhere else,' says she. 'Favors! It's you who are kind to let me stay here, an' not mind my tearin' your house all to pieces. Thomas is goin' to drive me up to Wallacetown this evenin' to see if we can find some mechanics'; an' she got up, an' kissed me, an' strolled off."

"Thomas thinks she's the eighth wonder of the world," said his father; "she can just wind him around her little finger."

"She's windin' us all," replied his wife, "an' we're standin' grateful-like, waitin' to be wound."

"That's so--all except Austin. Austin's mad as a hatter at what she got him to do Sunday morning; he doesn't like her, Mary."

"Humph!" said his wife.

CHAPTER III

G ood-bye, Mrs. Gray, I'm going for a ride."

"Good-bye, dearie; sure it ain't too hot?"

"Not a bit; it's rained so hard all this week that I haven't had a bit of exercise, and I'm getting cross."

"Cross! I'd like to see you once! It still looks kinder thunderous to me off in the West, so don't go far."

"I won't, I promise; I'll be back by supper-time. There's Austin, just up from the hayfield--I'll get him to saddle for me." And Sylvia ran quickly towards the barn.

"You don't mean to say you're going out this torrid day?" he demanded, lifting his head from the tin bucket in which he had submerged it as she voiced her request, and eyeing her black linen habit with disfavor.

"It's no hotter on the highroad than in the hayfield."

"Very true; but I have to go, and you don't. Being one of the favored few of this earth, there's no reason why you shouldn't sit on a shady porch all day, dressed in cool, pale-green muslin, and sipping iced drinks."

"Did you ever see me in a green muslin? I'll saddle Dolly myself, if you don't feel like it."

She spoke very quietly, but the immediate consciousness of his stupid break did not improve Austin's bad temper.

"Oh, I'll saddle for you, but the heat aside, I think you ought to understand that it isn't best for a woman to ride about on these lonely roads by herself. It was different a few years ago; but now, with all these Italian and Portuguese laborers around, it's a different story. I think you'd better stay at home."

The unwarranted and dictatorial tone of the last sentence spoiled the speech, which might otherwise, in spite of the surly manner in which it was uttered, have passed for an expression of solicitude. Sylvia, who was as headstrong as she was amiable, gathered up her reins quickly.

"By what right do you consider yourself in a position to dictate to me?" she demanded.

"By none at all; but it's only decent to tell you the risk you're running; now if you come to grief, I certainly shan't feel sorry."

"From your usual behavior, I shouldn't have supposed you would, anyway. Good-bye, Austin."

"Good-bye, Mrs. Cary."

"Why don't you call me Sylvia, as all the rest do?"

"It's not fitting."

"More dictation as to propriety! Well, as you please."

He watched her ride up the hill, almost with a feeling of satisfaction at having antagonized and hurt her, then turned to unharness and water his horses. He knew very well that his own behavior was the only blot on a summer, which but for that would have been almost perfect for every other member of the family, and yet he made no effort to alter it. In fact, only a few days before, his sullen resentment of the manner in which their long-prayed-for change of fortune had come had very nearly resulted disastrously for them all, and the more he brooded over it, the more sore and bitter he became.

*　　*　　*　　*　　*

By the first of August, the "Gray Homestead" had regained the proud distinction, which it had enjoyed in the days of its builder, of being one of the finest in the county. The house, with its wide and hospitable piazza, shone with white paint; the disorderly yard had become a smooth lawn; a flower-garden, riotous with color, stretched out towards the river, and the "back porch" was concealed with growing vines. Only the barns, which afforded Sylvia no reasonable excuse for meddling, remained as before, unsightly and dilapidated. Thomas, the practical farmer, had lamented this as he and Austin sat smoking their pipes one sultry evening after supper.

"Perhaps our credit has improved enough now so that we could borrow some money at the Wallacetown Bank," he said earnestly, "and if you and father weren't so averse to taking that good offer Weston made you last week for the south meadow, we'd have almost enough to rebuild, anyway. It's all very well to have this pride in 'keeping the whole farm just as grandfather left it to us,' but if we could sell part and take care of the rest properly, it would be a darned sight better business."

"Why don't you ask your precious Mrs. Cary for the money? She'd probably give it to you outright, same as she has for the house, and save you all that bother."

"Look here!" Thomas swung around sharply, laying a heavy hand on his brother's arm; "when you talk about her, you won't use that tone, if I know it."

Austin shrugged his shoulders. "Why shouldn't I? What do you know about her that justifies you in resenting it? Nothing, absolutely nothing! She's been here four months, and none of us have any idea to this day where she comes from, or where all this money comes from. Ask her, if you dare to."

He got no further, for Thomas, always the mildest of lads, struck him on the mouth so violently that he tottered backwards, and in doing so, fell straight under the feet of Sylvia, who stood in the doorway watching them, as if rooted to the spot, her blue eyes full of tears, and her face as white as when she had first come to them.

"Thomas, how **could** you?" she cried. "Can't you understand Austin at all, and make allowances? And, oh, Austin, how could **you**? Both of you? please forgive me for overhearing--I couldn't help it!" And she was gone.

Thomas was on his feet and after her in a second, but the was too quick for him; her sitting-room door was locked before he reached it, and repeated knocking and calling brought no answer. Mr. and Mrs. Gray, who slept in the chamber opening from the dining-room, and back of Sylvia's, reported the next morning that something must be troubling the "blessed girl," for they had heard soft sobbing far into the night; but, after all, that had happened before, and was to be expected from one "whose heart was buried in the grave." Their sons made no comment, but both were immeasurably relieved when, after an entire day spent in her room, during which each, in his own way, had suffered intensely, she reappeared at supper as if nothing had happened. It was a glorious night, and she suggested, as she left the table, that

Thomas might take her for a short paddle, a canoe being among the many things which had been gradually arriving for her all summer. Molly and Edith went with them, and Austin smoked alone with his bitter reflections.

*   *   *   *   *

The thunder was rumbling in good earnest when Howard Gray and Thomas came clattering up with their last load of hay for the night, and the three men pitched it hastily into place together, and hurried into the house. Mrs. Gray was bustling about slamming windows, and the girls were bringing in the red-cushioned hammocks and piazza, chairs, but the first great drops began to fall before they had finished, and the wind, seldom roused in the quiet valley, was blowing violently; Edith, stopping too long for a last pillow and a precious book, was drenched to the skin in an instant; the house was pitch dark before there was time to grope for lights, but was almost immediately illumined by a brilliant flash of lightning, followed by a loud report.

"My, but this storm is near! Usually, I don't mind 'em a bit, but, I declare, this is a regular rip-snorter! Edith, bring me--"

But Mrs. Gray was interrupted by the elements, and for fifteen minutes no one made any further effort to talk; the rain fell in sheets, the wind gathered greater and greater force, the lightning became constant and blinding, while each clap of thunder seemed nearer and more terrific than the one before it, when finally a deafening roar brought them all suddenly together, shouting frantically, "That certainly has struck here!"

It was true; before they could even reach it, the great north barn was in flames. There was no way of summoning outside help, even if any one could have reached them in such a storm, and the wind was blowing the fire straight in the direction of the house; in less than an hour, most of the old and rotten outbuildings had burnt like tinder, and the rest had collapsed under the fury of the sweeping gale; but by eight o'clock the stricken Grays, almost too exhausted and overcome to speak, were beginning to realize that though all their hay and most of their stock were destroyed, a change of wind, combined with their own mighty efforts, had saved the beloved old house; its window-panes were shattered, and its blinds were torn off, and its fresh paint smoked and defaced with wind-blown sand; but it was essentially unharmed. The hurricane changed to a steady downpour, the lightning grew dimmer and more distant, and vanished altogether; and Mrs. Gray, with a firm expression of countenance, in spite of the tears rolling down her cheeks, set about to finish the preparations for supper which the storm had so rudely interrupted three hours earlier.

"Eat an' keep up your strength, an' that'll help to keep up your courage," she said, patting her husband on the shoulder as she passed him. "Here, Katherine, take them biscuits out of the oven; an' Molly, go an' call the boys in; there ain't a mite of use in their stayin' out there any longer."

Austin was the last to appear; he opened the kitchen door, and stood for a moment leaning against the frame, a huge, gaunt figure, blackened with dirt and smoke, and so wet that the water dropped in little pools all about him. He glanced up and down the room, and gave a sharp exclamation.

"What's the matter, Austin?" asked his mother, stopping in the act of pouring out a steaming cup of tea. "Come an' get some supper; you'll feel better directly. It ain't so bad but what it might be a sight worse."

"*Come and get some supper*!" he cried, striding towards her, and once more looking wildly around. "The thunderstorm has been over nearly two hours, plenty of time for her to get home--she never minds rain--or to telephone if she had taken shelter anywhere; and can any one tell me--has any one even thought--I didn't, till five minutes ago-- *where is Sylvia*?"

CHAPTER IV

S ylvia! Sylvia! Sylvia!"
The musical name echoed and reechoed through the silent woods, but there was no other answer. Austin lighted a match, shielded it from the rain with his hand, and looked at his watch; it was just past midnight.

"Oh," he groaned, "where *can* she be? What has happened to her? If I only knew she was found, and unharmed, and safe at home again, I'd never ask for anything else as long as I lived."

He had knocked his lantern against a tree some time before, and broken it, and there was nothing to do but stumble blindly along in the darkness, hoping against hope. Howard Gray had gone north, Thomas east, and Austin south; before starting out, they had endeavored to telephone, but the storm had destroyed the wires in every direction. After travelling almost ten miles, Austin went home, thinking that by that time either his father or his brother must have been successful in his search, to be met only by the anxious despair of his mother and sisters.

"Don't you worry," he forced himself to say with a cheerfulness he was very far from feeling; "she may have gone down that old wood-road that leads out of the Elliotts' pasture. I heard her telling Thomas once that she loved to explore, that they must walk down there some Sunday afternoon; maybe she decided to go alone. I'll stop at the house, and see if Fred happened to see her pass."

Fred had not; but Mrs. Elliott had; there was little that escaped her eager eyes.

"My, yes, I see her go tearin' past before the storm so much as begun; she's sure the queerest actin' widow-woman I ever heard of; Sally says she goes swimmin' in a bathin'-suit just like a boy's, an' floats an' dives like a fish--nice actions for a grievin' lady, if you ask me! Do set a moment, Austin; set down an' tell me about the fire; I ain't had no details at all, an' I'm feelin' real bad--" But the door had already slammed behind Austin's hurrying figure.

"Sylvia, Sylvia, where are you?"

He ploughed along for what seemed like endless miles, calling as he went, and hearing his own voice come back to him, over and over again, like a mocking spirit. The wind, the rain, and the darkness conspired together to make what was rough travelling in the daytime almost impassable; strong as he was, Austin sank down more than once for a few minutes on some fallen log over which he stumbled. At these times the vision of Sylvia standing in the midst of the still-smoking ruins of the buildings, which had been, in spite of their wretched condition, dear to him because they were almost all he had in the world, seemed to rise before him with horrible reality: Sylvia, dressed in her black, black clothes, with her soft dark hair, and her deep-blue eyes, and her vivid red lips which so seldom either drooped or smiled but lay tightly closed together, a crimson line in her white face, which was no more sorrowful than it was mask-like. The expression was as pure and as sad and as gentle as that of a Mater Dolorosa he had chanced to see in a collection of prints at the Wallacetown Library, and yet--and yet--Austin knew instinctively that the dead husband, whoever he might have been, and his own brother Thomas were not the only men besides himself who had found it irresistibly alluring.

"I'm poorer than ever now," he groaned to himself, "and ignorant, and mean, and dirty, and a beast in every sense of the word; I can't ever atone for the way I've treated her--for the way I've--but if I could only find her and *try*, oh, I've got to! Sylvia, Sylvia, Sylvia--"

The rain struck about by the wind, which had risen again, lashed against the leaves of the trees, and the wet, swaying boughs struck against his face as he started on again; but the storm and his own footsteps were the only sounds he could hear.

It was growing rapidly colder, and he felt more than once in his pocket to make sure that the little flask of brandy he had brought with him was still safe, and tried to fasten his drenched coat more tightly about him. His teeth chattered, and he shivered; but this, he realized, was more with nervousness than with chill.

"If I'm cold, what must she be, in that linen habit? And she's so little and frail--" He pulled himself together. "I must stop worrying like this--of course, I'll find her,--alive and unharmed. Some things are too dreadful--they just can't happen. I've got to have a chance to beg her forgiveness for all I've said and done and thought; I've got to have something to give me courage to start all over again, and make a man of myself yet--to cleanse myself of ingratitude--and bitterness--and evil passions. Sylvia--Sylvia--Sylvia!"

It seemed as if he had called it a thousand times; suddenly he stopped short, listening, his heart beating like a hammer, then standing still in his breast. It couldn't be--but, oh, it was, it was--

"Austin! Is that you?"

"Yes, yes, yes, where are you?"

"I don't know, I'm sure--what a question!" And instantly a feeling of relief swept through him--she was *all right*--able to see the absurdity of his question more than he could have done! "But wherever I am, we can't be far apart; keep on calling, follow my voice--Austin--Austin--Austin--"

"All right--coming--tell me--are you hurt?"

"No--that is, not much."

"How much?"

"Dolly was frightened by the storm, bolted, and threw me off; I must have been stunned for a few minutes. I'm afraid I've sprained my ankle in falling, for I can't walk; and, oh, Austin, I'm awfully cold--and wet--and tired!"

"I know; it's--it's been just hellish for you. Keep on speaking to me, I'm getting nearer."

"I'll put out my hands, and then, when you get here, you won't stumble over me. I'm sure you're very near; your footsteps sound so."

"How long have you been here, should you think?"

"Oh, hours and hours. I was riding on the main road, when just what you predicted happened. It served me right--I ought to have listened to you. And so--oh, here you are-- *I knew, all the time*, you'd come."

He grasped the little cold, outstretched hands, and sank down beside her, chafing them in his own.

"Thank God, I've found you," he said huskily, and gulped hard, pressing his lips together; then forcing himself to speak quietly, he went on, "Sylvia--tell me exactly what happened--if you feel able; but first, you must drink some brandy--I've got some for you--"

"I don't believe I can. I was all right until a moment ago--but now everything seems to be going around--"

Austin put his arm around her, and forced the flask to her lips; then the soft head sank on his shoulder, and he realized that she had fainted. Very gently he laid her on the ground, and fumbled in the dark for the fastenings of her habit; when it was loosened, he pulled off his coat and flannel shirt, putting the coat over her, and the shirt under her head for a pillow; then listening anxiously for her breathing, felt again for her mouth, and poured more brandy between her lips. There were a few moments of anxious waiting; then she sighed, moved restlessly, and tried to sit up.

"Lie still, Sylvia; you fainted; you've got to keep very quiet for a few minutes."

"How stupid of me! But I'm all right now."

"I said, lie still."

"All right, all right, I will; but you'll frighten me out of my wits if you use that tone of voice."

"I didn't mean to frighten you; but you've got to keep quiet, for your own sake, Sylvia."

"I thought you said you wouldn't call me Sylvia."

"I've said a good many foolish things in the course of my life, and changed my mind about them afterwards."

"Or feel sorry if I came to grief--"

"And a good many untrue and wicked ones for which I have repented afterwards."

"Well, I did come to grief--or pretty nearly. I met three Polish workmen on the road. I think they were--intoxicated. Anyway, they tried to stop me. I was lucky in managing to turn in here--so quickly they didn't realize what I was going to do. If I hadn't been near the entrance to this wood-road--Austin, what makes you grip my hand so? You hurt."

"Promise me you'll never ride alone again," he said, his voice shaking.

"I certainly never shall."

"And could you possibly promise me, too, that you'll forgive the absolutely unforgivable way I've acted all summer, and give me a chance to show that I can do better-- *Sylvia*?"

"Oh, yes, *yes*! Please don't feel badly about that. I--I--never misunderstood at all. I know you've had an awfully hard row to hoe, and that's made you bitter, and--any man hates to have a woman help--financially. Besides"--she hesitated, and went on with a humility very different from her usual sweet imperiousness--"I've been pretty unhappy myself, and it's made *me* self-willed and obstinate and dictatorial."

"You! You're--more like an angel than I ever dreamed any woman could be."

"Oh, I'm not, I'm not--please don't think so for a minute. Because, if you do, we'll start out on a false basis, and not be real friends, the way I hope we're going to be now--"

"Yes--"

"And, please, may I sit up now? And really, my hands are warm"--he dropped them instantly--"and I would like to hear about the storm--whether it has done much damage, if you know."

"It has destroyed every building we owned except the house itself."

"Austin! You're not in earnest!"

"I never was more so."

"Oh, I'm sorry--more sorry than I can tell you!" One of the little hands that had been withdrawn a moment earlier groped for his in the darkness, and pressed it gently; she did not speak for some minutes, but finally she went on: "It seems a dreadful thing to say, but perhaps it may prove a blessing in disguise. I believe Thomas is right in thinking that a smaller farm, which you could manage easily and well without hiring help, would be more profitable; and now it will seem the most natural thing in the world to sell that great southern meadow to Mr. Weston."

"Yes, I suppose so; he offered us three thousand dollars for it; he doesn't care to buy the little brick cottage that goes with it--which isn't strange, for it has only five rooms, and is horribly out of repair. Grandfather used it for his foreman; but, of course, we've never needed it and never shall, so I wish he did want it."

"Oh, Austin--could *I* buy it? I've been *dying* for it ever since I first saw it! It could be made perfectly charming, and it's plenty big enough for me! I've sold my Fifth Avenue house, and I'm going to sell the one on Long Island too--great, hideous, barnlike places! Your mother won't want me forever, and I want a little place of my very own, and *I love* Hamstead--and the river--and the valley--I didn't dare suggest this--you all, except Thomas, seemed so averse to disposing of any of the property, but--'

"If we sell the meadow to Weston, I am sure you can have the cottage and as much land as you want around it; but the trouble is--"

"You need a great deal more money; of course, I know that. Have you any insurance?"

"Very little."

For some moments she sat turning things over in her mind, and was quiet for so long that Austin began to fear that she was more badly hurt than she had admitted, and found it an effort to talk.

"Is anything the matter?" he asked at last, anxiously. "Are you in pain?"

"No--only thinking. Austin--if you cannot secure a loan at some local bank, would you be very averse to borrowing the money from me--whatever the sum is that you need? I am investing all the time, and I will ask the regular rates of interest. Are you offended with me for making such a suggestion?"

"I am not. I was too much moved to answer for a minute, that is all. It is beyond my comprehension how you could bring yourself to do it, after overhearing what you heard me say the other evening."

"Then you'll accept?"

"If father and Thomas think best, I will; and thank you, too, for not calling it a gift."

"Are you likely to be offended if I go on, and suggest something further?"

"No; but I am likely to be so overwhelmed that I shall not be of much practical use to you."

"Well, then, I'd like you to take a thousand dollars more than you need for building, and spend it in travelling."

"In travelling!"

"Yes; Thomas is a born farmer, and the four years that he is going to have at the State Agricultural College are going to be exactly what he wants and needs. He isn't sensitive enough so that he'll mind being a little older than most of the fellows in his class. But, of course, for you, anything like that is entirely out of the question. How old are you, anyway?"

"Twenty-seven."

"Well, if you could get away from here for a time, and see other people, how they do things, how they make a little money go a long way, and a little land go still farther, how they work hard, and fail many times, and succeed in the end--not the science of farming that Thomas is going to learn, but the accomplished fact--I believe it would be the making of you. My Uncle Mat was one of the first import- ers of Holstein cattle in this country, and I'd like to have you do just what he did when he got through college. Of course, you can buy all the cows you want in the United States now, of every kind, sort, and description, and just as good as there are anywhere in the world; but I want you to go to Europe, nevertheless. Start right off while Thomas is still at home to help your father; take a steamer that goes direct to Holland; get into the interior with an interpreter. Then cross over to the Channel Islands. By that time you'll be in a position to decide whether you want to stock your farm with Holsteins, which have the strongest constitutions and give the most milk, or Jerseys, which give the richest. While you're over there, go to Paris and London for a few days--and see something besides cows. Come home by Liverpool. I know the United States Minister to the Netherlands very well, and no end of people in Paris. I'll give you some letters of introduction, and you'll have a good time besides getting a practical education. The whole trip needn't take you more than eight weeks. Then next spring visit a few of the big farms in New York and the Middle West, and go to one of those big cattle auctions they hold in Syracuse in July. Then--"

"For Heaven's sake, Sylvia! Where did you pick up all this information about farming?"

"From Uncle Mat--but I'll tell you all about that some other time. The question is now, 'Will you go?'"

"God bless you, *yes*!"

"That's settled, then," she cried happily. "I was fairly trembling with fear that you'd refuse. Why *is* it so hard for you to accept things?"

"I don't know. I've been bitter all my life because I've had to go without so much, and this summer I've been equally bitter because things were changing. It must be just natural cussedness--but I'm honestly going to try to do better."

"We've got to stay here until morning, haven't we?"

"I'm afraid we have. You can't walk, and even if you could, the chances are ten to one against our finding the highroad in this Egyptian darkness! When the sun comes up, I can pick my own way along through the underbrush all right, and carry you at the same time. You must weigh about ninety pounds."

"I weigh one hundred and ten! The idea!--There's really no chance, then, of our moving for several hours?"

"I'm sorry--but you must see there is not. Does it seem as if you couldn't bear being so dreadfully uncomfortable that much longer?"

"Not in the least. I'm all right. But--"

"Do you mind being here--alone with me?"

"No, *no, no*! Why on earth should I? Let me finish my sentence. I was only wondering if it might not help to pass the time if I told you a story? It's not a very pleasant one, but I think it might help you over some hard places yourself, if you heard it; and if you would tell part of it--as much as you think best--to your family after we get home, I should be very grateful. Some of it should, in all justice, have been told to you all long ago, since you were so good as to receive me when you knew nothing whatever about me, and the rest is--just for you."

"Is the telling going to be hard for you?"

"I don't think so--this way--in the dark--and alone. It has all seemed too unspeakably dreadful to talk about until just lately; but I've been growing so much happier--I think it may be a relief to tell some one now."

"Then do, by all means. I feel--"

"Yes--"

"More honored than I can tell you by your--confidence."

"Austin--when it's *in* you to say such nice things as you have several times to-night, *why* do you waste time saying disagreeable ones--the way you usually do to everybody?"

"I've just told you, I don't know, but I'm going to do better."

"Well--there was once a girl, whose father had died when she was a baby and who lived with her mother and a maid in a tiny flat in New York City. It was a pretty little flat, and they had plenty to eat and to wear, and a good many pleasant friends and acquaintances; but they didn't have much money--that is, compared to the other people they knew. This girl went to a school where all her mates had ten times as much spending money as she did, who possessed hundreds of things which she coveted, and who were constantly showering favors upon her which she had no way of returning. So, from the earliest time that she could remember, she felt discontented and dissatisfied, and regarded herself as having been picked out by Providence for unusual misfortunes; and her mother agreed with her.

"I fancy it is never very pleasant to be poor. But if one can be frankly poor, in calico and overalls, the way you've been, I don't believe it's quite so hard as it is to be poor and try 'to keep up appearances'; as the saying is. This girl learned very early the meaning of that convenient phrase. She gave parties, and went without proper food for a week afterwards; she had pretty dresses to wear to dances, and wore shabby finery about the house; she bought theatre tickets and candy, but never had a cent to give to charity; she usually stayed in the sweltering city all summer, because there was not enough money to go away for the summer, and still have some left for the next winter's season; and she spent two years at miserable little second-rate 'pensions' in Europe--that pet economy of fashionable Americans who would not for one moment, in their own country, put up with the bad food, and the unsanitary quarters, and the vulgar associates which they endure there.

"Before she was sixteen years old this girl began to be 'attractive to men,' as another stock phrase goes. I may be mistaken, and I'll never have a chance now to find out whether I am or not, but I believe if I had a daughter like that, it would be my earnest wish to bring her up in some quiet country place where she could dress simply, and spend much time outdoors, and not see too many people until she was nineteen or twenty. But the mother I have been talking about didn't feel that way. She taught her daughter to make the most of her looks--her eyes and her mouth, and her figure; she showed her how to arrange her dress in a way which should seem simple--and really be alluring; she drilled her in the art of being flippant without being pert, of appearing gentle when she was only sly, of saying the right thing at the right time, and--what is much more important--keeping still at the right time. The pupil was docile because she was eager to learn and she was clever. She made very few mistakes, and she never made the same one twice.

"Of course, all this education had one aim and end--a rich husband. 'I hope I've brought you up too sensibly,' the mother used to say, 'for you to even think of throwing yourself away on the first attractive boy that proposes to you. Your type is just the kind to appeal to some big, heavy, oversated millionaire. Keep your eyes open for him.' The daughter was as obedient in listening to this counsel as she had been in regard to the others, for it fell in exactly with her own wishes; she was tired of being poor, of scrimping and saving and 'keeping up appearances.' The innumerable young bank clerks and journalists and teachers and college students who fluttered about her burnt their moth-wings to no avail. But that **rara avis**, a really rich man, found her very kind to him.

"Well, you can guess the result. When she was not quite eighteen, a man who was beyond question a millionaire proposed to her, and she accepted him. He was nearly twenty years older than she was, and was certainly big, heavy, and oversated. Her uncle--her father's brother--came to her mother, and told her certain plain facts about this man, and his father and grandfather before him, and charged her to tell the child what she would be doing if she married him. Perhaps if the uncle had gone to the girl herself, it might have done some good--perhaps it wouldn't have-- you see she was so tired of being poor that she thought nothing else mattered. Anyway, he felt a woman could break these ugly facts to a young girl better than a man, and he was right. Only, you see, the mother never told at all; not that she really feared that her daughter would be foolish and play false to her excellent training- -but, still, it was just as well to be on the safe side. The millionaire was quite mad about his little fiancee; he was perfectly willing to pay--in advance--all the expenses for a big, fashionable wedding, with twelve bridesmaids and a wedding-breakfast at Sherry's; he was eager to load her with jewels, and settle a large sum of money upon her, and take her around the world for her honeymoon journey; he loved her little soft tricks of speech, the shy way in which she dropped her eyes, the curve of the simple white dress that fell away from her neck when she leaned towards him; and though she saw him drink--and drank with him more than once before her marriage--he took excellent care that it was not until several nights afterwards that she found him--really drunk; and they must have been married two months before she began to--really comprehend what she had done.

"There isn't much more to tell--that can be told. The woman who sells herself- -with or without a wedding ring--has probably always existed, and probably always will; but I doubt whether any one of them ever has told--or ever will--the full price which she pays in her turn. She deserves all the censure she gets, and more--but, oh! she does deserve a little pity with it! When this girl had been married nearly a year, she heard her husband coming upstairs one night long after midnight, in a condition she had learned to recognize--and fear. She locked her bedroom door.

When he discovered that, he was furiously angry; as I said before, he was a big man, and he was very strong. He knocked out a panel, put his hand through, and turned the key. When he reached her, he reminded her that she had been perfectly willing to marry him--that she was his wife, his property, anything you choose to call it; he struck her. The next day she was very ill, and the child which should have been born three months later came--and went--before evening. The next year she was not so fortunate; her second baby was born at the right time--her husband was away with another woman when it happened--a horrible, diseased little creature with staring, sightless eyes. Thank God! it lived only two weeks, and its mother, after a long period of suffering and agony during which she felt like a leper, recovered again, in time to see her husband die--after three nights, during which she got no sleep--of delirium tremens, leaving her with over two million dollars to spend as she chose--and the degradation of her body and the ruin of her soul to think of all the rest of her life!"

"Sylvia!"--the cry with which Austin broke his long silence came from the innermost depths of his being--"Sylvia, Sylvia, you shan't say such things--they're not true. Don't throw yourself on the ground and cry that way." He bent over her, vainly trying to keep his own voice from trembling. "If I could have guessed what--telling this--this hideous story would mean to you, I never should have let you do it. And it's all my fault that you felt you ought to do it--partly because of those vile speeches I made the other evening, partly because I've let you see how wickedly discontented I've been myself, partly because you must have heard me urging my own sister to make practically this same kind of a marriage. Oh, if it's any comfort to you to know it, you haven't told me in vain! Sylvia, do speak to me, and tell me that you believe me, and that you forgive me!"

She managed to give him the assurance he sought, her desperate, passionate voice grown gentle and quiet again. But she was too tired and spent to be comforted. For a long time she lay so still that he became alarmed, thinking she must have fainted again, and drew closer to her to listen to her breathing; at first there was a little catch in it, betraying sobs not yet wholly controlled, then gradually it grew calm and even; she had fallen asleep from sheer exhaustion.

Austin, sitting motionless beside her, found the night one of purification and dedication. To men of Thomas's type, slow of wit, steady and stolid and unemotional, the soil gives much of her own peaceful wholesomeness. But those like Austin, with finer intellects, higher ambitions, and stronger passions, often fare ill at her hands. Their struggles towards education and the refinements of life are balked by poverty and the utter fatigue which comes from overwork; while their search for pleasure often ends in a knowledge and experience of vices so crude and tawdry that men of greater wealth and more happy experience would turn from them in disgust, not because they were more moral, but because they could afford to be more fastidious. Between Broadway and the "main street" of Wallacetown, and other places of its type--small railroad or manufacturing centres, standing alone in an otherwise purely agricultural community--the odds in favor of virtue, not to say decency, are all in favor of Broadway; and Wallacetown, to the average youth of Hamstead, represents the one opportunity for a "show," "something to drink," and "life" in general. Sylvia had unlocked the door of material opportunity for Austin; but she had done far more than this. She had given him the vision of the higher things that lay beyond that, and the desire to attain them. Further than that, neither she nor any other woman could help him. The future, to make or mar, lay now within his own hands. And in the same spirit of consecration with which the knights of old prayed that they might attain true chivalry during the long vigil before their accolade, Austin kept his watch that night, and made his vow that the future, in spite of the discouragements and mistakes and failures which it must inevitably contain, should be undaunted by obstacles, and clean of lust and high of purpose.

The wind and rain ceased, the clouds grew less heavy, and at last, just before dawn, a few stars shone faintly in the clearing sky; then the sun rose in a blaze of glory. Sylvia had not moved, and lay with one arm under her dark head, the undried tears still on her cheeks. Austin lifted her gently, and started towards the highroad with her in his arms. She stirred slightly, opened her eyes and smiled, then lifted her hands and clasped them around his neck.

"It'll be easier to carry me that way," she murmured drowsily. "Austin--you're awfully good to me."

Her eyes closed again. A sheet of white fire, like that of which he had been conscious on the afternoon when they straightened out the yard together, only a thousand times more powerful, seemed to envelop him again. He looked down at the lovely, sleeping face, at the dark lashes curling over the white cheeks and the red, sweet lips. If he kissed her, what harm would be done--she would never even know--

Then he flung back his head. Sylvia was as far above him as those pale stars of the early dawn. It was clear to him that no one must ever guess how dearly he loved her; but he knew that it was far, far more essential that he, in his unworthiness, should not profane his own ideal. She was not for his touch, scarcely for his thoughts. The kiss which did not reach her lips burned into his soul instead, and cleansed it with its healing flame.

CHAPTER V

ylvia's sprain, as Austin had suspected, proved much more serious than she had admitted, but when the village doctor came about noon to dress her ankle, she insisted that she was none the worse for her long exposure, and that if she must lie still on a lounge for two weeks, the least the family could do would be to humor her in everything, and spend as much time as possible with her, or she would certainly die of boredom. She passed the entire day in making and unfolding plans, looking up the sailing dates of steamships, and writing letters of introduction for Austin. By night she had the satisfaction of knowing that Weston's offer for the south meadow had been accepted, that the Wallacetown Bank and the insurance money would furnish part of the needed funds, and that she was to be allowed to loan the rest, and that the little brick cottage belonged to her. The fact that Austin had had a long talk with his father and brother, and that his passage for Holland had been engaged by telegraph, seemed scarcely less of an achievement to her; but Mrs. Gray noticed, as she kissed her little benefactress after seeing her comfortably settled for the night, that her usually pale cheeks were very red and her eyes unnaturally bright, and worried over her all night long.

The next morning there could be no doubt of the fact that Sylvia was really ill, and two days later Dr. Wells shook his head with dissatisfaction after using his thermometer and stethoscope. He was a conscientious man who lacked self-confidence, and the look of things was disquieting to him.

"I think you ought to get a nurse," he said in the hall to Mrs. Gray as he went out, "and probably she would like to have her own doctor from the city in consultation, and some member of her family come to her. It looks to me very much as if we were in for bronchial pneumonia, and she's a delicate little thing at best."

Sylvia was laughing when Mrs. Gray, bent on being both firm and tactful, reentered her room. "Tell Dr. Wells he must make his stage-whispers softer if he doesn't want me to overhear him," she said, "and don't think of ordering the funeral flowers just yet. I'm not delicate--I'm strong as an ox--if I weren't I shouldn't be alive at all. Get a nurse by all means if it will make things easier for you--that's the only reason I need one. They're usually more bother than they're worth, but I know of two or three who might do fairly well, if any one of them is free. My doctor is an old fogey, and I won't have him around. As for family, I'm not as greatly blessed--numerically or otherwise--in that respect as the Grays, but my Uncle Mat would love to come, I feel sure, as he's rather hurt at my runaway conduct." She gave the necessary addresses, and still persisting that they were making a great fuss about nothing, turned over on her pillow in a violent fit of coughing.

Sylvia was right in one thing: she was much stronger than Dr. Wells guessed, and though the next week proved an anxious one for every member of the household except herself, it was not a dismal one. Even if she were flat on her back, her spirit and her vitality remained contagious. Thomas, whose state of mind was by this time quite apparent to the family, though he imagined it to be a well-concealed secret, hung about outside her door, positive that she was going to die, and brought offerings in the shape of flowers, early apples, and pet animals which he thought might distract her. Austin, who shared his room, insisted that he could not sleep because Thomas groaned and sighed so all night; Molly pertly asked him why he did not try rabbits, as kittens did not seem to appeal to Sylvia, and his mother bantered him half-seriously for thinking of "any one so far above him" whose heart, moreover, was buried "in the grave." Austin's somewhat expurgated version of Sylvia's story put an end to the latter part of the protest, but sent his hearers into a new ferment of excitement and sympathy. Sally, who was all ready to start for a "ball" in Wallacetown with Fred when she heard it, declared she couldn't go one step, it made her feel "that low in her spirits," and Fred replied, by gosh, he didn't blame her one mite; whereat they wandered off and spent the evening at a very comfortable distance from the house, but fairly close together, revelling in a wealth of gruesome facts and suppositions. Katherine said she certainly never would marry at all, men were such dreadful creatures, and Molly said, yes, indeed, but what else *could* a girl marry?--while Edith determined to devote the rest of *her* life to attending and adoring the lovely, sad, drooping widow, whose existence was to be one long poem of beautiful seclusion; and she was so pleased with her own ideas, and her manner of expressing them, that she wept scalding tears into the broth she was making for Sylvia as she stirred it over the stove.

The presence of "Uncle Mat," greatly dreaded beforehand, proved an unexpected source of solace and delight. He was a quiet, shrewd little man, not unlike Sylvia in many ways, but with a merry twinkle in his eye, and a brisk manner of speech which she did not possess. He sized up the Gray family quickly, and apparently with satisfaction, for he talked quite freely of his niece to them, and they saw that they were not alone in their estimate of her.

"It certainly was a great stroke of luck all round--for her as well as for you--when she blew in here," he said, "but if you knew what an awful hole we think she's left behind her in New York you'd think yourselves doubly lucky to have her all to yourselves. There's more than one young man, I can tell you"--with a sly look at Thomas--"watching out for her return. You should have seen her at a party I gave for her three years ago or more, dressed in a pink frock looped up with roses, and with cheeks to match! She wasn't always this pale little shadow, I can tell you. Well, the boys were around her that night like bees round a honeysuckle bush--no denying there's something almighty irresistible about these little, soft-looking girls, now, is there? Ah! her roses didn't last long, poor child. Now you've given her a good, healthful place to live in, and something to think about and do--she'd have lost her reason without them, after all she's been through. But when you're tired of her, I want her. I'm a poor, forlorn lonely old bachelor, and I need her a great deal more than any of you. What do you say to a little walk, Mr. Gray, before we turn in? I want to have a look at your fine farm. I have a farm myself--no such grand old place as this, of course, but a neat little toy not far from the city, where I can run down Sundays. Sylvia used to be very fond of going down with me. It's from my foreman, a queer, scientific chap--Jenkins his name is--that she's picked up all these notions she's been unloading on you. Pretty good, most of them, aren't they, though? You must run down there some time, boys, and look things over--it's well to go about a bit when one's thinking of building and branching out--Sylvia's idea, exactly, isn't it?"

Mr. Gray and Thomas did "run down," seizing the opportunity while Austin was still at home, and while there was practically no farm-work to be done. Jenkins did the honors of Mr. Stevens's little place handsomely, and they returned with magnificent plans, from the erection of silos and the laying of concrete floors to the proper feeding of poultry. When "Uncle Mat" was obliged to return to his business, after staying over two weeks with the Grays, Austin went with him, for he suggested that he would be glad to have the boy as his guest in New York for a few days before he sailed.

"You better have a glimpse of the 'neat little toy,' too," he said, "and perhaps see something of a rather neat little city, too! You'll want to do a little shopping and so on, and I might be of assistance in that way."

"I don't see how you can go," said Thomas to Austin the night before he left, as they were undressing, "while Sylvia is still in bed, and won't be around for another week at least. She's responsible for all your tremendous good fortune, and you'll leave without even saying thank you and good-bye. You're a darned queer ungrateful cuss, and always were."

"I know it," said Austin, "and such being the 'nature of the beast,' don't bother trying to make me over. You can be grateful and devoted enough for both of us. Now, do shut up and let me go to sleep--I sure will be thankful to get a room to myself, if I'm not for anything else."

"I don't see how any one can help being crazy over her," continued Thomas, thumping his pillow as if he would like to pummel any one who disagreed with him.

"Don't you?" asked Austin.

The next night he was in New York with Mr. Stevens, trying hard to feel natural in a tiny flat which was only one of fifty in the same great house. A colored butler served an elaborate dinner at eight o'clock in the evening, and brought black coffee, liqueurs, and cigars into the living-room afterwards, and, worst of all, unpacked all his scanty belongings and laid them about his room. Austin really suffered, and the cold perspiration ran down his back, but he watched his host carefully and waited from one moment to another to see what would be expected of him next; he managed, too, before he went to bed, to ask a question which had been on his mind for some time.

"Would you mind telling me, sir, where Sylvia's mother is?"

Uncle Mat shot one of his keen little glances in Austin's direction. "Why, no, not at all, as nearly as I can," he said. "My brother, Austin, made a most unfortunate match; his wife was a mean, mercenary, greedy woman, as hard as nails, and as tough as leather--but handsome, oh, very handsome, as a girl, and clever, I assure you. I have often been almost glad that my brother did not live long enough to see her in her real colors. She married, very soon after Sylvia herself, a worthless Englishman--discharged from the army, I believe, who had probably been her lover for some time. Cary gave her a check for a hundred thousand to get rid of her the day after his wedding to Sylvia, and the pair are probably living in great comfort on that at some second-rate French resort."

"Thank you for telling me; but it's rather awful, isn't it, that any one should have to think of her mother as Sylvia must? Why, my mother--" He stopped, flushing as he thought of how commonplace, how homely and ordinary, his mother had often seemed to him, how he had brooded over his father's "unfortunate match." "My mother has worked her fingers to the bone for all of us, and I believe she'd let herself be chopped in pieces to help us gladly any day."

"Yes," assented Mr. Stevens, "I know she would. There are--several different kinds of mothers in the world. It's a thousand pities Sylvia did not have a fair show at a job of that sort. She would have been one of the successful kind, I fancy."

"It would seem so," said Austin.

CHAPTER VI

New York City August 25

DEAR MOTHER AND FATHER:

I'm going to lay in a stock of picture post-cards to send you, for if things move at the same rate in Europe that they do in New York, I certainly shan't have time to write many letters. But I'll send a good long one to-night, anyhow. I always thought I'd like to live in the city, as you know, but a few days of this has already given me a sort of breathless feeling that I ought always to be on the move, whether there's anything special to do or not. The noise never stops for one minute, night or day, and the streets are perfect miracles of light and dirt and *hurry*. This whole flat could be put right into our dining-room, and we'd hardly notice it at that, and *hot!* Mr. Stevens says in the winter he nearly freezes to death, but I can't believe it.

All day Friday he kept me tearing from shop to shop, buying more clothes than I can wear out in a lifetime, I believe, lots of them things I'd never even seen or heard of before. Some of the suits had to be altered a little, so in the afternoon we went back to the same places we'd been to in the morning, and tried the blamed things on again. How women can like that sort of thing is beyond me--I'd rather dig potatoes all day. By five o'clock I was so tired that I was ready to lie right down on Fifth Avenue, and let the passing crowds walk over me, if they liked. But Mr. Stevens hustled me into a huge hotel called the Waldorf for a hair-cut and "tea" (which isn't a good square meal, but a little something to drink along with a piece of bread-and-butter as thick through as tissue-paper) and then out again to see a few sights before we went home to dress for "an early dinner" (*seven o'clock!*) and go to the theatre in the evening. "Dressing" meant struggling into my new dress-suit. I hoped it wouldn't arrive in time, but Mr. Stevens had had it marked "rush," and it did. I felt like a fool when I got it on, and a pretty hot, uncomfortable fool to boot.

Mr. Stevens apologized for the show, saying there was really nothing in town at this time of year, but you can imagine what it seemed like to me! I'd be almost willing to wear pink tights--same as a good many of the actresses did!--if it meant having such a glorious time.

It was almost ten o'clock Saturday morning when I waked up, and of course I felt like a fool again. But that is getting to be such a habitual state with me, that I don't need to keep wasting paper by mentioning it. By the time I was washed and shaved and dressed, Mr. Stevens had been to his office, transacted all the business necessary for the day, and was ready to see sights again. "It doesn't take long to do things when you get the hang of hustling," he said, referring to his own transactions; "come along. We've got a couple of hours before lunch, and then we'll take the 2.14 train down to my farm." So we shot downstairs about forty flights to the second in the elevator, hailed a passing taxicab, jumped in, and were tearing out Riverside Drive--much too fast to see anything--in no time. We had "lunch" at a big restaurant called Delmonico's, a great deal to eat and not half enough time to eat it in, then took another taxi and made our train by catching on to the last car.

I don't need to tell you about the farm, because you know all about that already. I never left Jenkins's heels one second, and he said I was much more of a nuisance than Thomas, because Thomas caught on to things naturally, and I asked questions all the time. I don't believe I'll see anything in Europe to beat that place. When we get to milking our cows, and separating our cream, and doing our cleaning by electricity, it'll be something like, won't it?

We took a seven o'clock train back to New York this morning, so that Mr. Stevens could get to his office by nine, and he had me go with him and wait around until he was at leisure again. I certainly thought the stenographers' fingers would fly off, and all the office boys moved with a hop, skip, and jump; really, the slowest things in the rooms were the electric fans whizzing around. By half-past eleven Mr. Stevens had dictated about two hundred and fifty letters, sold several million dollars' worth of property (he's a real-estate broker), and was all ready to go out with me to buy more socks, neckties, handkerchiefs, etc., having decided that I didn't have enough. We had "lunch" at Sherry's--another swell restaurant--and took a trip up the Hudson in the afternoon, getting back at half-past ten--"Just in time," said Mr. Stevens, "to look in at a roof-garden before we go to bed." So we "looked," and it sure was worth a passing glance, and then some. It's one o'clock in the morning now, and I sail at nine, so I'm writing at this hour in desperation, or you won't get any letter at all.

Much love to everybody. I picture you all peacefully sleeping--except Thomas, of course--with no such word as "hurry" in your minds.

AUSTIN

*   *   *   *   *

S.S. Amsterdam September 4

DEAR SALLY:

It doesn't seem possible that I'm going to land to-morrow! The first two days out were pretty dreadful, and I'll leave them to your imagination--there certainly wasn't much left of *me* except imagination! But by the third day I was beginning to sit up and take notice again, and by the fourth I was enjoying myself more than I ever did in all my life before.

There's a fellow on board named Arthur Brown, who has his sister Emily with him; they're both unmarried, and well over thirty, teachers in a small Western college, and are starting out on their "Sabbatical year." Seeing them together has made me think a lot about you, and wish you were along; they've very little money, and have never been to Europe before, and almost every night they sit down and figure out how they're going to get the most out of their trip, trying new plans and itineraries all the time. They get into such gales of laughter over it that you'd think being poor was the greatest fun in the world, and the tales they've told about working their way through high school and college, and saving up to come to Europe, would be pathetic if they weren't so screamingly funny. I haven't been gone very long yet, I know, but it's been long enough for me to decide that Sylvia sent me off, not primarily to buy cows and study agriculture, but to learn a few things that will be a darned sight better worth knowing than that even, and-- *to have a good time*! In the hope, of course, that I'll come home, not only less green, but less cussedly disagreeable.

Mr. Stevens has crossed on this boat twice, and introduced me to both the captain and the chief engineer before I started; they've both been awfully kind to me, and I've seen the "inwards and outwards" of the ship from garret to cellar, so to speak, and learned enough about navigation and machinery to make me want to learn a lot more. But even without all this, there would have been plenty to do. This isn't a "fashionable line," so they say, but it's a good deal more fashionable than anything we ever saw in Hamstead, Vermont! There's dancing every evening--not a bit like what we have at home, and it really made me gasp a little at first--you thought I was hard to shock, too, didn't you? Well, believe me, I blushed the first time I discovered that I was expected to hold my partner so tight that you couldn't get a sheet of paper between us. However, I soon stopped blushing, and bent all my energies to the agreeable task of learning instead, and the girls are all so friendly and jolly, that I believe I'm getting the hang of the new ways pretty well. There are no square dances at all and very few waltzes or two-steps, but two newer ones, the one-step and fox-trot, hold the floor, literally and figuratively! I wish I could describe the girls' dresses to you, they're so, pretty, but I can't a bit, except to say that they rather startled me at first, too; they appear to be made out of about one yard of material, and none of that yard goes to sleeves, and not much to waist. A very lively young lady sits next to me at the table, and I worried incessantly at first as to what would happen if her shoulder-straps should break: but apparently they are stronger than they look. When they--the girls, I mean--feel a little chilly on deck, they put on scarves of tulle--a gauzy stuff about half as thick as mosquito netting. I don't quite see why they're not all dead of pneumonia, but they seem to thrive.

I've also learned--or am trying to learn--to play a game of cards called "bridge"; it's along the same lines as good old bid-whist, but considerably dressed up. I like that, too, but feel pretty stupid at it, as most of the players can remember every two-spot for six hands back, and hold dreadful post-mortems of their opponents' mistakes at the end of the game. I've brought along the old French grammar I had in high school, as well as some new phrase-books that Mr. Stevens gave me, and take them to bed with me to study every night, for he told me that you could get along 'most anywhere if you knew French. There's a library aboard, too, so I've read several novels, and I'm getting used to my clothes--I don't believe I've got too many after all--and to taking a cold bath every morning and shaving at least once a day.

Make Fred toe the mark while I'm not there to look after you, but remember he's a good sort just the same; I was an awful fool ever to advise you not to stick to him, he's worth a dozen of his cousin. Tell Molly she'll have to do some practising to come up to the way some of the girls on this ship play, but I believe she's got more talent than all of them put together, if she'll only work hard enough to develop it. There's going to be an *extra* good time to-night, as it's the last one, and I'm looking forward to dancing my heels off. Love to you all, especially mother, and tell her I haven't seen a doughnut since I left home.

Affectionately your brother
AUSTIN

* * * * *

Paris, October 1
DEAR THOMAS:

I got here last night, and found the cable from father saying that the cattle and Dutch Peter had reached New York all right, and that he had met them there. I know you'll like Peter, and I hope we can keep him indefinitely, though I only hired him to take the cows over, and stay until those Holstein aristocrats were properly acclimated to the Homestead. I'm glad they've got there. And, gosh! I'm glad I've got *here!* I realize I've been a pretty poor correspondent, sending just picture post-cards, and now and then a note to mother, but, you see, I've crowded every minute so darned full, and then I've never had much practice. So before I start out to "do" Paris, I'll practice a little on you.

I landed at Rotterdam, had twenty-four hours there with Emily and Arthur Brown--that brother and sister I met on shipboard--then we separated, they going to Antwerp, and I heading straight for The Hague to present Sylvia's letter of introduction to Mr. Little, the American Minister, shaking in my shoes, and cold perspiration running down my back, of course. But I needn't "have shook and sweat," as our friend Mrs. Elliott says, for he was expecting me and was kindness itself. He found an interpreter to go through the farming district with me, and then he invited me to come and stay at his house for a few days before I started for the interior. He has a son about my age, who I imagine has suffered from the same form of heart disease with which you are afflicted at present, as he seemed to be somewhat affected every time Sylvia's name was mentioned; and a daughter Flora, an awfully friendly, jolly, pink-and-white creature. Fortunately she informed me promptly that she was engaged to a fellow in Paris, or I might have got heart disease, too. They kept me on the jump every minute--sight-seeing and parties, and excursions of all sorts, and one night we went to see a play of Shakespeare's, "The Two Gentlemen of Verona," given in Dutch. (I find that all Continentals admire him immensely, and give frequent performances of his works.) Get out our old copy and re-read it some rainy day; you're probably rusty on it, same as I was, but it's an interesting tale, and there's a song in it that can't help appealing to you. Here's the first verse:

"Who is Sylvia? What is she   That all the swains commend her? Holy, fair, and wise is she,   The heavens such grace did lend her That she might admired be."

I advise you to invest in doublet, hose, plumed hat, and guitar, and try the effect of a serenade under our Sylvia's--beg pardon, **your** Sylvia's window. The fellow in the play made a great hit, so there's no telling what you might accomplish.

I hated leaving the Littles', for the good time I had there sure beat the good time I had on shipboard "to a frazzle"; but I soon found out that the business part of the trip was going to be a good deal more interesting and absorbing than I had imagined it would be. My interpreter, Hans Roorda, a fellow several years younger than I am, can speak five languages, all equally well, and I kept him busy talking French to me. We were in the country almost three weeks. The farmers haven't half the mechanical conveniences that we considered absolutely necessary even in our least prosperous days, but are marvels of order and efficiency, for all that. I believe one of the greatest mistakes that we New England farmers have been making is to assume that farming is a mixture of three fourths muscle and one fourth brains--I'm beginning to think it's the other way around. As you have already learned, I followed Jenkins's advice, bought a dozen head of fine cattle, and hired Peter Kuyp, the son of one of the farmers I visited, to take care of them. Of course, this meant going back to Rotterdam to see them safely off, and I managed to get a glimpse of some of the other Dutch cities as well. When I got to Amsterdam I parted from Roorda with real regret, for I feel he's one of the many good friends I've already made. I found my first American mail in Amsterdam, among other letters one from you. The news from home in it was all fine. I'm glad father has sold that old Blue Hill pasture. It was too far off from the rest of our land to be of much real use to us, and I also think he was dead right to use the money he got from it to pay off old debts. Mr. Stevens writes me that he has sold Sylvia's Long Island house for her, and that her horses, carriages, sleighs, and motor are all going up to the Homestead. Now that the Holsteins are there, too, why don't you sell the few old cows and the two horses that we rescued from the fire, and use that money in paying off more debts? If the mortgage were only out of the way, with all the other improvements you speak of well started, I should think we were headed straight for millionaires' row.

I also found a letter from Mr. Little in Amsterdam, saying that Mrs. Little and Flora were about to start for Paris, and asking if I would care to act as their escort, since neither he nor his son could leave The Hague just then--simply a kind way of saying, "Here's another chance for you," of course! You can imagine the answer I telegraphed him! We "broke" the journey in Brussels and Antwerp, and I saw no end of new wonders, of course, and in Brussels we went to the opera. I did wish Molly was there, for she certainly would have thought she had struck Heaven, and I did, pretty nearly! I'm getting used to my dress-suit, and it isn't quite such an exquisite piece of torture to "do" my tie as it was at first, since Flora did it for me one night, and gave me some little hints for the future. She is really an awfully jolly girl.

We got to Paris late at night, and I never shall forget the long drive from the station, through the bright streets to the Fessendens' house, where the Littles were going to visit. Sylvia had given me a letter of introduction to them, too, but I didn't need to use it, for, of course, I got introduced to them then and there. There are three fellows--no girls--in the family, besides Mr. and Mrs. I knew beforehand that Flora was engaged to one of them, but I couldn't tell which, for they all fell upon her and embraced her with about equal enthusiasm. Then they all kissed Mrs. Little, and Mrs. Little and Mrs. Fessenden hugged each other, and Mr. Fessenden hugged Flora. I began to think that perhaps I might be included--by mistake--but all my hopes were in vain. I was invited to come to dinner the next night, however, and then I took my leave, and drove round for an hour--it seemed like an hour in Fairyland--before I went back to my hotel.

You must be getting settled in college now--it must have been an awful wrench to tear yourself away from the Homestead, I know, but you'll have a great time after you get over the first pangs of separation, I'm sure, and don't forget that "absence makes the heart grow fonder." I refer, of course, to Sylvia's heart because you've made it sufficiently plain to all of us that yours *can't*. Well, the best of luck go with you.

AUSTIN

*   *   *   *   *

Southampton, October 27

DEAR SYLVIA:

I had a feeling in my bones when I woke up this morning that something extra pleasant was going to happen; and when I got down to breakfast, and saw, on the top of my pile of mail, a letter postmarked Hamstead, but in a strange handwriting, I knew that it *had* happened.

You begin by scolding me because I haven't written mother oftener. I know I deserve it, and I'll write her from now on, every Sunday, at least; but then you go on by asking why I've never written you, except the little note I sent back by the pilot, which you say is not a note at all, "but a series of repetitions of unmerited thanks." I haven't written because I didn't feel that I you wanted to be bothered with me. And how can I write, and not say, "Thank you, thank you, thank you," with every line? Why, I've learned more, enjoyed more, *lived* more, in these two months since I came to Europe, than I had in all the rest of my life before! Sylvia--but I won't, if you don't like it!

Now, to answer your question, "What have I been doing all this time?" I feel sure you've seen what I have written, so you know what a wonderful trip I had from, The Hague to Paris. I'm glad I haven't got to try to describe Paris to you, for of course you know it much better than I do; but I hope some day, when my mind's a little calmer, I can describe it to the rest of the family. Just now I'm not in any state yet to separate the details from the wild, magnificent jumble of picture galleries and churches, tombs and palaces, parks and gardens, wonderful broad, bright streets, theatres, cafes, and dinner-parties. Of course, all your letters were the main reason that every one was so nice to me. My first day of sight-seeing ended with a perfectly uproarious dinner at the Fessendens'; I never in my life ran into such a jolly crowd.

I finally discovered which brother Flora belonged to--which had been puzzling me a good deal before--because about ten o'clock the other two suggested that we should go out and see if "we could have a little fun." I thought we were having a good deal right there, but of course I agreed, so we went; and we did.

Then--during the next ten days--I went to mass at the Madeleine, and to a ball at the American Embassy; I rode on the top of 'buses, and spun around in motors. We took some all-day trips out into the country, and saw not only the famous places, like Versailles and Fontainebleau, but lots of big, beautiful private estates with farms attached. There's none of the spotless shininess of Holland or the beautiful cattle there; but agriculture is developed to the nth degree for all that. Those French farmers wring more out of one acre than we do out of ten; but we're going to do some wringing in Hamstead, Vermont, in the future, I can tell you! The last night in Paris, I never went to bed at all. Twenty of us had dinner at the Cafe de la Paix--went to the theatre--saw the girls and fathers and mothers home--then went off with the other fellows to another show which lasted until three A.M. I had barely time to rush back to the hotel, collect my belongings, and catch my early train--for I'd made up my mind to do that so that I could stop off for two hours at Rouen on my way to Calais, and I was glad I did, though I must confess I yawned a good deal, even while I was looking at the Cathedral and the relics of Joan of Arc.

I had just a week in the Channel Islands, and though I didn't think beforehand that I could possibly get as much out of them as I did out of the country in Holland, of course, I found that I was mistaken. I bought six head of cattle, brought them to Southampton with me, and saw them safely embarked for America, as I cabled father. I suppose they've got there by now. They're beauties, but I believe I'm going to like the Holsteins better, just the same. They're larger and sturdier--less nervous--and give more milk, though it's not nearly so rich.

The Browns met me there, and I was awfully glad to see them again. I bought a knapsack, and, leaving all my good clothes behind me, started out with them on a week's walking trip through the Isle of Wight, getting back here only last night. We stopped overnight at any place we happened to be near, usually a farmhouse, and the next morning pursued our way again, with a lunch put up by our latest hostess in our pockets. Of course, the Browns didn't take the same interest in farming that I did, but they had a fine time, too. It's been a great thing for me to know them, especially Emily. She's not a bit pretty, or the sort that a fellow could get crazy over, or--well, I can't describe it, but you know what I mean. Every man who meets her must realize what a fine wife she'd make for somebody, and yet he wouldn't want her himself. But she's a wonderful friend. Do you know, I never had a woman friend before, or realized that there could be such a thing--for a man, I mean--unless there was some sentiment mixed up with it. This isn't the least of the valuable lessons I've learned.

After lunch to-day, we're going off again--not on foot this time, as it would take too long to see what we want to that way, but on hired bicycles. I'm sending my baggage ahead to London to "await arrival," but if the mild, though rather rainy, weather we've had so far holds, I hope to have two weeks more of *country* England before I go there; we have no definite plans, but expect to go to some of the cathedral towns, and to Oxford and Warwick at least.

And now I've overstayed the time you first thought I should be gone, already, and yet I'm going to close my letter by quoting the last lines in yours, "If you need more money, cable for it. (I don't; I haven't begun to spend all I had.) Don't hurry; see all you can comfortably and thoroughly; and if you decide you want to go somewhere that we didn't plan at first, or stay longer than you originally intended, please do. The family is well, the building going along finely, and Peter, your Dutch boy, most efficient--by the way, we all like him immensely. This is your chance. Take it."

Well, I'm going to. After the Browns leave London, they're going to Italy for the winter, and they want me to go with them, for a few weeks before I start home. I'll sail from Naples, getting home for Christmas, and what a Christmas it'll be! I know you'll tell me honestly if you think I ought not to do this, and I'll start for Liverpool at once, and without a regret; but if you cable "stay," I'll go towards Rome with an easy heart and a thankful soul.

I must stop, because I don't dare write any more. The "thank-you's" would surely begin to crop out.

Ever yours faithfully
AUSTIN GRAY

CHAPTER VII

The first of October found a very quiet household at the old Gray Homestead. Austin was in Europe; Thomas had gone to college at Burlington, Molly to the Conservatory of Music in Boston. Sally had prudently decided to teach for another year before getting married, and now that she could keep all her earnings, was happily saving them for her modest trousseau; she "boarded" in Wallacetown, where she taught, coming home only for Saturdays and Sundays, while Katherine and Edith were in high school, and gone all day. Mrs. Gray declared that she hardly knew what to do with herself, she had so much spare time on her hands with so many "modern improvements," and such a small family in the house. "Go with Mr. Gray on the 'fall excursion' to Boston," said Sylvia. "He told me that you hadn't been off together since you took your wedding trip. That will give you a chance to look in on Molly, too, and see how she's behaving--and you'll have a nice little spree besides. I'll look after the family, and Peter can look after the cows."

Sylvia had recovered rapidly from her illness, and her former shyness and aversion to seeing people were rapidly leaving her. She no longer lay in bed until noon, but was up with the rest of the family, insisting on doing her share in the housework, and proving a very apt pupil in learning that useful and wrongly despised art; when callers came she always dropped in to chat with them a little while, and even the mail-carrier of the "rural delivery, route number two," the errand-boy on the wagon from Harrington's General Store, and all the agents for flavoring extracts and celluloid toilet sets and Bibles for miles around, were not infrequently found lingering on the "back porch" passing the time of day with her, whether they had any excuse of mail or merchandise or not. Not infrequently she went to spend the day with Mrs. Elliott or with Ruth, and to church on Sunday with all the family;

and although perhaps she was not sorry at heart that her deep mourning gave her an excuse for not attending the village "parties" and "socials," she never said so. The Library, the Grange, and the Village Improvement Society all found her ready and eager to help them in their struggles to raise money, provide better quarters for themselves, or get up entertainments; and the Methodist minister was the first person to meet with a flat refusal to his demands upon her purse. He was far-famed as a successful "solicitor," and conceived the brilliant idea that Sylvia was probably sent by Providence to provide the needed repairs upon the church and parsonage and the increase in his own salary. He called upon her, and graciously informed her of his plan.

"The Lord has been pleased to make you the steward of great riches," he said unctuously, "and I feel sure there is no way you could spend them which would be more pleasing in his sight than that which I have just suggested."

"I agree with you perfectly that the church is in a disgraceful state of disrepair," said Sylvia calmly, "and that your salary is quite inadequate to live on properly. I have often wondered how your congregation could worship reverently in such a place, or allow their pastor to be so poorly housed. I believe the Bible commands us somewhere to do things decently and in order."

"You are quite right, Mrs. Cary, quite right. Then may I understand--"

"Wait just a minute. I have also wondered at the lack of proper pride your congregation seemed to show in such matters. It does not seem to me that it would really help matters very much if I, a complete outsider, not even a member of your communion, furnished all the necessary funds to do what you wish. Your flock would sit back harder than ever, and wait for some one else to turn up and do likewise when I have gone--and probably that second millionaire would never materialize, and you would be left worse off than before, even."

"My dear lady!" exclaimed the divine, amazed and distressed at the turn the conversation had taken, "most of the members of my congregation are in very moderate circumstances."

"I know--but they should do *their share*. And there are some, who, for a small village, are rich, and just plain stingy--why don't you go to them?"

"Unfortunately that would only result in the entire withdrawal of their support, I fear."

"And those are the worthy, struggling Christians whom you wish me to supply with everything to make their church beautiful and their minister comfortable--you want me to put a premium on stinginess! I shan't give you one cent under those conditions! Go to the three richest men in your church, and say to them, 'Whatever sum you will give, Mrs. Cary will double.' Appeal to your congregation as a whole, and tell it the same thing. Ask those who you know have no cash to spare to give some of their time, at whatever it is worth by the hour or the day. Set the children to arranging for a concert--I suppose you wouldn't approve of a little play--and see how the relatives and friends will flock to hear it. I'll gladly drill them. When you've tried all this, and the response has been generous and hearty, if still you haven't all you need, I'll gladly lend you the remainder of the sum without interest, and you may take your own time in discharging the debt."

"That is a young lady who gives a man much food for thought," remarked the minister to Mr. Gray, as, somewhat abashed, but greatly impressed, he was leaving the house a few minutes later.

"Very true--in more ways than one."

"Her person is not unpleasing and she seems to have an agile mind," continued Mr. Jessup.

Mr. Gray turned away to hide a smile. Later he teased Sylvia about her new conquest. "I am afraid," he said, his mouth twitching, "that you would flirt with a stone post."

"I didn't flirt with *him*" said Sylvia indignantly; "he ended the call by dropping on his knees, right there in my sitting-room, and saying, 'Let us pray--for new hearts!' Well, I've had lots of calls end with a prayer for a change of heart--"

"You little wretch! What did you do?"

"Do! I always strive to please! I knelt down beside him, of course, and then he took my hand, so I--Honestly, I don't care much what men *say*--if they only say it *right*--but I draw the line at being *stroked*! If that's your idea of a flirtation, it isn't mine!"

"Look out, my dear," warned Howard; "he's a widower and a famous beggar." And Sylvia laughed with him. During the first months she had never laughed. "I am getting to love that child as if she were my own," he said to his wife later. "Whatever shall we do when she goes away? It won't be long now, you'll see."

"Mercy! Don't you even speak of it!" rejoined Mrs. Gray. But she, too, was brooding over the possibility in secret. "Are you sure you're quite contented here, Sylvia?" she asked anxiously the next time they were alone.

Sylvia laid down the dish she was wiping, and came and laid her cheek, now growing softly pink again, against Mrs. Gray's. "Contented," she echoed; "why, I'm--I'm happy--I never was happy in my whole life before. But I shall freeze to death here this winter, unless you'll let me put a furnace in this great house; and I want to glass in part of the big piazza, and have a tiny little conservatory for your plants built off the dining-room. Do you mind if I tear up the place that much more--you've been so patient about it so far."

Mrs. Gray could only throw up her hands.

The "spree" to Boston took place, and proved wonderfully delightful, and then they all settled down quietly for the winter, looking forward to Christmas as the time that was to bring the entire family together again. For even James, the eldest son, had written that he was about to be married, and should come home with his bride for the holidays for his wedding trip; and as Sylvia still firmly refused to leave the farm, Mr. Stevens asked for permission to join Austin when he landed, and be with his niece over the great day. As the time drew near, the house was hung with garlands, and every window proudly displayed a great laurel wreath tied with a huge red bow. Sylvia moved all her belongings into her parlor, and decorated her bedroom for the bride and groom, and went about the house singing as she un-packed great boxes and trimmed a mammoth Christmas tree.

Four days before Christmas, Mr. and Mrs. James Gray arrived, and Mrs. James was promptly pronounced to be "all right" by her husband's family, though the poor girl, of course, underwent tortures before she was sure of their decision. Fred, who with his father and mother was to join in the great feast, brought Sally home from Wallacetown that same night, and took advantage of the mistletoe which Sylvia had hung up, right before them all. Thomas and Molly, both wonderfully citified already, appeared during the course of the next afternoon from opposite directions, and Molly played, and Thomas expounded scientific farming, to the wonder of them all. And finally Mr. Gray went to meet the midnight train from New York at Wallacetown the night before Christmas Eve, and found himself being squeezed half to pieces by the bear hugs of Austin and the hearty handshakes of Mr. Stevens.

"Pile right into the sleigh," he managed to say at last when he was partially released, but still gasping for breath; "we mustn't stand fooling around here, with the thermometer at twenty below zero, and a whole houseful waiting to treat you the same way you've treated me. Austin, seems as if you were bigger than ever, and you've got a different look, same as Thomas and Molly have, only yours is more different."

"There was more room for improvement in my case," his son laughed back, throwing his arm around him again. "My, but it's good to see you! Talk about changes! You look ten years younger, doesn't he, Mr. Stevens? How's mother? And--and Thomas, and the girls? And--and Peter?"

"Yes, how is *Peter*?" said Mr. Stevens.

"Why, Peter's all right," returned Mr. Gray soberly; "what makes you ask? That sort is never sick and he's as good and steady a boy as I ever saw."

"I'm so glad to hear it," murmured Mr. Stevens in an interested voice.

"And we had the biggest creamery check this month, Austin," went on his father, "that we *ever* had--with just those few cows you sent! Peter tends them as if they were young girls being dressed up for their sweethearts. The hens are laying well, too, right through this cold weather--the poultry house is so clean and warm, they don't seem to know that it's winter. We have enough eggs for our own use, and some to sell besides--I guess there won't be any to sell *this* week, will there? You'll like James's wife, I'm sure, Austin, and you, too, Mr. Stevens--she's a nice, healthy, jolly girl with good sense, I'm sure. She's not as pretty as my girls, but, then, few are, of course, in my eyes. It's plain to see they just set their eye-teeth by each other-- Sadie and James, I mean--and, of course, Fred is about most of the time; so with two pairs of lovers, it keeps things lively, I can tell you."

"Has Thomas recovered?" inquired Austin.

"Indeed, he hasn't! It's mean of us all to make fun of him--he's very much in earnest."

"How does Sylvia take it?" asked Sylvia's uncle.

"I don't think she notices."

"Oh, don't you?" said Mr. Stevens, in the same interested tone he had used before.

Mrs. Gray was standing in the door to receive them, even if it was twenty below zero, and was laughing and crying with her great boy in her arms before he was half out of the sleigh. The kissing that had taken place at the Fessendens' was nothing to that which now occurred at the Grays'; for when he had finished with his mother, Austin found all his sisters waiting for him, clamoring for the same welcome, and he ended with his new sister-in-law, and then began all over again. Meanwhile Mr. Stevens stood looking vainly about, and finally interrupted with "Where's *my* girl?"

"Oh, *there*, Mr. Stevens!" exclaimed Mrs. Gray, wiping her eyes, and settling her hair, "it was downright careless of me not to tell you right away, but I was so excited over Austin that I forgot all about it for a minute; of course, it's a dreadful disappointment to you, but it just couldn't seem to be helped. Frank--my son-in-law, you know, that lives in White Water--telephoned down this morning that the trained nurse had left, an' little Elsie was ailin', an' the hired girl so green, an' nothin' would do but that Sylvia must traipse up there to help Ruth before I could say 'Jack Robinson.'"

"What do you mean?" thundered Uncle Mat and Austin in the same breath; so Mrs. Gray tried again.

"Why, Ruth had a new baby a month ago, another little girl, an' the dearest child! They're all comin' home to-morrow, sure's the world, an' you'll see her then--they've named her Mary, for me, an' of course I'm real pleased. But as I was sayin'--it did seem as if some one had got to take hold an' help them get straightened out if they was goin' to put it through, an' of course, there's no one like Sylvia for jobs like that. Land! I don't know how we ever got along before she come! Anyway, she's up there now. Rode up with Hiram on the Rural Free Delivery--he was tickled most to death. She left her love, an' said maybe one of the boys would take the pair an' her big double sleigh, an' start up to get 'em all in real good season to-morrow mornin'."

"That means me, of course," said Thomas importantly.

"Of course," echoed both his brothers, quite unanimously.

Mr. Stevens said nothing, but calmly went up to bed, where he apparently slept well, as he did not reappear until after nine o'clock the following morning. He sought out Mrs. Gray in the sunny, shining kitchen, but did not evince as much surprise as she had expected when she told him, while she bustled about preparing fresh coffee and toast for him, that when Thomas, at seven o'clock, had gone to the barn to "hitch up" he had found that the double sleigh, the pair, and--Austin had all mysteriously vanished.

"Austin always was a dreadful tease," she ended, "but I can't help sayin' this is downright mean of him, when he knows how Thomas feels."

"My dear lady," said Mr. Stevens, cracking open the egg she had set before him with great care, "where are your eyes? What about Austin himself?"

Mrs. Gray set down the coffee-pot, looking at him in bewilderment. "What do you mean?" she asked. "I hope Austin is grateful to her now--an' that he'll *say* so. At first he didn't like her at all, an' he's never taken to her same as the rest of us have--seems to feel she's bossy an' meddlesome. Howard an' I have spoken of it a thousand times. He began by resenting everything she did, an' then got so he didn't even mention her name."

"Exactly. I've noticed that myself. I don't pretend to be an infallible judge of human nature, but mark my words, Austin has cared for my Sylvia since the first moment he ever set eyes on her. No man likes to feel that the woman he's in love with is doing everything for him and his family, and that he can't--as he sees it-- do anything in return. That's why he seems to resent her kindness, which I really think the rest of you have almost overestimated--if she's helped you in material ways, you've been her salvation in greater ways still. But there's still more to it than that: I think your son Austin has in him the makings of one of the finest men I ever knew, but he doesn't consider himself worthy of her. He'll try to conceal, and even to conquer, his feelings--just as long as he possibly can. I suppose he believes that'll be always. Of course, it won't. But naturally he can't bear to talk about her. Thomas has fallen in love with her face--which is pretty--and her manner--which is charm-ing--after the manner of most men. But Austin has fallen in love with her mind-- which is brilliant--and her soul--which, in spite of some little superficial faults that I believe he himself will unconsciously teach her to overcome, is beautiful--after the manner of very few men--and those men love but once, deeply and forever. And so, my dear Mrs. Gray, tease Thomas all you like, for Sylvia will refuse Thomas when he asks for her, and he will be engaged to another girl within a year; but she will run away from Austin before he brings himself to tell her how he feels--and it will be many a long day before his heart is light again."

CHAPTER VIII

I fairly dread to have Christmas come for one reason," had said Mrs. Gray to her husband beforehand.

"Why? I thought you were counting the days!"

"So I am. But I hate to think of all the presents Sylvia's likely to load us down with. Seems as if she'd done enough. I don't want to be beholden to her for any more."

"Don't worry, Mary. Sylvia's got good sense, and delicate feelings as well as an almighty generous little heart. She'll be the first to think how we'd feel, herself."

Mr. Gray was right. When Christmas came there was a simple, inexpensive trinket for each of the girls, and slightly costlier ones for the bride and Mrs. Gray; little pocket calendars, all just alike, for the men; that was all. Mr. Stevens had taken pleasure in bringing great baskets of candy, adorned with elaborate bows of ribbon, and bunches of violets as big as their heads, to all the "children," a fine plant to Mrs. Gray, and books to Howard and his sons; and Austin's suit-case bulged with all sorts of little treasures, which tumbled out from between his clothes in the most unexpected places, as he unpacked it in the living-room, to the great delight of them all.

"Here's a dress-length of gray silk from Venice for mother," he said, tossing the shimmering bundle into her lap; "I want her to have it made up to wear at Sally's wedding. And here's lace for Sadie and Sally both--the bride and the bride-to-be. Nothing much for the rest of you"--and out came strings of corals and beads, handkerchiefs and photographs, silk stockings and filagree work, until the floor was strewn with pretty things. After all the presents were distributed, it was time to begin to get dinner, and to decorate the great table laid for sixteen. There was a turkey, of course, and a huge chicken pie as well, not to mention mince pies and squash pies and apple pies, a plum pudding and vanilla ice-cream; angel cakes and fruit cakes and chocolate cakes; coffee and cider and blackberry cordial; and after they had all eaten until they could not hold another mouthful, and had "rested up" a little, Sylvia played while they danced the Virginia Reel, Mr. Stevens leading off with Mrs. Gray, and Mr. Gray with Sadie. And finally they all gathered around the piano and sang the good old carols, until it was time for the Elliotts to go home, and for Ruth to carry the sleepy babies up to bed.

Since early fall it had been Sylvia's custom to sit with the family for a time after the early supper was over, and the "dishes done up"; then she went to her own parlor, lighted her open fire, and sat down by herself to read or write letters. But she always left her door wide open, and it was understood that any one who wished to come to her was welcome. Austin was the last to start to bed on Christmas night, and seeing Sylvia still at her desk as he passed her room, he stopped and asked:

"Is it too late, or are you too tired and busy to let me come in for a few minutes?"

She glanced at the clock, smiling. "It isn't very late, I'm not a bit tired, and in a minute I shan't be too busy; I've been working over some stupid documents that I was bound to get through with to-night, but I'm all done now. Throw that rubbish into the fire for me, will you?" she continued, pointing to a pile of torn-up letters and printed matter, "and draw up two chairs in front of the fire. I'll join you in a minute."

He obeyed, then stood watching her as she straightened out her silver desk fixtures, gravely putting everything in perfect order before she turned to him.

"What a beau cavalier you have become," she said, smiling again, as he drew back to let her pass in front of him, and turned her chair to an angle at which the fire could not scorch her face; "what's become of the old Austin? I can't seem to find him at all!"

"Oh, I left him in the woods the night of the fire, I hope," returned Austin, laughing, "while you were asleep. I'm sure neither you nor any one else wants him back."

Sylvia settled herself comfortably, and smoothed out the folds of her dull-black silk dress. "Wouldn't you like to smoke?" she asked; "it's an awfully comfortable feeling--to watch a man smoking, in front of an open fire!"

"I'd love to, if you're sure you don't mind. I don't want to make the air in here heavy--for I suppose you've got to sleep here on this sofa, having allowed yourself to be turned out of your good bed."

She laughed. "I'm so small that I can curl up and sleep on almost anything, like a kitten," she said. "And it's fine to think of being able to give my room to James and Sadie--they're so nice, and so happy together. I can open the windows wide for a few minutes after you've gone, and there won't be a trace of tobacco smoke left. If there were, I shouldn't mind it. Now, what is it, Austin?"

"I want to talk. I haven't seen you a single minute alone. And though the others are all interested, it isn't like telling things to a person who's done all the wonderful things and seen all the wonderful places that I just have. I've simply got to let loose on some one."

"Of course, you have. I thought that was it. Talk away, but not too loud. We mustn't disturb the others, who are all trying to go to sleep by this time. Tell me--which of the Italian cities did you like best--Rome--or Florence--or Naples?"

"Will you think me awfully queer if I say none of them, but after Venice, the little ones, like Assisi, Perugia, and Sienna. I'm so glad we took the time for them. Oh, *Sylvia*--" And he was off. The little clock on the mantel struck several times, unnoticed by either of them, and it was after one, when, glancing inadvertently at it, Austin sprang to his feet, apologizing for having kept her awake so long, and hastily bade her good-night.

"May I come again some evening and talk more?" he asked, with his hand on the door-handle, "or have I bored and tired you to death? You're a wonderful listener."

"Come as often as you like--I've been learning things, too, that I want to tell you about."

"For instance?"

"Oh, how to cook and sweep and sew--and how to be well and happy and at peace," she added in a lower voice. Then, speaking lightly again, "We'll try to keep up that French you've worked so hard at, together--I'm dreadfully out of practice, myself--and read some of Browning's Italian poems, if you would care to. Good-night, and again, Merry Christmas."

He left her, almost in a daze of excitement and happiness; and mounted the stairs, turning over everything that had been said and done during the two hours since he entered her room. As he reached the top, a sudden suspicion shot through him. He stopped short, almost breathlessly, then stood for several moments as if uncertain what to do, the suspicion gaining ground with every second; then suddenly, unable to bear the suspense it had created, ran down the stairs again. Sylvia's door was closed; he knocked.

"All right, just a minute," came the ready answer. A minute later the door was thrown open, and Sylvia stood in it, wrapped in a white satin dressing-gown edged with soft fur, her dark hair falling over her shoulders, her neck and arms bare. She drew back, the quick red color flooding her cheeks.

"*Austin!*" she exclaimed; "I never thought of your coming back--I supposed, of course, it was one of the girls. I can't--you mustn't--" But Sylvia was too much mistress of herself and woman of the world to remain embarrassed long in any situation. She recovered herself before Austin did.

"What has happened?" she asked quickly; "is any one ill?"

"No--Sylvia--what were those papers you gave me to burn?"

"Waste--rubbish. Go to bed, Austin, and don't frighten me out of my wits again by coming and asking me silly questions."

"What kind of waste paper? Please be a little more explicit."

"How did you happen to come back to ask me such a thing--what made you think of it?"

"I don't know--I just did. Tell me instantly, please."

"Don't dictate to me--the last time you did you were sorry."

"Yes--and you were sorry that you didn't listen to me, weren't you?"

"No!" she cried, "I wasn't--not in the end. If I hadn't gone out to ride that day, you never would have gone to Europe--and come back the man you have!"

She turned away from him, her eyes full of tears, her voice shaking. He was quite at a loss to understand her emotion, almost too excited himself to notice it; but he could not help being conscious of the tensity of the moment. He spoke more gently.

"Sylvia--don't think me presuming--I don't mean it that way; and you and I mustn't quarrel again. But I believe I have a right to ask what that document you gave me to burn up was. If you'll give me your word of honor that I haven't--I can only beg your forgiveness for having intruded upon you, and for my rudeness in speaking as I did."

She turned again slowly, and faced him. He wondered if it was the unshed tears that made her eyes so soft.

"You have a right," she said, "and *I* shouldn't have spoken as I did. You were fair, and I wasn't, as usual. I'll tell you. And will you promise me just to--to give this little slip of paper to your father--and never refer to the matter again, or let him?"

"I promise."

"Well, then," she went on hurriedly, "about a month ago I bought the mortgage on this farm. It seemed to me the only thing that stood in the way of your prosperity now--it hung around your father's neck like a millstone--just the thought that he couldn't feel that this wonderful old place was wholly his, the last years of his life, and that he couldn't leave it intact for you and Thomas and your children after you when he died. So I made up my mind it should be destroyed to-day, as my real Christmas present to you all. The transfer papers were all properly made out and recorded--this little memorandum will show you when and where. But Hiram Hutt's title to the property, and mine--and all the correspondence about them--are in that fireplace. That burden was too heavy for your father to carry--thank God, I've been the one to help lift it!"

In the moment of electrified silence that followed, Sylvia misinterpreted Austin's silence, just as he had failed to understand her tears. She came nearer to him, holding out her hands.

"Please don't be angry," she whispered; "I'll never give any of you anything again, if you don't want me to. I know you don't want--and you don't need--charity; but you did need and want--some one to help just a little--when things had been going badly with you for so long that it seemed as if they never could go right again. You'd lost your grip because there didn't seem to be anything to hang on to! It's meant new courage and hope and *life* to me to be able to stay here--I'd lost my grip, too. I don't think I could have held on much longer--to my *reason* even--if I hadn't had this respite. If I can accept all that from you, can't you accept the clear title to a few acres from me? Austin--don't stand there looking at me like that--tell me I haven't presumed too far."

"What made you think I was angry?" he said hoarsely. "Do men dare to be angry with angels sent from Heaven?" He took the little slip of paper which she still held in her extended hand. "I thought you had done something like this--that was why you made me burn the papers myself--in the name of my father--and of my children--God bless you." Without taking his eyes off her face, he drew a tiny box from his pocket. "Sylvia--would you take a present from *me*?"

"Why, yes. What--"

"It isn't really a present at all, of course, for it was bought with your money, and perhaps you won't like it, for I've noticed you never wear any jewelry. But I couldn't bear to come home without a single thing for you--and this represents--what you've been to me."

As he spoke, he slipped into her hand a delicate chain of gold, on which hung a tiny star; she turned it over two or three times without speaking, and her eyes filled with tears again. Then she said:

"It *is* a present, for this means you travelled third-class, and stayed at cheap hotels, and went without your lunches--or you couldn't have bought it. You had only enough money for the trip we originally planned, without those six weeks in Italy. I'll wear *this* piece of jewelry--and it will represent what *you've* been to *me*, in my mind. Will you put it on yourself?"

She held it towards him, bending forward, her head down. It seemed to Austin that her loveliness was like the fragrance of a flower. Involuntarily, the hands which clasped the little chain around her white throat, touching the warm, soft skin, fell to her shoulders, and drew her closer.

The swift and terrible change that went over Sylvia's face sent a thrust of horror through him. She shut her eyes, and shrank away, trembling all over, her face grown ashy white. Instantly he realized that the gesture must have replied to her some ghastly experience in the past; that perhaps she had more than once been tricked into an embrace by a gift; that a man's love had meant but one thing to her, and that she now thought herself face to face with that thing again, from one whom she had helped and trusted. For an instant the grief with which this realization filled him, the fresh compassion for all she had suffered, the renewed love for all her goodness, were too much for him. He tried to speak, to take away his hands, to leave her. He seemed to be powerless. Then, blessedly, the realization of what he should do came to him.

"Open your eyes, Sylvia," he commanded.

Too startled to disobey, she did so. He looked into them for a full minute, smiling, and shook his head.

"You did not understand, dear lady," he said. And dropping on his knees before her, he took her hands, laid them against his cheek for a minute, touched them with his lips, and left her.

CHAPTER IX

Uncle Mat made a determined effort to persuade Sylvia to return to New York with him; and though he was not successful, he was not altogether discouraged by her reply.

"I *have* been thinking of it," she said, "but I promised Mrs. Gray I'd stay here through the winter, and she'd be hurt and disappointed now if I didn't; besides, I don't feel quite ready for New York myself yet. I realize that I've remained--nearly long enough--and as soon as the warm weather comes, I'm going to have my own little house remodelled and put in order, and move there for the summer. It'll be such fun--just like doll's housekeeping! Then in the fall--I wont promise--but perhaps if you still want me, I'll come to you, at least until I decide what to do next."

"Come now for a visit, if you won't for the rest of the winter."

"Not yet; by spring I'm afraid I'll have to have some new clothes--I've had nothing since I came here except a fur coat, which arrived by parcel post! Sally wants to go away in the Easter vacation, and if you can squeeze us both into your little guest-room, perhaps we'll come together then."

"You're determined to have some sort of a bodyguard in the shape of your new friends to protect you from your old ones?"

"Not quite that. I'll come alone if you prefer it," said Sylvia quickly.

"No, no, my dear; I should be glad to have Sally. How about Austin, too? He could sleep on the living-room sofa, you know, and that would make four of us to go about together, which is always a pleasant number. Thomas would be home at that time, and Austin could probably leave more easily than at any other."

"Ask him by all means. I think he would be glad to go."

Austin was accordingly invited, and accepted with enthusiasm. Uncle Mat found him in the barn, where he was separating cream with the new electric separator, but he nodded, with a smile which showed all his white teeth, as his voice could not be heard above the noise of the machine.

"Indeed, I will," he said heartily, when the current was switched off again. "How unfortunate that Easter comes so late this year--but that will give us all the longer to look forward to it in! I hate to have you go back, Mr. Stevens, but I suppose the inevitable call of the siren city is too much for your easily tempted nature!"

Mr. Stevens laughed, and assented. "How that boy has changed!" he said to himself as he walked back to the house. "He fairly radiates enthusiasm and wholesomeness. Well, I'm sorry for him. I wish Sylvia would leave now instead of in the spring, in spite of her promises and scruples and what-not. And I wish, darn it all, that she were as easy to read as he is."

Austin's existence, just at that time, seemed even more rose-colored than Uncle Mat could suspect. The day after Christmas he pondered for a long time on the events of the night before, and gave some very anxious thought to his future line of conduct. At first he decided that it would be best to avoid Sylvia altogether, and thus show her that she had nothing to dread from him, for her sudden fear had been very hard to bear; but before night another and wiser course presented itself to him--the idea of going on exactly as if nothing had happened that was in the least extraordinary, and prove to her that he was to be trusted. Accordingly, assuming a calmness which he was very far from feeling, he stopped at her door again before going upstairs, saying cheerfully:

"Tell me to go away if you want to; if not, I've come for my first French lesson."

Sylvia looked up with a smile from the book she was reading. "Entrez, monsieur," she said gayly; "avez-vous apporte votre livre, votre cahier, et votre plume? Comment va l'oncle de votre ami? Le chat de votre mere, est-il noir?"

Austin burst out laughing at her mimicry of the typical conversation in a beginner's grammar, and she joined him. The critical moment had passed. He saw that he was welcome, that he had risen and not fallen in her regard, though he was far from guessing how much, and opening his book, drew another chair near the fire and sat down beside her.

"You must have some romances as well as this dry stuff," she said, when he had pegged away at Chardenal for over an hour. "We'll read Dumas together, begin-ning with the Valois romances, and going straight along in the proper order. You'll learn a lot of history, as well as considerable French. Some of it is rather indiscreet but--"

"Which of us do you think it is most likely to shock?" he asked, with such an expression of mock-alarm that they both burst out laughing again; and when they had sobered down, "Now may we have some Browning, please?"

So Sylvia reached for a volume from her shelf, and began to read aloud, while Austin smoked; she read extremely well, and she loved it. She went from "The Last Duchess" to "The Statue and the Bust," from "Fra Filippo Lippi" to "Andrea del Sarto." And Austin sat before the fire, smoking and listening, until the little clock again roused them to consciousness by striking twelve.

"This will never do!" he exclaimed, jumping up. "I must have regular hours, like any schoolboy. What do you say to Monday, Wednesday, and Friday evenings, from seven-thirty to ten? The other nights I'll bend my energies to preparing my lessons."

"A capital idea. Good-night, Austin."

"Good-night, Sylvia."

There were, however, no more French lessons that week. The next evening twenty young people went off together in sleighs, got their supper at White Water, danced there until midnight, and did not reach home until three in the morning. The following night there was a "show" in Wallacetown, and although they had all declared at their respective breakfast-tables--for breakfast is served anywhere from five-thirty to six-thirty in Hamstead, Vermont--that nothing would keep them out of bed after supper *that* night, off they all went again. A "ball" followed the "show," and the memory of the first sleigh-ride proved so agreeable that another was under-taken. And finally, on New Year's Eve the Grays themselves gave a party, opening wide the doors of the fine old house for the first time in many years. Sylvia played for the others to dance on this occasion, as she had done at Christmas, but in the rest of the merry-making she naturally could take no part. Austin, however, proved the most enthusiastic reveller of all, put through his work like chain lightning, and was out and off before the plodding Thomas had fairly begun. Manlike, it did not occur to him to give up any of these festivities because Sylvia could not join in them. For years he had hungered and thirsted, as most boys do, for "a good time"--and done so in vain. For years his work had seemed so endless and yet so futile--for what was it all leading to?--that it had been heartlessly and hopelessly done, and when it was finished, it had left him so weary that he had no spirit for anything else much of the time. Now the old order had, indeed, changed, yielding place to new. Good looks, good health, and a good mind he had always possessed, but they had availed him little, as they have many another person, until good courage and high ideals had been added to them. He scarcely saw Sylvia for several days, and did not even realize it, they seemed so full and so delightful; then coming out of the house early one afternoon intending to go to the barn to do some little odd jobs of cleaning up, he met her, coming towards him on snowshoes, her cheeks glowing, and her eyes sparkling. She waved her hand and hurried towards him.

"Oh, *Austin*! Are you awfully busy?"

"No, not at all. Why?"

"I've just been over to my house, for the first time--you know in the fall, I couldn't walk, and then I lost the key, and--well, one thing after another has kept me away--lately the deep snow. But these last few days I got to thinking about it--you've all been gone so much I've been alone, you see--so I decided to try getting there on snowshoes--just think of having a house that's so quiet that there isn't even a *road* to it any more! It was quite a tramp, but I made it and went in, and, oh! it's so *wonderful*--so exactly like what I hoped it was going to be--that I hurried back to see if you wouldn't come and see it too, and let me tell you everything I'm planning to do to it?"

She stopped, entirely out of breath. In a flash, Austin realized, first, that she had been lonely and neglected in the midst of the good times that all the others had been having; realized, too, that he had never before seen her so full of vitality and enthusiasm; and then, that, without being even conscious of it, she had come instinctively to him to share her new-found joy, while he had almost forgotten her in his. He was not sufficiently versed in the study of human nature to know that it has always been thus with men and women, since Eve tried to share her apple with Adam and only got blamed for her pains. Austin blamed himself, bitterly and resentfully, and decided afresh that he was the most utterly ungrateful and unworthy of men. His reflections made him slow in answering.

"Don't you *want* to come?"

"Of course I want to come! I was just thinking--wait a second, I'll get my snow-shoes."

"I'm going to tear down a partition," she went on excitedly as they ploughed through the snow together, "and have one big living-room on the left of the front door; on the right of it a big bedroom--I've always *pined* for a downstairs bed-room--I don't know why, but I never had one till I came to your house--with a bathroom and dressing-room behind it; the dining-room and kitchen will be in the ell. I'm sure I can make that unfinished attic into three more bedrooms, and another bathroom, but I want to see what you think. I'm going to have a great deep piazza all around it, and a flower-garden--and--"

She could hardly wait to get there. Her enthusiasm was contagious. Austin soon found himself making suggestions, helping her in her plans. They went through every nook and corner of the tiny cottage; he had not dreamed that it possessed the possibilities that Sylvia immediately found in it. They stayed a long time, and walked home over fields of snow which the sinking sun was turning rosy in its glowing light. That evening Austin came for his lesson again.

By the second of January, the last of the visitors had gone, and the old Gray place was restored to the order and quiet which had reigned before the holidays be-gan. Mrs. Gray was lonely, but her mind was at ease. She had been watching Austin closely, and it seemed quite clear to her that Uncle Mat was mistaken about him. The idea that her favorite son was going to be made unhappy was quickly dismissed; and in her rejoicing over the first payment on their debt at the bank, and in the new position of importance and consequence which her husband was beginning to occupy in the neighborhood, it was soon completely forgotten. The succeed-ing months seemed to prove her right; and the all-absorbing interest in the family was Mr. Gray's election to the Presidency of the Cooperative Creamery Association of Hamstead, and his probable chances of being nominated as First Selectman--in place of Silas Jones, recently deceased--at March Town Meeting.

CHAPTER X

Wallacetown, the railroad centre which lay five miles south of Hamstead across the Connecticut River, was generally regarded by the agricultural community in its vicinity as a den of iniquity. This opinion was not deserved. Wallacetown was progressive and prosperous; its high school ranked with the best in the State, its shops were excellent, its buildings, both public and private, neat and attractive. There were several reasons, however, for the "slams" which its neighbors gave it. Its population, instead of being composed largely of farmers, the sons, grandsons, and great-grandsons of the "old families" who had first settled the valley, was made up of railway employees and officials, and of merchants who had come there at a later date. Close team-work between them and the dwellers in Hamstead, White Water, and other villages near at hand, would have worked out for the advantage of both. But unfortunately they did not realize this. Wallacetown was also the only town in the vicinity where a man "could raise a thirst" as Austin put it, Vermont being "dry," and New Hampshire, at this time, "local option." Probably, from the earliest era, young men have been thirsty, and their parents have bemoaned the fact. It is not hard to imagine Eve wringing her hands over Cain and Abel when they first sampled generously the beverage they had made from the purple grapes which grew so plentifully near the Garden of Eden. Wallacetown also offered "balls," not occasionally, but two or three times a week. The Elks Hall, the Opera House, and even the Parish House were constantly being thrown open, and a local orchestra flourished. These "balls" were usually quite as innocent as those that took place in larger cities, under more elegant and exclusive surroundings; but the stricter Methodists and Congregationalists of the countryside did not believe in dancing at all, especially when there might be a "ginger-ale high-ball" or a glass of ale connected with it. Besides, there were two poolrooms and a wide street paved with asphalt, and brilliantly lighted down both sides. Trains ran--and stopped--by night as well as by day, and Sundays as well as week-days. In short, Wallacetown was up-to-date. That alone, in the eyes of Hamstead, was enough to condemn it. And when an enterprising citizen opened a Moving-Picture Palace, and promptly made an enormous success of it, Mrs. Elliott could no longer restrain herself.

"It's something scandalous," she declared, "to see the boys an' girls who would be goin' to Christian Endeavor or Epworth League if they'd ben brought up right, crowdin' 'round the entrance doors lookin' at the posters, an' payin' out good money that ought to go into the missionary boxes for the heathen in the Sandwich Islands, to go an' see filums of wimmen without half enough clothes on. We read in the **Wallacetown Bugle** that there was goin' to be a picture called 'The Serpent of the Nile' an' Joe an' I thought we could risk that, it sounded kinder geographical an' instructive. Of course we went mostly to see the new buildin' an' who else would be there, anyway. But land! the serpent was a girl dressed in the main in beads an' a pleasant smile. She loafed around on hard-lookin' sofas that was set right out in the open air, an' seemed to have more beaux than wimmen-friends. I'm always suspicious of that kind of a woman. I wanted to leave right away, as soon as I see what it was goin' to be like, but Joe wouldn't. He wanted to set right there until it was over. He seemed to feel afraid some one might see us comin' out, an' that maybe we better stay until the very end, so's we wouldn't be noticed, slippin' out with the crowd.-- Have you took cold, Sylvia? You seem to have a real bad cough."

Sylvia, who had been sewing peacefully beside the sunny kitchen window filled with geraniums, rose hastily, and left Mrs. Gray alone with her friend. Having gained the hall in safety, she sank down on the stairs, and laughed until the tears rolled down her cheeks. And here Austin, coming in a moment later, found her.

"What on earth--?" he began, and then, without even pursuing his question, sat down beside her and joined in her laugh. "What would you do?" he said at last, when some semblance of order had been restored, "without Mrs. Elliott? Considering the quiet life you lead, you must be simply pining for amusement."

"I am," said Sylvia. "Austin--let's go to the movies in Wallacetown to-morrow night."

Austin, suddenly grave, shook his head. "Shows" in Wallacetown were associated in his mind with a period in his life when he had very nearly broken his mother's heart, and which he had now put definitely behind him. The idea of connecting Sylvia, even in the most remote way, with that period, was abhorrent to him.

"Why not?" she asked defiantly.

"Well, for one thing, the roads are awful. This combination in March of melting snow and mud is worse than anything I know of--ruts and holes and slush. It would take us over an hour to get there."

"And three to get back, I suppose," said Sylvia pertly; "we could go in my motor."

"I haven't taken out the new license for this year yet. Besides, though I believe the movies are very good for a place the size of Wallacetown, of course, they can't be equal to what you'll be seeing in New York pretty soon. Wait and go there."

"I won't!" said Sylvia, springing up. "I'll get Thomas to take me. You always have some excuse when I want you to do anything. Why don't you say right out that you don't care to go?"

Sylvia expected denials and protestations. She was disappointed. Thomas had arrived home for his long spring vacation a few days before, and had promptly begun to follow Sylvia about like a shadow. Austin, who never sought her out except for his French lessons, had endeavored to remonstrate with his younger brother. The boy flared up, with such unusual and unreasonable anger, that Austin had decided it was wiser not to try to spare him any longer, but to let "him make a fool of himself and have it over with." When Sylvia made her tart speech, it suddenly flashed through his mind that a ten-mile ride, without possibility of interruption, was an excellent opportunity for this. He therefore grinned so cheerfully that Sylvia was more puzzled and piqued than ever.

"I'm sure Thomas would be tickled to death to take you," he said enthusiastically; "I'll get the car registered the first thing in the morning, and he can spend the afternoon washing and oiling it. It really needs a pretty thorough going-over. It'll do my heart good to see him in his old clothes for once. He seems to have entirely overlooked the fact that he was to spend this vacation being pretty useful on the farm, and not sighing at your heels dressed in the height of fashion as he understands it. He's wearing out the mat in front of the bureau, he stands there so much, and I've hardly had a chance for a shave or a tub since he got here. He locks himself in the bathroom and spends hours manicuring his nails and putting bay-rum on his hair. He--All right, I won't if you say so! But, Sylvia, you ought to make a real spree of this, and go in to the drug-store for an ice-cream soda after the show."

"Is that the usual thing?"

"It's the most usual thing that I should recommend to you. Of course, there are others--

"Austin, you are really getting to be the limit. Go tell Thomas I want him."

"With pleasure. I haven't," murmured Austin, "had a chance to tell him that so far. He's never been far enough off--except when he was getting ready to come. That's probably what he's doing now. I'll go upstairs and see."

Austin had guessed right. Thomas stood in front of the mirror, shining with cleanliness, knotting a red silk tie. He had reached that stage in a young man's life when clothes were temporarily of supreme importance. Gone was the shy and shabby ploughboy of a year before. This self-assertive young gentleman was clad in a checked suit in which green was a predominating color, a black-and-white striped shirt, and chocolate-colored shoes. His hair, still dripping with moisture, was brushed straight back from his forehead and the smell of perfumed soap hung heavy about him.

"Hullo," he said, eyeing his brother's intrusion with disfavor, "how dirty you are!"

Austin, whose khaki and corduroy garments made him look more than ever like a splendid bronze statue, nodded cheerfully.

"I know. But some one's got to work. We can't have two lilies of the field on the same farm.--Sylvia wants to speak to you."

"Do you know why?" asked Thomas, promptly displaying more dispatch.

"I think she intends to suggest that you should take her to the moving-pictures in Wallacetown to-morrow night. She doesn't get much amusement here, and now that she's feeling so much stronger again, I think she rather craves it."

"Of course she does," said Thomas, "and if you weren't the most selfish, pig-headed, blind bat that ever flew, you'd have seen that she got it, long before this. Where is she?"

It seemed to the impatient Thomas that the next evening would never arrive. All night, and all the next day, he planned for it exultantly. He was to have the chance which the ungrateful Austin had seen fit to cast away. He would show Sylvia how much he appreciated it. Through the long afternoon, suddenly grown unseasonably warm, he toiled on the motor until it was spick and span from top to bottom and from end to end. He was careful to start his labors early enough to allow a full hour to dress before supper, cautioned his mother a dozen times to be sure there was enough hot water left in the boiler for a deep bath, and laid out fresh and gorgeous garments on the bed before he began his ablutions. He was amazed to find, when he came downstairs, that Sylvia, who had tramped over to the brick cottage that afternoon, was still in the short muddy skirt and woolly sweater that she had worn then, poking around in the yard testing the earth for possibilities of early gardening.

"The frost has come out a good deal to-day," she said, wiping grimy little hands on an equally grimy handkerchief; "I expect the mud will be awful these next few weeks, but I can get in sweet peas and ever-bearing strawberries pretty soon now."

"We'll have to start right after supper," said Thomas, by way of a delicate hint. He did not feel that it was proper for him to suggest to Sylvia that her present costume was scarcely suitable to wear if she were to accompany him to a "show."

"Start?" Sylvia looked puzzled. Then she remembered that in a moment of pique with Austin she had arranged to go to Wallacetown with Thomas. As she thought it over, it appealed to her less and less. "You mean to Wallacetown? I'm afraid I'd forgotten all about it, I've been so busy to-day. I wonder if we'd better try it? The warmth to-day won't have improved the roads any, and they were pretty bad before."

Thomas felt as if he should choke. That she should treat so casually the evening towards which he had been counting the moments for twenty-four hours seemed almost unbearable. He strove, however, to maintain his dignified composure.

"Just as you say, of course," he replied with hurt coolness.

Sylvia glanced at him covertly, and the corners of her mouth twitched.

"I suppose we may as well try it," she said. "Do you suppose some of the others would like to come with us? There's plenty of room for everybody."

Again Thomas choked. This was the last thing that he desired. How was he to disclose to Sylvia the wonderful secret that he adored her with the whole family sitting on the back seat?

"I don't believe they could get ready now," he said; "they didn't know you expected them to go, you see, and there's really awfully little time." He took out his watch.

Sylvia fled. Twenty minutes later she appeared at the supper-table, clad in a soft black lace dress, slightly low in the neck, her arms only partially concealed by transparent, flowing sleeves, her waving hair coiled about her head like a crown. She had on no jewels--only the little star that Austin had given her--and the gown was the sort of demi-toilette which two years before she would have considered hardly elaborate enough for dinner alone in her own house. To the Grays, however, her costume represented the zenith of elegance, and Thomas began vaguely to feel that there was something the matter with his own appearance.

"Ought I to have put on my dress-suit?" he asked Austin in a stage-whisper, as Sylvia left the room to get her wraps.

The mere thought of a dress-suit at the Wallacetown "movies" was comic to the last degree, but the merciless Austin jumped at the suggestion.

"Why don't you? You won't be very late if you change quickly. You won't need to take another bath, will you? I'll bring round the car."

He showed himself, indeed, all that was helpful and amiable. He not only brought around the car, he went up and helped Thomas with stubborn studs and a refractory tie. He stood respectfully aside to let his brother wrap Sylvia's coat around her, and held open the door of the car.

"Have a good time!" he shouted after them, as they plunged out of sight, somewhat jerkily, for Thomas, who had not driven a great deal, was not a master of gear-shifting. His mother looked at him anxiously.

"I can't help feelin' you're up to some deviltry, Austin," she said uneasily, "though I don't know just what 'tis. I'm kinder nervous about this plan of them goin' off to Wallacetown."

"I'm not," said Austin with a wicked grin, and took out his French dictionary.

The first part of the evening, however, seemed to indicate that Mrs. Gray's fears were groundless. Sylvia and Thomas reached the Moving-Picture Palace without mishap, though they had left the Homestead so late owing to the latter's change of attire and the slow rate at which the mud and his lack of skill had obliged them to ride, that the audience was already assembled, and "The Terror of the Plains," a stirring tale of an imaginary West, was in full progress before they were seated. Thomas's dress-suit did not fail to attract immediate attention and equally immediate remarks, and Sylvia, who hated to be conspicuous, felt her cheeks beginning to burn. But--more sincerely than Mr. Elliott--she decided that it was better to wait until the entertainment was over than to attract further notice by going out at once. Thomas, less sensitive than she, enjoyed himself thoroughly.

"We have splendid pictures in Burlington," he announced, "but this is good for a place of this size, isn't it, Sylvia?"

"Yes. Don't talk so loudly."

"I can't talk any softer and have you hear unless I put my head up closer. Can I?"

"Of course, you may not. Don't be so silly."

"I didn't mean to be fresh. You're not cross, are you, Sylvia?"

It seemed to her as if the "show" would never end. Chagrin and resentment overcame her. What had possessed her to come to this hot, stuffy place with Thomas, instead of reading French in her peaceful, pleasant sitting-room with Austin? Why didn't Austin show more eagerness to be with her, anyway? She liked to be with him--ever and ever so much--didn't see half so much of him as she wanted to. There was no use beating about the bush. It was perfectly true. She was growing fonder of him, and more dependent on him, every day. And every other man she had ever known had been grateful for her least favor, while he--Her hurt pride seemed to stifle her. She was very close to tears. She was jerked back to composure by the happy voice of Thomas.

"My, but that was a thriller! Come on over to the drug-store, Sylvia, and have an ice-cream cone."

"I'm not hungry," said Sylvia, rising, "and it must be getting awfully late. I'd rather go straight home."

Thomas, though disappointed, saw no choice. But once off the brilliantly lighted "Main Street," and lumbering down the road towards Hamstead, he decided not to put off the great moment, for which he had been waiting, any longer. Wondering why his stomach seemed to be caving in so, he tactfully began.

"Did you know I was going to be twenty-one next month, Sylvia?" he asked.

"No," said Sylvia absently; "that is, I had forgotten. You seem more like eighteen to me."

This was a somewhat crushing beginning. But Thomas was not daunted.

"I suppose that is because I was older than most when I went to college," he said cheerfully, "but though you're a little bit older, I'm nearer your age than any of the others--much nearer than Austin. Had you ever thought of that?"

"No," said Sylvia again, still more absently. "Why should I? I feel about a thousand."

"Well, you *look* about sixteen! Honest, Sylvia, no one would guess you're a day over that, you're so pretty. Has any one ever told you how pretty you are?"

"Well, it has been mentioned," said Sylvia dryly, "but I have always thought that it was one of those things that was greatly overestimated."

"Why, it couldn't be! You're perfectly lovely! There isn't a girl in Burlington that can hold a candle to you. I've been going out, socially, a lot all winter, and I know. I've been to hops and whist-parties and church-suppers. The girls over there have made quite a little of me, Sylvia, but I've never--"

There was a deafening report. Thomas, cursing inwardly, interrupted himself.

"We must have had a blow-out," he said, bringing the car to a noisy stop. "Wait a second, while I get out and see."

It was all too true. A large nail had passed straight through one of the front tires. He stripped off his ulster, and the coat of his dress-suit, and turned up his immaculate trousers.

"You'll have to get up for a minute, while I get the tools from under the seat, Sylvia. I'm awfully sorry.--It's pretty dark, isn't it?--I never changed a tire but once before. Austin's always done that."

"Austin's always done almost everything," snapped Sylvia. Then, peering around to the back of the car, "Why don't *you do* something? What *is* the matter now?"

"The lock on the extra wheel's rusted--you see it hasn't been undone all winter. I can't get it off."

"Well, *smash* it, then! We can't stay here all night."

"I haven't got anything to smash it *with*. I must have forgotten to put part of the tools back when I cleaned the car."

"Oh, Thomas, you are the most *inefficient* boy about everything except farming that I ever saw! Let me see if I can't help."

She jumped out, her feet, clad in silk stockings and satin slippers, sinking into the mud as she did so. Together for fifteen minutes, rapidly growing hot and angry, they wrestled with the refractory lock. At the end of that time they were no nearer success than they had been in the beginning.

"We'll have to crawl home on a flat tire," she said at last disgustedly; "I hope we'll get there for breakfast."

Thomas had never seen her temper ruffled before. Her imperiousness was always sweet, and it was Heaven to be dictated to by her. The fact that he believed her to be comparing him in her mind to Austin did not help matters. Austin, as he knew very well, would have managed some way to get that tire changed. For some time they rode along in silence, the mud churning up on either side of the guards with every rod that they advanced. At last, realizing that his precious moments were slipping rapidly away, and that though, in Sylvia's present mood, it was hardly a favorable time to go on with his declaration, the morrow would be even less so, Thomas summoned up his courage once more.

"Is your back tired?" he asked. "It's awfully jolty, going over these ruts. I could steer all right with one hand, if you would let me put my other arm around you."

"You're not steering any too well as it is," remarked Sylvia tartly. "*Thomas*! What are you thinking of? Don't you touch me!--There, now you've done it!"

Thomas certainly had "done it." Sylvia, at his first movement, had slapped him in the face with no gentle tap. And Thomas, with only one hand on the wheel, and too amazed to keep his wits about him, had allowed the car to slide down the side of the road into the deep, muddy gutter, straight in front of the Elliotts' house.

Late as it was, a light was snapped on in the entrance without delay. Electricity had been installed here before any other place in the village had been blessed with it, for the owners never missed a chance of seeing anything, and Mrs. Elliott seemed to sleep with one eye and one ear open. She appeared now in the doorway, dressed in a long, gray flannel "wrapper," her hair securely fastened in metal clasps all about her head, against the "crimps" for the next day.

"Who is it?" she cried sharply--"and what do you want?"

Of all persons in the world, this was the last one whom either Sylvia or Thomas desired to see. Neither answered. Nothing dismayed, Mrs. Elliott advanced down the walk. Her carpet-slippers flapped as she came.

"Come on, Joe," she called over her shoulder to her less intrepid spouse. "Are you goin' to leave me alone to face these desperate drunkards, lurchin' around in the dead of night, an' makin' the road unsafe for doctors who might be out on some errand of mercy--they're the only *respectable* people who wouldn't be abed at this hour of the night. You better get right to the telephone, an' notify Jack Weston. He ain't much of a police officer, to be sure, but I guess he can deal with bums like these--too stewed to answer me, even!" Then, as she drew nearer, she gave a shriek that might well have been heard almost as far off as Wallacetown, "Land of mercy! It's Sylvia an' Thomas!"

Thomas cowered. No other word could express it. But Sylvia got out, slamming the door behind her.

"We've been to Wallacetown to a moving-picture show," she said with a dignity which she was very far from feeling, "and we've been unfortunate in having tire-trouble on the way home. And now we seem to be stuck in the mud. I had no idea the roads were in such a condition, or of course I shouldn't have gone. We can't possibly pry the motor up in this darkness, so I think we may as well leave it where it is, first as last until morning, and walk the rest of the way home. Come on, Thomas."

"I wouldn't ha' b'lieved," said Mrs. Elliott severely, "that you would ha' done such a thing. Prayer-meetin' night, too! Well, it's fortunate no one seen you but me an' Joe. If I was gossipy, like some, it would be all over town in no time, but you know I never open my lips. But, land sakes! here comes a *team*. Who can this be?"

Eagerly she peered out through the darkness. Then she turned again to the unfortunate pair.

"It's Austin in the carryall," she cried excitedly; "now, ain't that a piece of luck? You won't have to walk home, after all. Though what *he's* out for, either, at this hour--"

Austin reined in his horse. "Because I knew Sylvia and Thomas must have got into some difficulty," he said quietly. Considering the pitch at which it had been uttered, it had not been hard to overhear Mrs. Elliott's speech. "Pretty bad travelling, wasn't it? I'm sorry. Tires, too? Well, that was hard luck. But we'll be home in no time now, and of course the show was worth it. You didn't hurt your dress-suit any, did you, Thomas? I worried a little about that. You drive--I'll get in on the back seat with Sylvia, and make sure the robe's tucked around her all right. It seems to be coming off cold again, doesn't it? Good-night, Mrs. Elliott--thank you for your sympathy."

Conversation languished. Austin, unseen by the miserable Thomas on the front seat, and unreproved by the weary and chilly Sylvia, "tucked the robe around her" and then, apparently, forgot to take his arm away. Moreover, he searched in the darkness for her small, cold fingers, and gathered them into his free hand, which was warm and big and strong. As they neared the house, he spoke to her.

"The next time you want to go to 'a show' I guess I'd better take you myself, after all," he whispered. "You'll find a hot-water bag in your bed, and hot lemonade in the thermos bottle on the little table beside it. I put a small 'stick' in it--oh, just a twig! And I've kept the kitchen fire up. The water in the tank's almost boiling, if you happen to feel like a good tub--"

He helped her out, and held open the front door for her gravely. Then, closing it behind her, he turned to Thomas.

"You'd better run along, too," he said, with a slight drawl; "I'll put the horse up."

"Oh, go to hell!" sobbed Thomas.

CHAPTER XI

"So you refused Weston's offer of three hundred dollars for Frieda?"

"Yes, father. Do you think I was wrong?"

"Well, I don't know. That's a good deal of money, Austin."

"I know, but think what she cost to import, and the record she's making! I told him he might have two of the brand-new bull calves at seventy-five apiece."

"What did he say?"

"Jumped at the chance. He's coming *for* the calves, and **with** the cash early to-morrow morning. I said he might have a look at Dorothy, too. Peter thinks she isn't quite up to our standard, and I'm inclined to agree with him, though I imagine his opinion is based partly on the fact that she's a Jersey! If Weston will give three hundred for *her*, right on the spot, I think we'd better let her go."

"Did you do any other special business in Wallacetown?"

"I took ten dozen more eggs to Hassan's Grocery, and he paid me for the last two months. Thirty dollars. Pretty good, but we ought to do better yet, though, of course, we eat a great many ourselves. How's the tax assessing coming along? I suppose you've been out all day, too."

"Yes. I'm so green at it I find it rather hard work. It's hard luck that both of the listers should be sick just now, though in New Hampshire the selectmen always have to do the assessing. But I've had some funny experiences to-day. I found one woman terribly distressed because her husband wasn't at home. 'He waited 'round all yesterday afternoon for you, thinkin' you'd probably be here,' she said, 'but he's gone to White Water to-day.' 'Well,' I said, 'let's see if we can't get along just as well without him. Have you a horse?' 'Yes, but he's over age--he can't be taxed.' 'Any cows?' 'Just two heifers--they're too young.' 'Any money on deposit?' 'Lord, no!' 'Then there's only the poll-tax?' I suggested. 'Bless you, he's seventy-six years old--there ain't no poll-tax!' she rejoined. And the long and short of it was that they weren't taxable for a single thing!"

Austin laughed. "How much longer are you going to be at this, father?" he asked, as he turned to go away.

"All through April, I'm afraid. I'm sorry it makes things so much harder for you on the farm, Austin, but it means three dollars a day. I'm so glad Katherine and Edith could go on the high school trip to Washington--your mother had her first letter this noon. You'll want to read it--they're having a wonderful time. I'm trying to figure out whether we can possibly let Katherine go to Wellesley next year. She's got her heart just set on it, and Edith seems perfectly willing to stay at home, so we shan't be put to any extra expense for her."

"I guess when the time comes we can find a way to help Katherine if she helps herself as much as Thomas and Molly are doing. By the way, has it occurred to you that there may be some reason for Edith's sudden turn towards domesticity?"

"Why, no--what do you mean?"

"Peter."

"Peter!" echoed Mr. Gray, aghast; "why the child isn't seventeen yet, and he can't be more than a couple of years older!"

"I know. But such things do sometimes happen."

"You don't consider Peter a suitable match for one of your sisters?" went on the horrified father; "why, she's oceans above him."

"Any farther than Sylvia is above Thomas? You seem to be taking that rather hard."

For Thomas, in spite of Austin's warnings, and his chastening experience on the night of the expedition to the Moving-Picture Palace, had broken bounds again and openly declared himself. Sylvia, who already reproached herself for her ill-temper on that occasion, was very kind and very sweet, and had the tact and wisdom not to treat the matter as a joke; but she was as definite and firm in her "no" as she was considerate in the way she put it. Thomas was as usual quite unable to conceal his feelings, and his parents were grieving for him almost as much as he was for him-self, although they had never expected any other outcome to his first love-affair, and were somewhat amazed at his presumption.

"You never thought of this yourself," went on the bewildered parent, ignoring

Austin's last remark, feeling that his children were treating him most unfairly by indulging in so many affairs of the heart which could not possibly have a fortunate outcome. "*I* haven't noticed a thing, and I'm sure your mother hasn't, or she would have spoken about it to me. Why, Edith's hardly out of her cradle."

"It would take a pretty flexible cradle to hold Edith nowadays," returned Austin dryly; "she's running around all over the countryside, and she has more partners at a dance than all the other girls put together. She isn't as nice as Molly, or half so interesting as Katherine, but she has a little way with her that--well, I don't know just *what* it is, but I see the attraction myself. I thought I'd tell you so that if you didn't like it, we could try to scrimp a little harder, and send her off for a year or so, too--she never could get into college, but she might go to some school of Domestic Science. No--I didn't notice Peter's state of mind myself at first."

"Sylvia!" said his father sharply. "She didn't approve, of course."

"On the contrary, very highly. She says that the sooner a girl of Edith's type is married--to the right sort of a man, of course--the better, and I'm inclined to think that she's right. Then she pointed out that Peter had gone doggedly to school all winter, struggling with a foreign language, and enduring the gibes he gets from being in a class with boys much younger than himself, with very good grace. She mentioned how faithful and competent he was in his work, and how interested in it; asked if I had noticed the excellency of his handwriting, his accounts--and his manners! And finally she said that a boy who would promise his mother to go to church once a fortnight at least, and keep the promise, was doing pretty well."

"Speaking of church," said Mr. Gray uneasily, as if forced to agree with all Austin said, yet anxious to change the subject, "Mr. Jessup is calling. He comes pretty frequently."

"Yes--I had noticed *that* for myself! I don't think Sylvia particularly likes it."

"Then I imagine she can stop it without much outside help," said his father, somewhat ruefully. "Well, we must get to work, and not sit here talking all the rest of the afternoon--not that there's so very much afternoon left! What are you going to do next, Austin?"

"Change my clothes, and then start burning the rubbish-pile--there's a good moon, so I can finish it after the milking's done."

"That means you'll be up until midnight--and you were out in the barn at five!"

exclaimed Mr. Gray. "I don't see where you get all your energy."

"From ambition!" laughed Austin, starting away. "This is going to be the finest farm in the county again, if I have anything to do about it." As he entered the house, and went through the hall, he could hear voices in Sylvia's parlor, and though the door was ajar, he went past it, contrary to his custom. His father was right. If she did not like the minister's visits, she was quite competent to stop them without outside help. Was it possible-- *could* it be?--that she *did* like them? He flung off his business clothes and got into his overalls with a sort of savage haste--after all, what difference ought it to make to him whether she liked them or not? She was going away almost immediately, would inevitably marry some one before very long, Mr. Jessup at least held a dignified position and possessed a good education, and if she married him, she would come back to Hamstead, they could see her once in a while--Having tried to comfort himself with these cheering reflections, he started down the stairs, inwardly cursing. Then he heard something which made him stop short.

"Please go away," Sylvia was saying, in the low, penetrating voice he knew so well, "and I think it would be better if you didn't come any more. How dare you speak to me like that! And how can a clergyman so lose his sense of dignity as to behave like any common fortune-hunter?"

Austin pushed open the door without stopping to knock, and walked in.

"Good-afternoon, Mr. Jessup," he said coolly, "my father told me we were having the pleasure of a call from you. I'm just going out to milk--won't you come with me, and see the cattle? They're really a fine sight, tied up ready for the night."

Mr. Jessup picked up his hat, and Austin held the door open for him to pass out, leaving Sylvia standing, an erect, scornful little black figure, with very red cheeks, her angry eyes growing rapidly soft as she looked straight past the minister at Austin.

The results of Mr. Jessup's visit were several. The most immediate one was that Austin's work was so delayed by the interruption it received that it was nearly nine o'clock before he was able to start his bonfire. Thomas joined him, but after an hour declared he was too sleepy to work another minute, and strolled off to bed. Austin's next visitor was his father, who merely came to see how things were getting along and to say good-night. And finally, when he had settled down to a period of laborious solitude, he was amazed to see Sylvia open and shut the front door very quietly, and come towards him in the moonlight, carrying a white bundle so large that she could hardly manage it.

"For Heaven's sake!" he exclaimed, hurrying to help her, "you ought to have been asleep hours ago! What have you got here?"

"Something to add to your bonfire," she said savagely, and as he took the great package from her, the white wrapping fell open, showing the contents to be inky black. "All the crepe I own! I won't wear it another day! I've been respectful to death--even if I couldn't be to the dead--and to convention long enough. I've swathed myself in that stuff for nearly fifteen months! I won't be such a hypocrite as to wear it another day! And if Thomas--and--and--Mr. Jessup and--and everybody--are going to pester the life out of me, I might just as well be in New York as here. I'm glad I'm going away."

"No one else is going to pester you," said Austin quietly, "and they won't any more. But you'll have a good time in New York--I think it's fine that you're going." He tossed the bundle into the very midst of the burning pile, and tried to speak lightly, pretending not to notice the excitement of her manner and the undried tears on her flushed cheeks. "I think you're just right about that stuff, too. Will this mean all sorts of fluffy pink and blue things, like what Flora Little wears? I should think you would look great in them!"

"No--but it means lots and lots of pure white dresses and plain black suits and hats, without any crepe. Then in the fall, lavender, and gray, and so on."

"I see--a gradual improvement. Won't you sit down a few minutes? It's a wonderful night."

"Thank you. Austin--you and Sally will have to help me shop when I get to New York--Heaven knows what I can wear to travel down in."

Austin stopped raking, and flung himself down on the grass beside her. "Sylvia," he said quickly, "I'm awfully sorry, but I can't go."

"Can't go! Why not?" she exclaimed, with so much disappointment in her voice that he was amazed.

"Father's a selectman now, you know, and away all day just at this time on town business. There's too much farmwork for Thomas and Peter to manage alone. I didn't foresee this, of course, when I accepted your uncle's invitation. I can't tell you how much it means to me to give it up, but you must see that I've got to."

"Yes, I see," she said gravely, and sat silently for some minutes, fingering the frill on her sleeve. Then she went on: "Uncle Mat wants me to stay a month or six weeks with him, and I think I ought to, after. deserting him for so long. When I come back, my own little house will be ready for me, and it will be warm enough for me to move in there, so I think these last few days will be 'good-bye.' Your family has let me stay a year--the happiest year of all my life--and I know your mother loves me--almost as much as I love her--and hates to have me go. But all families are better off by themselves, and in one way I think I've stayed too long already."

"You mean Thomas?"

She nodded, her eyes full of tears. "I ought to have gone before it happened," she said penitently; "any woman with a grain of sense can usually see that--that sort of thing coming, and ward it off beforehand. But I didn't think he was quite so serious, or expect it quite so soon."

"The young donkey! To annoy you so!"

"*Annoy* me! Surely you don't think *Thomas* was thinking of the money?"

"Good Lord, no, it never entered his head! Neither did it enter his head what an unpardonable piece of presumption it was on his part to ask you to marry him. A great, ignorant, overgrown, farmer boy!"

"You are mistaken," said Sylvia quietly; "I do not love Thomas, but if I did, the answer would have had to be 'no' just the same. The presumption would be all on my part, if I allowed any clean, wholesome, honest boy, in a moment of passion, to throw away his life on a woman like me. Thomas must marry a girl, as fresh as he is himself--not a woman with a past like mine behind her."

For nearly a year Austin had exercised a good deal of self-control for a man little trained in that valuable quality. At Sylvia's speech it gave way suddenly, and without warning. Entirely forgetting his resolution never to touch her, he leaned forward, seizing her arm, and speaking vehemently.

"I wish you would get rid of your false, gloomy thoughts about yourself as easily as you have got rid of your false, gloomy clothing," he said, passionately. "The mother and husband who made your life what it was are both where they can never hurt you again. Your character they never did touch, except in the most superficial way. When you told me your story, that night in the woods, you tried to make me think that you did voluntarily--what you did. You lied to me. I thought so then. I know it now. You were flattered and bullied, cajoled and coerced--a girl scarcely older than my sister Edith, whom we consider a child, whose father is distressed to even think of her as marriageable. It is time to stop feeling repentance for sins you never committed, and to look at yourself sanely and happily--if you must be introspective at all. No braver, lovelier, purer woman ever lived, or one more obviously intended to be a wife and mother. The sooner you become both, the better."

There was a moment of tense silence. Sylvia made no effort to draw away from him; at last she asked, in a voice which was almost pleading in its quality:

"Is that what you think of me?"

Austin dropped his hand. "Good God, Sylvia!" he said hoarsely; "don't you know by this time what I think of you?"

"Then you mean--that you want me to marry you?"

"No, no, no!" he cried. "Why are you so bound to misunderstand and misjudge me? I beg you not to ride by yourself, and you tell me I am 'dictating.' I go for months without hearing from you for fear of annoying you, and you accuse me of 'indifference.' I bring you a gift as a vassal might have done to his liege lady--and you shrink away from me in terror. I try to show you what manner of woman you really are, and you believe that I am displaying the same presumption which I have just condemned in my own brother. Are you so warped and embittered by one experience--a horrible one, but, thank Heaven, quickly and safely over with!--that you cannot believe me when I tell you that the best part of a decent man's love is not passion, but reverence? His greatest desire, not possession, but protection? His ultimate aim, not gratification, but sacrifice?"

He bent over her. She was sitting quite motionless, her head bowed, her face hidden in her hands; she was trembling from head to foot. He put his arm around her.

"Don't!" he said, his voice breaking; "don't, Sylvia. I've been rough and violent--lost my grip on myself--but it's all over now--I give you my word of honor that it is. Please lift your head up, and tell me that you forgive me!" He waited until it seemed as if his very reason would leave him if she did not answer him; then at last she dropped her hands, and raised her head. The moon shone full on her upturned face, and the look that Austin saw there was not one of forgiveness, but of something so much greater that he caught his breath before she moved or spoke to him.

"Are you blind?" she whispered. "Can't you see how I have felt--since Christmas night, even if you couldn't long before that? Don't you know why I just couldn't go away? But I thought you didn't care for me--that you couldn't possibly have kept away from me so long if you did--that you thought I wasn't good enough--Oh, my dear, my dear--" She laid both hands on his shoulders.

The next instant she was in his arms, his lips against hers, all the sorrow and bitterness of their lives lost forever in the glory of their first kiss.

CHAPTER XII

When, two days later, Sylvia and Sally left for New York, none of the Grays had been told, much less had they suspected, what had happened. A certain new shyness, which Austin found very attractive, had come over Sylvia, and she seemed to wish to keep their engagement a secret for a time, and also to keep to her plan of going away, with the added reason that she now "wanted a chance to think things over."

"To think whether you really love me?" asked Austin gravely.

"Haven't I convinced you that I don't need to think that over any more?" she said, with a look and a blush that expressed so much that the conversation was near to being abruptly ended.

Austin controlled himself, however, and merely said:

"I'm going down to our little cemetery this afternoon to put it in good order for the spring; I know you've always said you didn't want to go there, but perhaps you'll feel differently now. All the Grays are buried there, and no one else, and in spite of all the other things we've neglected, we've kept that as it should be kept; and it's so peaceful and pretty--always shady in summer, when it's hot, and sheltered in winter, when it's cold! I thought you could take a blanket and a book, and sit and read while I worked. Afterwards we can walk over to your house if you like--you may want to give me some final directions about the work that's to be done there while you're gone."

"I'd love to go to the cemetery--or anywhere else, for that matter--with you," said Sylvia, "and afterwards--to *our* house. Perhaps you'll want to give some directions yourself!"

The tiny graveyard lay in the hollow of one of the wooded slopes which broke the great, undulating meadow which stretched from the Homestead to the river, a wall made of the stones picked up on the place around it, a plain granite shaft erected by the first Gray in the centre, and grouped about the shaft the quaint tablets of the century before, with old-fashioned names spelled in an old-fashioned manner, and with homely rhymes and trite sayings underneath; farther off, the newer gravestones, more ornate and less appealing. The elms were just beginning to bud, and the cold April wind whistled through them, but the pines were as green and sheltering as always, and Sylvia spread her blanket under one of them, and worked away at the sewing she had brought instead of a book, while Austin burned the grass and dug and pruned, whistling under his breath all the time. He stopped once to call her attention to a robin, the first they had seen that spring, and finally, when the sacred little place was in perfect order, came with a handful of trailing arbutus for her, and sat down beside her.

"I thought I remembered seeing some of this on the bank," he said; "it's always grown there--will you take it for your 'bouquet des fiancailles,' Sylvia? I remember how surprised we all were last year because you liked the little wild flowers best, and went around searching for them, when your rooms were full of carnations and hothouse roses. And because you used to go out to walk, just to see the sunsets. Do you still love sunsets, too?"

"Yes, more than ever. In the fall while you were gone, I used to go down to the river nearly every afternoon, and watch the color spread over the fields. There's something about a sunset in the late autumn that's unlike those at any other time of year--have you ever noticed? It's not rosy, but a deep, deep golden yellow--spreading over the dull, bare earth like the glory from the diadem of a saint--one of those gray Fathers of early Italy, for instance."

"I know what you mean--but they seem to me more like the glory that comes into any dull, bare life," said Austin,--"the kind of glory you've been to me. It worries me to hear you say you want to go away to 'think things over.' What is there to think over--if you're sure you care?"

"There are lots of details to a thing of this sort."

"A thing of what sort?"

"Oh, Austin, how stupid you are! A--a marriage, of course."

"I thought all that was necessary were two willing victims, a license, and a parson."

"Well, there's a good deal more to it than that. Besides, your family would surely guess if I stayed here. I want to keep it just to ourselves for a little while."

"I see. It's all right, dear. Take all the time you want."

"What would you tell them, anyway?" she went on lightly,--"that I proposed to you, and that you accepted me? Or, to be more exact, that you didn't accept me, but said, 'No, no, no!' most decidedly, and went on repeating it, with variations, until I threw myself into your arms? It was an awful blow to my pride--considering that heretofore I've certainly had my fair share of attention, and even a little more than that--to have to do *all* the love-making, and I'm certainly not going to go brag about it--' This time the conversation really did get interrupted, for Austin would not for one instant submit to such a "garbling of statistics" and took the quickest means in his power to put an end to it."

He had the wisdom, however, greater, perhaps, than might have been expect- ed, not to oppose any of her wishes just then, and it was Sylvia herself who at the last minute felt her heart beginning to fail her, and called him to the farther end of the station platform, on the pretext of consulting him about some baggage.

"I don't see how I can say good-bye--in just an ordinary way," she whispered, "and I'm beginning to miss you dreadfully already. If I can't stand it, away from you, you must arrange to come down for at least a day or two."

It was beginning to sprinkle, and, taking her umbrella, he opened it and handed it to her, leaning forward and kissing her as soon as she was hidden by it.

"I never meant to say good-bye 'in an ordinary way,'" he said cheerfully, "what- ever your intentions were! And, of course, I'll manage to come to town for a day or two, if you find you really want me. Fred would be glad to help me out for that long, I'm sure. On the other hand, if it's a relief to be rid of me for a while, and New York looks pretty good to you, don't hurry back--you've been away for a whole year, remember. I'll understand."

In spite of his cheerful words and matter-of-course manner, Austin stood watching the train go out with a heavy heart. He was very sincere in feeling that his presumption had been great, and that he had taken advantage of feelings which mere youth and loneliness might have awakened in Sylvia, and from which she would recover as soon as she was with her own friends again. And yet he loved her so dearly that it was hard--even though he acknowledged that it was best--to let her go back to the world by whose standards he felt he fell short in every way.

"If I lose her," he said to himself, "I must remember that--of course I ought to. King Cophetua and the beggar maid makes a very pretty story--but it doesn't sound so well the other way around. And then she's given me such a tremendous amount already--if I never get any more, I must be thankful for that."

Sally spent a rapturous week in New York, and came home with her modest trousseau all bought and glowing accounts of the good times she had had.

"The very first thing Sylvia did, the morning after we got there," she said, "was to buy a new limousine and hire a man to run it. My, you ought to see it! It's lined with pearl gray, and Sylvia keeps a gold vase with orchids--fresh ones every day--in it! She helped me choose all my things, and I never could have got half so much for my money, or had half such pretty things if she hadn't; and she began right off to get the most *elegant* clothes for herself, too! I knew Sylvia was pretty, but I never knew *how* pretty until I saw her in a low-necked white dress! We went to the theatre almost every evening, and saw all the sights, besides--it didn't take long to get around in that automobile, I can tell you! Perfect rafts of people kept coming to see her all the time, telling her how glad they were to see her back, and teasing her to do things with them. I bet she'll get married again in no time--there were *dozens* of men, all awfully rich and attractive and apparently just *crazy* about her! We went out twice to lunch, and once to dinner, at the grandest houses I ever even imagined, and every one was lovely to me, too, but of course it was only Sylvia they really cared about. I was about wild, I got so excited, but it didn't make any more impression on Sylvia than water rolling off a duck's back--she didn't seem the least bit different from when she was here, helping mother wash the supper dishes, and teaching Austin French. She took it all as a matter of course. I guess we didn't any of us realize how important she was."

"I did," said Austin.

"You!" exclaimed his sister, with withering scorn. "You've never been even civil to her, much less respectful or attentive! If you could see the way other men treat her--"

"I don't want to," said Austin, with more truth than his sister guessed.

A young, lovely, and agreeable widow, with a great deal of money, and no "impediments" in the way of either parents or children, is apt to find life made extremely pleasant for her by her friends; and every one felt, moreover, that "Sylvia had behaved so very well." For two months after her husband's death, she had lived in the greatest seclusion, too ill, too disillusioned and horror-stricken, too shattered in body and soul--as they all knew only too well--to see even her dearest friends. Then she had gone to the country, remaining there quietly for a year, regaining her health and spirits, and had now returned to her uncle's home, lightening her mourning, going out a little, taking up her old interests again one by one--a fitting and dignified prelude for a new establishment of her own. She could not help being pleased and gratified at the warmth of her reception; and she found, as Austin had predicted, that "New York looked pretty good to her." It is doubtful whether the taste for luxury, once acquired, is ever wholly lost, even though it may be temporarily cast aside; and Sylvia was too young and too human, as well as too healthy and happy again, not to enjoy herself very much, indeed.

For nearly a month she found each day so full and so delightful as it came, that she had no time to be lonely, and no thought of going away; but gradually she came to a realization of the fact that the days were *too* full; that there were no opportunities for resting and reading and "thinking things over"; that the quiet little dinners and luncheons of four and six, given in her honor, were gradually but surely becoming larger, more formal and more elaborate; that her circle of callers was no longer confined to her most intimate friends; that her telephone rang in and out of season; that the city was growing hot and dusty and tawdry, and that she herself was getting tired and nervous again. And when she waked one morning at eleven o'clock, after being up most of the night before, her head aching, her whole being weary and confused, it needed neither the insistent and disagreeable memory of a little incident of the previous evening, nor the letter from Austin that her maid brought in on her breakfast-tray, to make her realize that the tinsel of her gayety was getting tarnished.

* * * * *

DEAREST (the letter ran):

It is midnight, and--as you know--I am always up at five, but I must send you just a few words before I go to bed, for these last two days have been so full that it has seemed to be impossible to find a moment in which to write you. "Business is rushing" at the Gray Homestead these days, and everything going finely. The chickens and ducklings are all coming along well--about four hundred of them-- and we've had three beautiful new heifer calves this week. Peter is beside himself with joy, for they're all Holsteins. I went to Wallacetown yesterday afternoon, and made another $200 payment on our note at the bank--at this rate we'll have that halfway behind us soon.

To-day I've been over at your house every minute that I could spare and suc- ceeded in getting the last workman out--for good--at eight o'clock this evening. (I bribed him to stay overtime. There are a few little odd jobs left, but I can work those in myself in odd moments.) There is no reason now why you shouldn't begin to send furniture any time you like. I never would have believed that it would be possible to get three such good bedrooms--not to mention a bathroom and closets-- out of the attic, or that tearing out partitions and unblocking fireplaces would work such wonders downstairs. It's all just as you planned it that first day we tramped over in the snow to see it--do you remember?--and it's all lovely, especially your bedroom on the right of the front door, and the big living-room on the left. The papers you chose are exactly right for the walls, and the white paint looks so fresh and clean, and I'm sure the piazza is deep enough to suit even you. I've ploughed and planted your flower- and vegetable-gardens, as well as those at the Homestead, and this warm, early spring is helping along the vegetation finely, so I think things will soon be coming up. We've decided to try both wheat and alfalfa as experiments this year, and I can hardly wait to see whether they'll turn out all right.

Katherine graduates from high school the eighteenth of June, and as Sally's teaching ends the same day, and Fred's patience has finally given out with a bang, she has fixed the twenty-fifth for her wedding. Won't she be busy, with just one week to get ready to be a bride, after she stops being a schoolmarm? But, of course, we'll all turn to and help her, and Molly will be home from the Conservatory ten days before that--you know how efficient she is. By the way, has she written you the good news about her scholarship? We may have a famous musician in the family yet, if some mere man doesn't step in and intervene. Speaking of lovers, Peter is teaching Edith Dutch! And when mother remonstrated with her, she flared up and asked if it was any different from having you teach me French! (I sometimes believe "the baby" is "onto us," though all the others are still entirely unsuspicious, and keep right on telling me I never half appreciated you!) So they spend a good deal of time at the living-room table, with their heads rather close together, but I haven't yet heard Edith conversing fluently in that useful and musical foreign language which she is supposed to be acquiring.

I haven't had a letter from you in nearly a week, but I'm sure, if you weren't well and happy, Mr. Stevens would let us know. I'm glad you're having such a good time--you certainly deserve it after being cooped up so long. Sorry you think it isn't suitable for you to dance yet, for, of course, you would enjoy that a lot, but you can pretty soon, can't you?

Good-night, darling. God bless you always!
AUSTIN

*   *   *   *   *

There was something in the quiet, restrained tone of the letter, with its details of homely, everyday news, and the tidings of his care and interest in her little house, that touched Sylvia far more than many pages of passionate outpouring of loneliness and longing could have done. She knew that the loneliness and longing were there, even though he would not say so, and she turned from the great bunch of American Beauties which had also come in with her breakfast-tray, with something akin almost to disgust as she thought of Austin's tiny bunch of arbutus--his "bouquet des fiancailles," as he had called it--the only thing, besides the little star, that he had ever given her. She called her maid, and announced that in the future she would never be at home to a certain caller; then she reached for the telephone beside her bed and cancelled all her engagements for the next few days, on the plea of not feeling well, which was perfectly true; and then she called up Western Union, and dispatched a long telegram, after which she indulged in a comforting and salutary outburst of tears.

"It will serve me quite right if he won't come," she sobbed. "I wouldn't if I were he, not one step--and he's just as stubborn as I am. I never was half good enough for him, and now I've neglected him, and frittered away my time, and even flirted with other men--when I'd scratch out the eyes of any other woman if she dared to look at him. It's to be hoped that he doesn't find out what a frivolous, empty-headed, silly, vain little fool I am--though it probably would be better for him in the end if he did."

Sylvia passed a very unhappy day, as she richly deserved to do. For the woman who gives a man a new ideal to live for, and then, carelessly, herself falls short of the standard she has set for him, often does as great and incalculable harm as the woman who has no standards at all.

Uncle Mat received a distinct shock when he reached his apartment that night, to find that his niece, dressed in a severely plain black gown, was dining at home alone with him. Before he finished his soup he received another shock.

"Austin Gray is coming to New York," she said, coolly, buttering a cracker; "I have just had a telegram saying he will take a night train, and get in early in the morning--eight o'clock, I believe. I think I'll go and meet him at the station. Are you willing he should come here, and sleep on the living-room sofa, as you suggested once before, or shall I take him to a hotel?"

"Bring him here by all means," returned her bewildered relative; "I like that boy immensely. What streak of good luck is setting him loose? I thought he was tied hand and foot by bucolic occupations."

"Apparently he has found some means of escape," said Sylvia; "would you care to read aloud to me this evening?"

CHAPTER XIII

W hy, Sylvia, my dear! I never dreamed that you would come to meet me!"

Austin was, indeed, almost beside himself with surprise and delight when, as he left the train and walked down the long platform in the Grand Central Station, he saw Sylvia, dressed in pure white serge, standing near the gate. He waved his hat like a schoolboy, and hurried forward, setting down his suitcase to grip her hands in both of his.

"Have you had any breakfast?" she asked, as they started off.

"Yes, indeed, an hour ago."

"Then where would you like to go first? I have the motor here, and we're both entirely at your disposal."

He hesitated a moment, and then said, laughing, "It didn't occur to me that you'd come to the station, and I fully intended to go somewhere and get a hair-cut that wouldn't proclaim me as coming straight from Hamstead, Vermont, and replenish the wardrobe that looked so inexhaustible to me last fall, before I presented myself to you."

Sylvia joined in his laugh. "Go ahead. I'll sit in the motor and wait for you. Afterwards we'll go shopping together."

"To buy things like these?" he asked, eyeing her costume with approval.

"No. I have enough clothes now. I was going to begin choosing our furniture--and thought you might be interested. Get in, dear, this is ours," she said, walking up to the limousine which Sally had described with such enthusiasm, and which now stood waiting for her, its door held open by a French chauffeur, who was smiling with true Gallic appreciation of his mistress's "affaire de coeur," "and here," she added, after they were comfortably seated inside, taking a gardenia from the flower-holder, "is a posy I've got for you."

"Thank you. Have you anything else?" he asked, folding his hand over hers as she pinned it on.

"Oh, Austin, you're such a funny lover!"

"Why?"

"Because you nearly always--ask beforehand. Why don't you take what you've a perfect right to--if you want it?"

"Possibly because I don't feel I have a perfect right to--or sure that I have any right at all," he answered gravely, "and I can't believe it's really real yet, anyway. You see, I only had two days with you--the new way--before you left, and I had no means of knowing when I should have any more--and a good deal of doubt as to whether I deserved any."

There was no reproach in the words at all, but so much genuine humility and patience that Sylvia realized more keenly than ever how selfish she had been.

"You'll make me cry if you talk to me like that!" she said quickly. "Oh, Austin, I've countless things to say to you, but first of all I want to tell you that I'll never leave you like this again, that it's--just as real as *I am*, that you can have just as many days as you care to now, and that I'll spend them all showing you how much right you have!" And she threw her arms around his neck and drew his face down to hers, oblivious alike of Andre on the front seat and all the passing crowds on Fifth Avenue.

"Don't," Austin said after a moment. "We mustn't kiss each other like that when some one might see us--I forgot, for a minute, that there *was* any one else in the world! Besides, I'm afraid, if we do, I'll let myself go more than I mean to--it's all been stifled inside me so long--and be almost rough, and startle or hurt you. I couldn't bear to have that happen to you--again. I want you always to feel safe and shielded with me."

"Safe! I hope I'll be as safe in heaven as I am with you! Don't you think I know what you've been through this last year?"

"No, I don't," he said passionately; "I hope not, anyway. And that was before I ever touched you, besides. It's different now. I shan't kiss you again to-day, my dear, except"--raising her hand to his lips--"like this. Are you going to wait for me here?" he ended quietly, as the motor began to slow down in front of the Waldorf.

"No," she said, her voice trembling; "I'm going to church, 'to thank God, kneeling, for a good man's love.' Come for me there, when you're ready."

"Are you in earnest?"

"I never was more so."

He joined her at St. Bartholomew's an hour later, and seeking her out, knelt beside her in the quiet, dim church, empty except for themselves. She felt for his hand, and gripping it hard, whispered with downcast eyes and flushed cheeks:

"Austin, I have a confession to make."

"Of course, you have--I knew that from the moment I got your telegram. Well, how bad is it?" he said, trying to make his voice sound as light as possible. But her courage had apparently failed her, for she did not answer, so at last he went on:

"You didn't miss me much, at first, did you? When you thought of me I seemed a little--not much, of course, but quite an important little--out of focus on the only horizon that your own world sees. Well, I knew that was bound to happen, and that if you really cared for me as much as you thought you did at the farm, it was just as well that it should--for you'd soon find out how much your own horizon had broadened and beautified. Don't blame yourself too much for that. I suppose the worst confession, however, is that something occurred to make you long, just a little, to have me with you again--just as you were glad to see me come into the room the last day our minister called. What was it?"

"Austin! How can you guess so much?"

"Because I care so much. Go on."

"People began to make love to me," she faltered, "and at first I did--like it. I--flirted just a little. Then--oh, Austin, don't make me tell you!"

"I never imagined," he said grimly, "that Thomas and Mr. Jessup were the only men who would ever look at you twice. I suppose I've got to expect that men are going to *try* to make love to you always--unless I lock you up where no one but me can see you, and that doesn't seem very practical in this day and generation! But I don't see any reason--if you love me--why you should *let* them. You have certainly got to tell me, Sylvia."

"I will not, if you speak to me that way," she flashed back. "Why should I? You wouldn't tell me all the foolish things you ever did!"

"Yes, Sylvia, I will," he said gravely, "as far as I can without incriminating anybody else--no man has a right to kiss--or do more than that--and tell, in such a way as to betray any woman--no matter what sort she is. Some of the things I've done wouldn't be pleasant, either to say or to hear; for a man who is as hopeless as I was before you came to us is often weak enough to be perilously near being wicked. But if you wish to be told, you have every right to. And so have I a right to an answer to my question. No one knows better than I do that I'm not worthy of you in any way. But you must think I am or you wouldn't marry me, and if you're going to be my wife, you've got to help me to keep you--as sacred to me as you are now. Shall I tell first, or will you? A church is a wonderful place for a confession, you know, and it would be much better to have it behind us."

"You needn't tell at all," she said, lifting her face and showing as she did so the tears rolling down her cheeks. "*Weak*! You're as strong as steel! If all men were like you, there wouldn't be anything for me to tell either. But they're not. The night before I telegraphed you, an old friend brought me home after a dinner and theatre party. We had all had an awfully gay time, and--well, I think it was a little *too* gay. This man wanted to marry me long ago, and I think, perhaps, I would have accepted him once--if he'd--had any money. But he didn't then--he's made a lot since. He began to pay me a good deal of attention again the instant I got back to New York, and I was glad to see him again, and--Of course, I ought to have told him about you right off, but some way, I didn't. I always liked him a lot, and I enjoyed--just having him round again. I thought that if he began to show signs of--getting restive--I could tell him I was engaged, and that would put an end to it. But he didn't show any signs--any *preliminary* signs, I mean, the way men usually do. He simply--suddenly broke loose on the way home that night, and when I refused him, he said most dreadful things to me, and--"

"Took you in his arms by force, and kissed you, in spite of yourself." Austin finished the sentence for her speaking very quietly.

"Oh, Austin, *please* don't look at me like that! I couldn't help it!"

"Couldn't help it! No, I suppose you struggled and fought and called him all kinds of hard names, and then you sent for me, expecting me to go to him and do the same. Well, I shan't do anything of the sort. I think you were twice as much to blame as he was. And if you ever--let yourself in for such an experience again, I'll never kiss you again--that's perfectly certain."

"*Austin!*"

"Well, I mean it--just that. I don't know much about society, but I know some-thing about women. There are women who are just plain bad, and women who are harmless enough, and attractive, in a way, but so cheap and tawdry that they never attract very deeply or very long, and women who are good as gold, but who haven't a particle of--allure--I don't know how else to put it--Emily Brown's one of them. Then there are women like you, who are fine, and pure, and--irresistibly lovely as well; who never do or say or even think anything that is indelicate, but whom no man can look at without--wanting--and who--consciously or unconsciously--I hope the latter--tempt him all the time. You apparently feel free to--play with fire--feeling sure you won't get even scorched yourself, and not caring a rap whether any one else gets burnt; and then you're awfully surprised and insulted and all that if the--the victim of the fire, in his first pain, turns on you. 'Said dreadful things to you'--I should think he would have, poor devil! Perhaps young girls don't real-ize; but a woman over twenty, especially if she's been married, has only herself to blame if a man loses his head. Were you sweet and tender and--*aloof*, just be-cause you were sick and disgusted and disillusioned, instead of because that was the real *you*--are you going to prove true to your mother's training, after all, now that you're happy and well and safe again? If you have shown me heaven--only to prove to me that it was a mirage--you might much better have left me in what I knew was hell!"

He left her, so abruptly that she could not tell in which direction he had turned, nor at first believe that he had really gone. Then she knelt for what seemed to her like hours, the knowledge of the justice of all he had said growing clearer every minute, the grief that she had hurt him so growing more and more intolerable, the hopelessness of asking his forgiveness seeming greater and greater It did not oc-cur to her to try to find him, or to expect that he would come back--she must stay there until she could control her tears, and then she must go home. A few women, taking advantage of the blessed custom which keeps nearly all Anglican and Ro-man churches open all day for rest, meditation, and prayer, came in, stayed a few minutes, and left again. At eleven o'clock there was a short service, the daily Morn-ing Prayer, sparsely attended. Sylvia knelt and stood, mechanically, with the other worshippers. Then suddenly, just before the benediction was pronounced, Austin slid into the seat beside her, and groped for her hand. Neither spoke, nor could have spoken; indeed, there seemed no need of words between them. A very great love is usually too powerful to brook the interference of a question of forgiveness. The clergyman's voice rose clear and comforting over them:

"'The grace of our Lord Jesus Christ, and the love of God, and the fellowship of the Holy Ghost, be with us all ever more. Amen.'"

"Is there a flower-shop near here?" was the perfectly commonplace question Austin asked as they went down the church steps together into the spring sunshine.

"Yes, just a few steps away. Why?"

"I want to buy you some violets--the biggest bunch I can get."

"Aren't you rather extravagant?"

"Not at all. The truth is, I've come into a large fortune!"

"Austin! What do you mean?"

He evaded her question, smiling, bought her an enormous bouquet, and then suggested that if her destination was not too far away they should walk. She dismissed the smiling Andre, and walked beside Austin in silence for a few minutes hoping that he would explain without being asked again.

"Did you say you were going to Tiffany's to buy furniture--I thought Tiffany's was a jewelry store, and in the opposite direction?"

"It is. I'm going to the Tiffany Studios--quite a different place. Austin--don't tease me--do tell me what you mean?"

"Why? Surely you're not marrying me for my money!"

"Good gracious, you plague like a little boy! Please!"

"Well, a great-aunt who lived in Seattle, and whom I haven't seen in ten years, has died and left me all her property!"

"How much?"

"Mercy, Sylvia, how mercenary you are! Enough so you won't have to buy my cigars and shoe-strings--aren't you glad?"

"Of course, but I wish you'd stop fooling and tell me all about it."

"Well, I shan't--if I did you'd make fun of me, because it would seem so small to you, and I want to be just as lavish and extravagant as I like with it all the time I'm in New York--you'll have to let me 'treat' now! And just think! I'll be able to pay my own expenses when I take that trip to Syracuse which you seem to think is going to complete my agricultural education. Peter's going with me, and I imagine we'll be a cheerful couple!"

"How are things going in that quarter?"

"Rather rapidly, I imagine. I've given father one warning, and I shan't interfere again, bless their hearts! I caught him kissing her on the back stairs the other night, but I walked straight on and pretended not to see."

"Thereby earning their everlasting gratitude, of course, poor babies!"

"How many years older than Edith are you?"

"Never mind, you saucy boy! Here we are--have you any suggestions you may not care to make before the clerks as to what kind of furniture I shall buy?"

"None at all. I want to see for myself how much sense you have in certain directions, and if I don't like your selections, I warn you beforehand that the offending articles will be used for kindling wood."

"Do be careful what you say. They know me here."

"Careful what *I* say! I shall be a regular wooden image. They'll think I'm your second cousin from Minnesota, being shown the sights."

He did, indeed, display such stony indifference, and maintain such an expression of stolid stupidity, that Sylvia could hardly keep her face straight, and having chosen a big sofa and a rug for her living-room, and her dining-room table, she announced that she "would come in again" and graciously departed.

"I have a good mind to shake you!" she said as they went down the steps. "I had no idea you were such a good actor--we'll have to get up some dramatics when we get home. Did you like my selections?"

"Very much, as far as they went. Where are you going now--I see that your grinning Frenchman and upholstered palace on wheels are waiting for you again."

"Well, I can't walk *all* day--I'm going to Macy's to buy kitchen-ware. You'd better do something else--I'm afraid you'll criticize my brooms and saucepans!"

"All right, go alone. I'm going to the real Tiffany's."

"What for?"

"To squander my fortune, Pauline Pry. I'll meet you at Sherry's at one-thirty. I suppose some kindly policeman will guide my faltering footsteps in the right direction. Good-bye." And he closed the door of the car in her radiant face.

They had a merry lunch an hour later, Austin ordering the meal and paying for it with such evident pleasure that Sylvia could not help being touched at his joy over his little legacy. Then he proposed that, although they were a little late, they might go to a matinee, and afterwards insisted on walking up Fifth Avenue and stopping for tea at the Plaza.

"I've seen more beautiful cities than New York," he said, as they sauntered along, much more slowly than most of the hurrying throng,--"Paris, for instance-- fairly alive with loveliness! But I don't believe there's a place in the world that gives you the feeling of *power* that this does--especially just at this time of day, when the lights are coming on, and all these multitudes of people going home after their day's work or pleasure. It's tremendous--lifts you right off your feet--do you know what I mean?"

They reached home a little after six, to find Uncle Mat, whose existence they had completely forgotten, waiting for them with his eyes glued to the clock.

"I was about to have the Hudson River dragged for you two," he said, as Austin wrung his hand and Sylvia kissed him penitently. "Where *have* you been? I came home to lunch, and made several appointments to introduce Austin to some very influential men, who I think would make valuable acquaintances for him. It's inexcusable, Sylvia, for you to monopolize him this way."

The happy culprits exchanged glances, and then Sylvia linked her arm in Austin's and got down on her knees, dragging him after her.

"I suppose we may as well confess," she said, "because you'd guess it inside of five minutes, anyway. Please don't be very angry with us."

"What *are* you talking about? Austin, can you explain? Has Sylvia taken leave of her senses?"

"I'm afraid so, sir," said Austin, with mock gravity; "it certainly looks that way. For about six weeks ago she told me that--some time in the dim future, of course-- she might possibly be prevailed upon to marry me!"

Uncle Mat declared afterwards that this last shock was too much for him, and that he swooned away. But all that Austin and Sylvia could remember was that after a moment of electrified silence, he embraced them both, exclaiming, "Bless my stars! I never for one moment suspected that she had that much sense!"

CHAPTER XIV

Are you two young idiots going out again this evening?" asked Uncle Mat as the three were eating their dessert, glancing from Sylvia's low-necked white gown to Austin's immaculate dress-suit.

"No. This is entirely in each other's honor. But I hope you are, for I want to talk to Austin."

"Good gracious! What have you been doing all day? What do you expect *me* to do?"

"You can go to your club and have five nice long rubbers of bridge," said Sylvia mercilessly, "and when you come back, please cough in the hall."

"I want to write a few lines to my mother, after I've had a little talk with Mr. Stevens--then I'm entirely at your disposal," said Austin, as she lighted their cigars and rose to leave them.

"I'm glad some one wants to talk to me," murmured Uncle Mat meekly.

Sylvia hugged him and kissed the top of his head. "You dear jealous old thing! I've got some telephoning and notes to attend to myself. Come and knock on my door when you're ready, Austin."

"You have a good deal of courage," remarked Uncle Mat, nodding in Sylvia's direction as she went down the hall.

"Perhaps you think effrontery would be the better word."

"Not at all, my dear boy--you misunderstand me completely. Sylvia's the dearest thing in the world to me, and I've been worrying a good deal about her remarriage, which I knew was bound to come sooner or later. I'm more than satisfied and pleased at her choice--I'm relieved."

"Thank you. It's good to know you feel that way, even if I don't deserve it."

"You do deserve it. In speaking of courage, I meant that the poor husband of a rich wife always has a good deal to contend with; and aside from the money question, you're supersensitive about what you consider your lack of advantages and polish--though Heaven knows you don't need to be!" he added, glancing with satisfaction at the handsome, well-groomed figure stretched out before him. "I never saw any one pick up the veneer of good society, so called, as rapidly as you have. It shows that real good breeding was back of it all the time."

"I guess I'd better go and write my letter," laughed Austin, "before you flatter me into having an awfully swelled head. But I want to tell you first--I'm not a pauper any more. I've got twenty thousand dollars of my own--an old aunt has died and left most of her will in my favor. I've taken capital, and paid off all our debts--except what we owe to Sylvia. She can give me that for a wedding present if she wants to. It's queer how much less sore I am about her money now that I've got a little of my own! There are one or two things that I want to buy for her, and I want to pay my own expenses and Peter's on a trip through western New York farms this summer. The rest I must invest as well as I can, to bring me in a little regular income. I'm sure, now that the farm and the family are perfectly free of debt, that I can earn enough to add quite a little to it every year. If Sylvia lost every cent she had, we could get married just the same, and though she'd have to live simply and quietly, she wouldn't suffer. I thought you would help me with investments--or take me to some other man who would."

"I will, indeed--if you don't spend *all* your time, as Sylvia fully intends you shall, making love to her. This changes the outlook wonderfully--clears the sky for both of you! It's bad for a man to be wholly dependent on his wife, and scarcely less bad for her. But there's another matter--"

"Yes, sir?"

"I don't want you to think I'm meddling--or underestimating Sylvia--"

"I won't think that, no matter what you say."

"How long have you and she been in love with each other? Wasn't it pretty nearly a case of 'first sight'?"

Austin flushed. "It certainly was with me," he said quietly.

"And haven't you--quarrelled from the very beginning, too?"

The boy's flush deepened. "Yes," he said, still more quietly, "we seemed to misunderstand--and antagonize each other."

"Even to-day?"--Then as Austin did not answer, "Now, tell me truthfully--whose fault is it?"

"The first time it was mine," said Austin quickly. "She made me clean up the yard--it needed it, too!--and I was furious! And I was rude--worse than rude--to her for a long time. But since then--"

"You needn't be afraid to say it was hers," remarked Sylvia's uncle dryly. "She wants an absolutely free hand, which isn't good for her to have--she's only twenty-two now, pretty as a picture, and still absolutely inexperienced about many things. She can't bear the thought of dictation, and you're both young and self-willed and proud, and very much in love--which makes the whole thing harder, and not easier, as I suppose you imagine. Now, some women, even in these days, aren't fit to live with until--figuratively speaking--they've been beaten over the head with a club. Sylvia's not that kind. She's not only got to respect her husband's wishes, she's got to *want* to--and I believe you can make her want to! I think you're absolutely just--and unusually decent. If I didn't I shouldn't dare say all this to you--or let you have her at all, if I could help it. And besides being fair, you know how to express yourself--which some poor fellows unfortunately can't do--they're absolutely tongue-tied. In fact, you're perfectly capable of taking things into your own hands every way, and making a success of it--and if you don't before you're married, neither of you can possibly hope to be happy afterwards."

"There's one thing you're overlooking, Mr. Stevens, which I should have had to tell you to-night, anyway."

"What is it?"

"I'm not worthy of tying up Sylvia's shoes--much less of marrying her. I've been straight as a string since she came to the farm, but before that--any one in Hamstead would tell you. It was town talk. I can't, knowing that, act as I would if I--didn't have that to remember. It's all very well to say that a man--*gets through* with all that, absolutely--I've heard them say it dozens of times! But how can he be sure he is through--that the old sins won't crop up again? I love Sylvia more than--than I can possibly talk about, and I'm *afraid*--afraid that I won't be worthy of her, and that if she gave in absolutely--that I'd abuse my position."

Uncle Mat glanced up quietly from his cigar. There were tears in the boy's eyes, his voice trembled. The older man, for a moment, felt powerless to speak before the penitent sincerity of Austin's confession, the humility of his bared soul.

"As long as you feel that way," he said at last, a trifle huskily, "I don't believe there's very much danger--for either of you. And remember this--lots of good people make mistakes, but if they're made of the right stuff, they don't make the same mistake but once. And sometimes they gain more than they lose from a slip-up. You certainly are made of the right stuff. Perhaps you will go through some experience like what you're dreading, though I can't foresee what form it will take. Meanwhile remember that Sylvia's been through an awful ordeal, and be very gentle with her, though you take the reins in your hands, as you should do. I'm thankful that she has such a bright prospect for happiness ahead of her now--but don't forget that you have a right to be happy, too. Don't be too grateful and too humble. She's done you some favors in the past, but she isn't doing you one now--she never would have accepted you if she hadn't been head over heels in love with you. Now write your letter, and then go to her. But to-morrow I want you all the morning--we must look into the acquaintances I spoke about, and the investments you spoke about. Meanwhile, the best of luck--you deserve it!"

Austin smoked thoughtfully for some minutes after Uncle Mat left him, and finally, roused from his brown study by the striking of a clock, went hurriedly to the desk and began his letter. Before he had finished, Sylvia's patience had quite given out, and she came and stood behind him, with her arm over his shoulder as he wrote. He acknowledged the caress with a nod and a smile, but went on writing, and did not speak until the letter was sealed and stamped.

"Sorry to have kept you waiting, dear. Now, then, what is it?"

"I've been thinking things over."

"So I supposed. Well, what have you thought, honey?"

"First, that I want you to have these. I've been going through my jewelry lately, and have had Uncle Mat sell everything except a few little trinkets I had before I--was married, and the pearls he gave me then. In my sorting process, I came across these things that were my father's. I never offered them to--to--any one before. But I want you to wear them, if you will."

She handed him a little worn leather box as she spoke, and on opening it he found, besides a few pins and studs of no great value, a handsome, old-fashioned watch and a signet ring.

"Thank you very much, dear. I'll wear them with great pride and pleasure, and this will be an exchange of gifts, for I've got something for you, too--that's what my shopping was this morning."

He took her left hand in his, slipped off her wedding ring, and slid another on her finger--a circle of beautiful diamonds sunk in a platinum band delicately chased.

"*Austin!* How exquisite! I never had--such a lovely ring! How did you happen to choose--just this?"

"Largely because I thought you could use it for both an engagement ring now, and a wedding ring when we get married--which was what I wanted." And without another word, he took the discarded gold circle and threw it into the fire. "And partly," he went on quite calmly--as if nothing unusual had happened, and as if it was an everyday occurrence to burn up ladies' property without consulting them--"because I thought it was beautiful, and--suitable, like the little star."

"And you expect me to wear it, publicly, now?"

"I shall put it a little stronger than that--I shall insist upon your doing so."

She looked up in surprise, her cheeks flushing at his tone, but he went on quietly:

"I've just written my mother, and asked her to tell the rest of the family, that we are engaged. They have as much right to know as your uncle. You can do as you please about telling other people, of course. But you can't wear another man's ring any longer. And it seems to me, as we shall no longer be living in the same house, and as I shall be coming constantly to see you after you come back to Hamstead, that it would be much more dignified if I could do so openly, in the role of your prospective husband. While as far as your friends here are concerned--after what you told me this morning--I think you must agree with me that it is much fairer to let them know at once how things stand with you, and introduce me to them."

"I don't want to use up these few precious days giving parties. I want you to myself."

"I know, dear--that's what I'd prefer, in one way, too. But I have got to take some time for business, and later on your friends will feel that you were ashamed of me--and be justified in feeling so--when they learn that we are to be married, and that you were not willing to have me meet them when I was here."

Sylvia did not answer, but sat with her eyes downcast, biting her lips, and pulling the new ring back and forth on her finger.

"That is, of course, unless you *are* ashamed--are you perfectly sure of your own mind? If not, my letter isn't posted yet, and it is very easy to tell your uncle that you have found you were mistaken in your feelings."

"What would you do if I should?" she asked defiantly.

"Do? Why, nothing. Tell him the same thing, of course, pack my suit-case, and start back to Hamstead as soon as I had met the men I came to see on business."

"Oh, Austin, how can you talk so! I don't believe you really want me, after all!"

"Don't you?" he asked in an absolutely expressionless voice, and pushing back his chair he walked over to the window, turning his back on her completely.

She was beside him in an instant, promising to do whatever he wished and begging his forgiveness. But it was so long before he answered her, or even looked at her, that she knew that for the second time that day she had wounded him almost beyond endurance.

"If you ever say that to me again, no power on earth will make me marry you," he said, in a voice that was not in the least threatening, but so decisive that there could be no doubt that he meant what he said; "and we've got to think up some way of getting along together without quarrelling all the time unless you have your own way about everything, whether it's fair that you should or not. Now, tell me what you wanted to talk to me about, and we'll try to do better--those troublesome details you mentioned before you left the farm? Perhaps I can straighten out some of them for you, if you'll only let me."

"The first one is--money."

"I thought so. It's a rather large obstacle, I admit. But things are not going to be so hard to adjust in that quarter as I feared. I'll tell you now about the little legacy I mentioned this morning." And he repeated his conversation with Uncle Mat. "You can do what you please with your own money, of course--take care of your own personal expenses, and run the house, and give all the presents you like to the girls--but you can't ever give me another cent, unless you want to call the family indebtedness to you your wedding present to me."

"You can't get everything you want on the income of ten thousand dollars--

which is about all the capital you'll have left when you've paid all these first expenses you mention."

"I can have everything I *need*--with that and what I'll earn. What's your next 'detail'?"

"I suppose I'll have to give in about the money--but will you mind, very much, if we have--a long engagement?"

"I certainly shall. As I told you before, I think too much has been sacrificed to convention already."

"It isn't that."

"What, then?"

"I don't know how to tell you, and still have you believe I love you dearly."

"You mean, that for some reason, you're not ready to marry me yet?" And as she nodded without speaking, her eyes filling with tears, he asked very gently, "Why not, Sylvia?"

"I'm afraid."

"Afraid-- *of me?*"

"No--that is, not of you personally--but of marriage itself. I can't bear yet--the thought of facing--passion."

The hand that had been stroking her hair dropped suddenly, and she felt him draw away from her, with something almost like a groan, and put her arms around his neck, clinging to him with all her strength.

" *Don't*--I love you--and love you--and *love you*--oh, can't I make you see? Are you very angry with me, Austin?"

"No, darling, I'm not angry at all. How could I be? But I'm just beginning to realize--though I thought I knew before--what a perfect hell you've been through--and wondering if I can ever make it up to you."

"Then this doesn't seem to you dreadful--to have me ask for this?"

"Not half so dreadful as it would to have you look at me as you did on Christmas night."

He began stroking her hair again, speaking reassuringly, his voice full of sympathy.

"Don't cry, dearest--it's all right. There's nothing to worry over. It's right that you should have your way about this--it's *my* way, too, as long as you feel like this.

I hope you won't *too* long--for--I love you, and want you, and--and need you so much--and--I've waited a year for you already. But I promise never to force--or even urge--you in any way, if you'll promise me that when you *are* ready--you'll tell me."

"I will," she sobbed, with her head hidden on his shoulder.

"Then that's settled, and needn't even be brought up again. Don't cry so, honey. Is there anything else?"

"Just one thing more; and in a way, it's the hardest to say of any."

"Well, tell me, anyway; perhaps I may be able to help."

"My baby," she said, speaking with great difficulty, "the poor little thing that only lived two weeks. It's buried in the same lot with--its father--at Greenwood. I never can go near that place again. I've paid some one to take care of it, and Uncle Mat has promised me to see that it's done. I think some day you and I--will have a son--more than one, I hope--and he will *live*! But if this--this baby--could be taken away from where he is now, and buried in that little cemetery, you know--I could go sometimes, quite happily, and stay with him, and put flowers on his little grave; and later on there could be a stone which said, merely, 'Harold, infant son of Sylvia--Gray.'"

Apparently Austin forgot what he had said that morning, for long before she had finished he took her in his arms; but the kisses with which he covered her face and hair were like those he would have given to a little child, and there was no need of an answer this time. For a long while she lay there, clinging to him and crying, until she was utterly spent with emotion, as she had been on the night when they had stayed in the wood; and at last, just as she had done then, she dropped suddenly and quietly to sleep. Through the tears which still blinded his own eyes, Austin half-smiled, remembering how he had longed to kiss her as he carried her home, rejoicing that his conscience no longer needed to stand like an iron barrier between his lips and hers. He waited until he was sure that she was sleeping so soundly that there would be little danger of waking her, then lifted her, took her down the hall to her room, and laid her on the big, four-posted bed.

"That's the second time you've been to sleep in my arms, darling," he whispered, bending over to kiss her before he left her; "the third time will be on our wedding might--God grant that isn't very far away!"

CHAPTER XV

"Graduation from high school" ranks second in importance only to a wedding in rural New England families. For not only the "Graduating Exercises" themselves, with their "Salutatory" and "Valedictory" addresses, their "Class History" and "Class Prophecy," their essays and songs, constitute a great occasion, but there is also the all-day excursion of picnic character; the "Baccalaureate Sermon" in the largest church; the "Prize Speaking" in the nearest "Opera House"; and last, but not least, the "Graduation Ball" in the Town Hall. The boys suffer agonies in patent-leather boots, high, stiff collars and blue serge suits; the girls suffer torments of jealousy over the fortunate few whose white organdie dresses come "ready-made" straight from Boston. The Valedictorian, the winner at "Prize Speaking," the belle of the parties, are great and glorious beings somewhat set apart from the rest of the graduates; and long after housework and farming are peacefully resumed again, the success of "our class" is a topic of enduring interest.

A wedding brings even more in its train. The bride's house, where the marriage service, as well as the wedding reception, generally takes place, must be swept and scoured from attic to cellar, and, if possible, painted and papered as well. Guestrooms must be set in order for visiting members of the family, and the bridal feast prepared and served without the help of caterers. The express office is haunted for incoming wedding presents, and though the destination of "the trip"--generally to Montreal or Niagara Falls if the happy pair can afford it--is a well-guarded secret, the trousseau and the gifts, as they arrive, stand in proud display for the neighbors to run in and admire, and the prospective bride and groom, self-conscious and blushing, attend divine service together in the face of a smiling and whispering congregation.

It was small wonder, then, that the Gray family, with the prospect of a graduation and a wedding within a few days of each other before it, was thrown into a ferment of excitement compared to which the hilarity of the Christmas holidays was but a mild ripple. Molly had won a scholarship at the Conservatory, and was beginning to show some talent for musical composition; Katherine was the Valedictorian of her class; Edith had every dance engaged for the ball; and though Thomas had not distinguished himself in any special way, he had kept a good average all the year in his studies, and managed to be very nearly self-supporting by the outside "chores" he had done at college, and it was felt that he, too, deserved much credit, and that his home-coming would be a joyful event. He was trying out "practical experiments" with his class, and could promise only to arrive "just in time"; but Molly, who headed her letters with the notes of the wedding march, and said that she was practising it every night, wrote that she would be home *plenty* long enough beforehand to help with *everything*, and that mother *simply mustn't* get all worn out working too hard with the house-cleaning; Sadie and James were coming home for a week, to take in both festivities, though Sadie must be "careful not to overdo just now." Katherine was entirely absorbed in her determination to get "over ninety" in every one of her final examinations; and Mr. and Mrs. Gray were both so busy and so preoccupied that Edith and Peter were left to pursue the course of true love unobserved and undisturbed.

The effect which Austin's letter to his mother, written the night after he reached New York, produced in a household already pitched so high, may readily be imagined. A thunderbolt casually exploding in their midst could not have effected half such a shock of surprise, or the gift of all the riches of the Orient so much joy. And when, a week later, he came home bringing Sylvia with him--a new Sylvia, laughing, crying, blushing, as shy as a girl surprised at her first tete-a-tete, Mr. and Mrs. Gray welcomed the little lady they loved so well as their daughter.

Those were great days for Mrs. Elliott, who, as mother of the prospective bridegroom, as well as Mrs. Gray's most intimate friend, enjoyed especial privileges; and as she was not averse to sharing her information and experiences, the entire village joyfully fell upon the morsels of choice gossip with which she regaled them.

"I don't believe any house in the village ever held so many elegant clothes at once," she declared. "For besides all Sally's things, which are just too sweet for anything, there's Katherine's graduation dress an' ball-dress, an' a third one, mind, to wear when she's bridesmaid--most girls would think they was pretty lucky to have any one of the three! Edith has a bridesmaid's dress just like hers, an' a bright yellow one for the ball, an' Molly's maid-of-honor's outfit is handsomest of all--pale pink silk, draped over kind of careless-like with chif*fon*, an' shoes an' silk stockin's to match. An' Mis' Gray, besides that pearl-colored satin Austin brought her from Europe, has a lavender brocade! 'I didn't feel to need it at all,' she told me, 'but Sylvia just insisted. "Two nice dresses aren't a bit too many for you to have," says Sylvia; "the gray one will be lovely for church all summer, an' after Sally's weddin', you can put away the lavender for--Austin's," she finished up, blushin' like a rose.' 'Have you any idea when that's goin' to be?' I couldn't help askin'. 'No,' says Mis' Gray, 'I wish I had. Howard an' I tried to persuade her to be married the same night as Sally! I've always admired a double-weddin'. But she wouldn't hear of it, an' I must say I was surprised to see her so set against it, an' that Austin didn't urge her a bit, either, for they just set their eyes by each other, any one can see that, an' there ain't a thing to hinder 'em from gettin' married to-morrow, that I know of, if they want to--unless perhaps they think it's too soon,' she ended up, kinder meanin'-like."

"The presents are somethin' wonderful," Mrs. Elliott related on another occasion. "Sally's uncle out in Seattle--widower of her that left Austin all that money--has sent her a whole dinner-set, white with pink roses on it--twelve dozen pieces in all, countin' vegetable dishes, bone-plates, an' a soup-tureen. She's had sixteen pickle-forks, ten bon-bon spoons, an' eight cut-glass whipped-cream bowls, but I dare say they'll all come in handy, one way or another, an' it makes you feel good to have so many generous friends. Austin's insisted on givin' her one of them Holst**een** cows he fetched over from Holland, an' Fred says it's one of the most valuable things she's got, though I should feel as if any good bossy, raised right here in Hamstead, would probably do 'em just as well, an' that he might have chosen somethin' a little more tasty. Ain't men queer? Sylvia? Oh, she's given her a whackin' big check--enough so Sally can pay all her 'personal expenses,' as she calls 'em all her life, an' never touch the principal at that; an' a big box of knives an' forks an' spoons--'a chest of flat silver' she calls it, an' a silver tea-set to match--awful plain pattern they are, but Sally likes 'em. Yes, it's nice of her, but it ain't any more than I expected. She's got plenty of money--why shouldn't she spend it?"

Only once did Mrs. Elliott say anything unpleasant, and the village, knowing her usually sharp tongue, thought she did remarkably well, and took but little stock in this particular speech.

"I'm glad it's Sally Fred picked out, an' not one of the other girls," she declared; "she's twenty-nine years old now--a good, sensible age--pleasant an' easy-goin', same's her mother is, an' yet real capable. Ruth always was a silly, incompetent little thing--she has to hire help most of the time, with nothin' in the world to do but cook for Frank, look after that little tiny house, take care of them two babies, an' go into the store off an' on when business is rushin'. Molly's head is full of nothin' but music, an' Katherine's of books. As to that pretty little fool, Edith, I'm glad she ain't my daughter, runnin' round all the time with that Dutch boy, an' her parents both so possessed with the idea that she ain't out of her cradle yet--she bein' the youngest--that they can't see it. Peter ain't the only one she keeps company with either--if he was, it wouldn't be so bad, for I guess he's a good enough boy, though I can't understand a mortal word he says, an' them foreigners all have a kinder vacant look, to me. But the other night I was took awful sudden with one of them horrible attacks of indigestion I'm subject to--we'd had rhubarb pie for supper, an' 'twas just elegant, but I guess I ate too much of it, an' the telephone wouldn't work on account of the thunderstorm we'd had that day--seems like that there'd been a lot of them this season--so Joe had to hitch up an' go for the doctor. As he went past the cemetery, he see Edith leanin' over the fence with that no-count Jack Weston--an' it was past midnight, too!"

In the midst of such general satisfaction, it was perhaps inevitable that at least one person should not be pleased. And that person, as will be readily guessed, was Thomas. Sylvia, thinking the blow might fall more bearably from his brother's hand than from hers, relegated the task of writing him to Austin; and Austin, with a wicked twinkle in his eye, wrote him in this wise:

DEAR THOMAS:

When you made that little break that I warned you against this spring, Sylvia probably offered to be a sister to you. I believe that is usual on such occasions. You have doubtless noticed that she is exceptionally truthful for a girl, so--largely to keep her word to you, perhaps--she decided a little while ago to marry me. Of course, I tried to dissuade her from this plan, but you know she is also stubborn.

There seems to be nothing for me to do but to fall in with it. I don't know yet when the execution is going to take place, and though, of course, it would be a relief in a way if I did, I am not finding the death sentence without its compensations. Why don't you come home over some Sunday, and see how well I am bearing up? Sylvia told me to ask you, with her love, or I should not bother, for I am naturally a little loath, even now, to have so dangerous a rival, as you proved yourself in your spring vacation, too much in evidence.

Your affectionate brother
AUSTIN

P.S. Have you taken any more ladies to Moving-Picture Palaces lately?

Needless to say, if Sylvia had seen this epistle, it would not have gone. But she did not. Austin took good care of that. And Thomas did come home--without waiting for Sunday. He rushed to the Dean's office, and told him there had been a death in the family. It is probable that, at the moment, he felt that this was true. At any rate, the Dean, looking at the boy's flushed cheeks and heavy eyes, did not doubt it for an instant.

"Of course, you must go home at once," he said kindly; "wait a minute, my Ford's at the door. I'll run you down to the station--you can just catch the one o'clock. I'll tell one of the fellows to express a suit-case to you this evening."

Travel on the Central Vermont Railroad is safe, but its best friend cannot maintain that it is swift. To get from Lake Champlain to the Connecticut River requires several changes, much patient waiting in small and uninteresting stations for connections, and the consumption of considerable time. It was a little after seven when Thomas, dinnerless and supperless, reached Hamstead, and plodding doggedly up the road in a heavy rain, met Mr. and Mrs. Elliott just starting out in their buggy for Thursday evening prayer meeting.

"Pull up, Joe," the latter said excitedly, as she spied the boy advancing towards them. "I do declare, there's Thomas Gray comin' up the road. I wonder if he's been expelled, or only suspended. I must find out, so's I can tell the folks about it after meetin', an' go down an' comfort Mary the first thing in the mornin' after I get them tomato plants set out. I always thought Thomas was some steadier than Austin, but Burlington's a gay place, an' he's probably got in with wild companions up there. Do you suppose it's some cheap little show girl, or gettin' in liquor by express from over in New York State, or forgin' a check on account of gamblin' debts? I know how boys spend their time while they're gettin' educated, you can't tell me. Or maybe he hasn't passed some examination. He never was extra bright. Failed everything, probably.--Good-evenin', Thomas, it's nice to see you back, but quite a surprise, it not bein' vacation time or nothin'. I suppose everything's goin' fine at college, ain't it?"

Thomas had never loved Mrs. Elliott, and lately he had come as near hating her as he was capable of hating anybody. He longed inexpressibly to cast a withering scowl in her direction, and pass on without answering. But his inborn civility was greater than his aversion. He pulled off his cap and stopped.

"Yes, everything's all right--I guess," he said, rather stupidly. Then a brilliant inspiration struck him. "I've been doing so well in my studies that they've given me a few days off to come home. That doesn't often happen--they made an exception in my case."

It was seldom that the slow-witted Thomas was blessed with one of these flights of fancy. For a minute he felt almost cheered. Mrs. Elliott was baffled.

"Do tell," she exclaimed. "It must be a rare thing--I never hear the like of it before. I'm most surprised you didn't take advantage of such a chance to go down to Boston an' see Molly. Didn't feel's you could afford it, I suppose. I guess she's kinder lonely down there. She don't seem to get acquainted real fast. You'd think, with all the people there *are* in Boston, she wouldn't ha' had much trouble, but then Molly's manner ain't in her favor, an' I suppose folks in the city is real busy--must be awful hard to keep house, livin' the way they do. I don't think much of city life. The last time Joe an' I went down on the excursion, we see the Charles River, an' the Old Ladies' Home, an' the Chamber of Horrors down on Washington Street, but we was real glad to come home. There was somethin' the matter with the lock to our suit-case, an' we couldn't get it undone all the time we was there, but fortunately it was real warm weather, so we really didn't suffer none. I thought by this time Molly might have a beau, but then, Molly's real plain. If the looks could ha' ben divided up more even between her an' Edith, same's the brains between you an' Austin, 'twould ha' ben a good thing, wouldn't it? But then you say you're gettin' on well now, an' in time some man may marry her, so's he can set an' listen to her play when he comes in tired from his chores at night. I've heard of sech things. An' then there's quite a bunch of love-affairs in the family already, ain't there?"

"Yes," said Thomas angrily, "there is."

Mrs. Elliott was quick to mark his tone. She nudged her husband.

"Well, well," she said playfully, "Austin's cut you out, ain't he? Mr. Jessup was in the race for a while, too, an' I thought he was runnin' pretty good, but you know we read in the Bible it don't always go to the swift. An' Austin may not get her af-ter all--I hear there's several in New York as well an' she might change her mind. I never set much stock in young men marryin' widows myself. Seems like there's plenty of nice girls as ought to have a chance. An' Sylvia's awful high-toned, an' stubborn as a mule--I dunno's she an' Austin will be able to stick it out, he's some set himself. I shouldn't wonder if it all got broke off, an' I'm not sayin' it mightn't be for the best if it was. But I don't deny Sylvia's real pretty an' generous, an' I like her spunk. I was tellin' Joe only yesterday--"

"I'm afraid I'm keeping you from meeting," said Thomas desperately, and strode off down the road.

The barn--the beautiful new barn that Sylvia had made possible and that had filled his heart with such joy and pride--was still lighted. He walked straight to it, and met Peter coming out of the door. Peter stared his surprise.

"Where's my brother?" asked Thomas roughly.

"Mr. Gray ben still in the barn vorking. It's too bad he haf so much to do--he don't get much time mit de missus--den she tink he don't vant to come. I'm glad you're back, Mr. Thomas. I vas yust gon in to get ve herd book for him. I took it in to show Edit' someting I vant to explain to her, and left it in ve house. Most dum."

"You needn't bring it back. I want to see him alone."

Peter nodded, his bewilderment growing, and disappeared. Thomas flung him-self down the long stable, without once glancing at the row of beautiful cows, his footsteps echoing on the concrete, to the office at the farther end. The door was open, and Austin sat at the roll-top desk, which was littered with account books, transfer sheets, and pedigree cards, typewriting vigorously. He sprang up in sur-prise.

"Why, Thomas!" he exclaimed cordially. "Where did you drop from? I'm awfully glad to see you!"

"You damned mean deceitful skunk!" cried the boy, slamming the door behind him, and ignoring his brother's outstretched hand. "I'd like to smash every bone in your body until there wasn't a piece as big as a toothpick left of you! You made me think you didn't care a rap about her--you said I wasn't worthy of her--that I was an ignorant farmer and she was a great lady. That's true enough--but I'm just as good as you are, every bit! I know you've done all sorts of rotten things I never have! But just the same this is the first time I ever thought that you--or any Gray-- wasn't *square*! And then you write me a letter about her like that--as if she'd flung herself at your head-- *Sylvia*!"

Austin's conscience smote him. He had never seen Thomas's side before; and neither he nor any other member of the family had guessed how much their incessant teasing had hurt, or how hard the younger brother had been hit. In the extremely unsentimental way common in New England, these two were very fond of each other, and he realized that Thomas's affection, which was very precious to him, would be gone forever if he did not set him right at once.

"Look here," he said, forcing Thomas into the swivel chair, and seating himself on the desk, ignoring the papers that fell fluttering to the floor, "you listen to me. You've got everything crooked, and it's my fault, and I'm darned sorry. I never told you I cared for Sylvia, not because I wanted to deceive you, but because I cared so everlasting *much*, from the first moment I set eyes on her, that I couldn't talk about it. No one else guessed either--you weren't the only one. The funny part of it is, that *she* didn't! She thought, because I steered pretty clear of her, out of a sense of duty, that I didn't like her especially. Imagine--not liking Sylvia! Ever hear of any one who didn't like roses, Thomas? But I never dreamed that she'd have me--or even of asking her to! As to throwing herself at my head--well, she put it that way herself once, and I shut her up pretty quick--you'll find out how to do it yourself some day, with some other girl, though, of course, it doesn't look that way to you now--but I can't give you that treatment! I guess I'll have to tell you--though I never expected to tell a living soul--just how it did happen. It's--it's the sort of thing that is too sacred to share with any one, even any one that I think as much of as I do of you--but I've got to make you believe that, five minutes beforehand, I had no idea it was going to occur." And as briefly and honestly as he could, he told Thomas how Sylvia had come to him while he was making his bonfire, and what had taken place afterwards. Then, with still greater feeling in his voice, he went on: "There's something else I haven't told any one else either, and that is, that I can't for a single instant get away from the thought that, even now, I'm not going to get her. I know I haven't any right to her and I don't feel sure that I can make her happy--that she can respect me as much as a girl ought to respect the man she's going to marry. I certainly don't think I'm any worthier of her than you--or as worthy--never did for a minute. I *have* done lots of rotten things, and you've always been as straight as a string--and you'd better thank the Lord you have! When you get engaged you won't have to go through what I have! But you see the difference is, as far as Sylvia and you and I are concerned"--he hesitated, his throat growing rough, his ready eloquence checked--"Sylvia likes you ever so much; she thinks you're a fine boy, and that by and by you'll want to marry a fine girl; but I'm a man already, and young as she is, Sylvia's a woman--and God knows why--she loves me!"

Austin glanced at Thomas. The anger was dying out of the boy's face, and unashamed tears were standing in his eyes.

"A lot," added Austin huskily. Then, after a long pause: "Won't you have a whiskey-and-soda with me--I've got some in the cupboard here for emergencies, while we talk over some of this business I was deep in when you came in? There are any number of things I've been anxious to get your opinion on--you've got lots of practical ability and good judgment in places where I'm weak, and I miss you no end when you're where I can't get at you--I certainly shall be glad when you're through your course, and home for good! And after we get this mess straightened out"--he bent over to pick up the scattered sheets--"we'd better go in together and find Sylvia, hadn't we?"

CHAPTER XVI

Strangely enough, Sylvia and Austin were perhaps less happy at this time than any of the other dwellers at the Homestead. After the first day, the week in New York had been a period of great happiness to both of them, and Austin had proved such an immediate success, both among Sylvia's friends and Uncle Mat's business associates, that both were immensely gratified. But after the return to the country, matters seemed to go less and less well. During the year in which they had "loved and longed in secret," each had exalted the other to the position of a martyr and a saint. The intimacy of their engagement was rapidly revealing the fact that, after all, they were merely ordinary human beings, and the discovery was something of a shock to both. Austin had thought over Uncle Mat's advice, and found it good; he was gentle and considerate, and showed himself perfectly willing to submit to Sylvia's wishes in most important decisions, but he refused to be dictated to in little things. She was so accustomed, by this time, to having her slightest whim not only respected, but admired, by all the adoring Gray family, and most of her world at large besides, that she was apt to behave like a spoiled child when Austin thwarted her. She nearly always had to admit, afterwards, that he had been right, and this did not make it any easier for her. His "incessant obstinacy," as she called it, was rapidly "getting on her nerves," while it seemed to him that they could never meet that she did not have some fresh grievance, or disagree with him radically about something. She wanted him at her side all the time; he had a thousand other interests. She saw no reason why, after they were married, they should live in the country all the year, and every year; he saw no reason why they should do anything else. And so it went with every subject that arose.

If Sylvia had been less idle, she would have had no time to think about "nerves." But the manservant and his wife whom she had installed in the little brick house were well-trained and competent to the last degree, and the menage ran like clock-work without any help from her. She was debarred from riding or driving alone, and the girls at the farm had no time to go with her, and it was still an almost unheard-of thing in that locality for a woman to run a motor. She could not fill an hour a day working in her little garden, and she had no special taste for sewing. The only thing for her to do seemed to be to sit around and wait for Austin to appear, and Austin was not only very busy, but extremely absorbed in his work. It was impossible for him to come to see her every night, and when he did come, he was so thoroughly and wholesomely tired and sleepy, that his visits were short. On Sundays he had more leisure; but Mr. and Mrs. Gray seemed to take it for granted that Sylvia would still go to church with them in the morning, and spend the rest of the day at their house. She could not bring herself to the point of disappointing them, though she rebelled inwardly; but she complained to Austin, as they were walking back to her house together after a day spent in this manner, that she never saw him alone at all.

"It's not only the family," she said, "but Peter, and Fred, and Mr. and Mrs. Elliott are around all the time, and to-day there were Ruth and Frank and those two fussy babies needing something done for them every single minute besides! It was perfect bedlam. I want you to myself once in a while."

"You can have me to yourself, for good and all, whenever you want me," replied Austin.

This was so undeniable a statement that Sylvia changed the subject abruptly.

"There is no earthly need of your working so hard, and you know it."

"But Sylvia, I like to work; and I'm awfully anxious to make a success of things, now that we've got such a wonderful start at last."

"Are you more interested in this stupid old farm than you are in me?"

"Why, Sylvia, it isn't a 'stupid old farm' to me! It's the place my great-grand-father built, and that all the Grays have lived in and loved for four generations! I thought you liked it, too."

"I do, but I'm jealous of it."

"You ought not to be. You know that there's nothing in the world so dear to me as you are."

"Then let me pay for another hired man, so that you'll have more time for yourself--and for me."

"Indeed, I will not. You'll never pay for another thing on this farm if I can help it. No one could be more grateful than I am for all you've done, but the time is over for that."

"Won't you come in?" she asked, as, they reached her garden, and she noticed that he stopped at the gate.

"Not to-night--we've had a good walk together, and you know I have to get up pretty early in the morning. Good-night, dear," and he raised her fingers to his lips.

She snatched them away, lifting her lovely face. "Oh, Austin!" she cried, "how can you be so calm and cold? I think sometimes you're made of stone! If you must go, don't say good-night like that--act as if you were made of flesh and blood!"

"I'm acting in the only sane way for both of us. If you don't like it, I had better not come at all."

And he went home without giving her even the caress he had originally intended, and slept soundly and well all night; but Sylvia tossed about for hours, and finally, at dawn, cried herself to sleep.

The first serious disagreement, however, came just before Katherine's graduation. Austin, who loved to dance, was looking forward to his clever sister's "ball" with a great deal of pride and pleasure, and was genuinely amazed when Sylvia objected violently to his going, saying that as she could not dance, and as all the rest of the family would be there, Katherine did not need him, and that he had much better stay at home with her.

"But, Sylvia," protested Austin, "I *want* to go. I'm awfully proud of Katherine, and I wouldn't miss it for anything. Why don't you come, too? I don't see any reason why you shouldn't."

"Of course you don't. You weren't brought up among people who know what's proper in such matters."

"I know it, Sylvia. But if that's going to trouble you, you should have thought of it sooner. My knowledge of etiquette is very slight, I admit, but my common-sense tells me that announcing one's engagement should be equivalent to stopping all former observances of mourning."

"I didn't want to announce it. It was you that insisted upon that, too."

"Well, you know why," said Austin with some meaning.

"All right, then," burst out Sylvia angrily, "go to your old ball. You seem to think you are an authority on everything. I'm sure I don't want to go, anyway, and dance with a lot of awkward farmers who smell of the cow-stable. I shouldn't think you would care about it either, now that you've had a chance to see things properly done."

"I care a good deal about my sister, Sylvia, and about my friends here, too. There are no better people on the face of the earth--I've heard you say so, yourself! It's only a chance that I'm a little less awkward than some of the others."

The result of this conversation was that Austin did not go near Sylvia for several days. He was deeply hurt, but that was not all. He began to wonder, even more than he ever had before, whether his comparative poverty, his lack of education, his farmer family and traditions and friends, were not very real barriers between himself and a girl like Sylvia. What was more, he questioned whether a strong, passionate, determined man, who felt that he knew his own best course and proposed to take it, could ever make such a delicate, self-willed little creature happy, even if there were no other obstacles in their path than those of warring disposition.

Something of his old sullenness of manner returned, and his mother, after worrying in silence over him for a time finally asked him what the trouble was. At first he denied that there was anything, next stubbornly refused to tell her what it was, and at last, like a hurt schoolboy, blurted out his grievance. To his amazement and grief, Mrs. Gray took Sylvia's part. This was the last straw. He jerked himself away from her, and went out, slamming the front door after him. It was evening, and he was tired and hot and dirty. The rest of the family had almost finished supper when he reached the table, an unexpected delay having arisen in the barn, and he had eaten the unappetizing scraps that remained hurriedly, without taking time to shave and bathe and change his clothes. He had never gone to Sylvia in this manner before; but he strode down the path to her house with a bitter satisfaction in his heart that she was to see him when he was looking and feeling his worst, and that she would have to take him as he was, or not at all. He found her in her garden cutting roses, a picture of dainty elegance in her delicate white fabrics. She greeted him somewhat coolly, as if to punish him for his lack of deference to her on his last visit, and his subsequent neglect, and glanced at his costume with a disapproval which she was at no pains to conceal. Then with a sarcasm and lack of tact which she had never shown before, she gave voice to her general dissatisfaction.

"*Really, Austin*, don't come near me, please; you're altogether too *barny*. Don't you think you're carrying your devotion to the nobility of labor a little too far, and your devotion to me--if you still have any--not quite far enough? You're slipping straight back to your old slovenly, disagreeable ways--without the excuse that you formerly had that they were practically the only ways open to you. If you're too proud to accept my money and the freedom that it can give you, and so stubborn that you make a scene and then won't come near me for days because I refuse to go to a cheap little public dance with you--"

She got no farther. Austin interrupted her with a violence of which she would not have believed him capable.

"*If*! If you're too stubborn to go with me to my sister's *graduation ball*, and too proud to accept the fact that I'm a *farmer*, with a farmer's friends and family and work, and that *I'm damned glad of it*, and won't give them up, or be supported by any woman on the face of the earth, or let her make a pet lap-dog of me, you can go straight back to the life you came from, for all me! You seem to prefer it, after all, and I believe it's all you deserve. If you don't--don't ask my forgiveness for the things you've said the last two times I've seen you, and say *you'll go to that party* with me, and be just as darned pleasant to every one there as you know how to be--and promise to stop quarrelling, and keep your promise--I'll never come near you again. You're making my life utterly miserable. You won't marry me, and yet you are bound to have me make love to you all the time, when I'm doing my best to keep my hands off you--and I'd rather be shot *than* marry you, on the terms you're putting up to me at present! You've got two days to think it over in, and if you don't send for me before it's time to start for the ball, and tell me you're sorry, you won't get another chance to send for me again as long as you live. I'm either not worth having at all, or I'm worth treating better than you've seen fit to do lately!"

He left her, without even looking at her again, in a white heat of fury. But before the hot dawn of another June day had given him an excuse to get up and try to work off his feelings with the most strenuous labor that he could find, he had spent a horrible sleepless night which he was never to forget as long as he lived. His anger gave way first to misery, and then to a panic of fear. Suppose she took him literally--

though he had meant every word when he said it--suppose he lost her? What would the rest of his life be worth to him, alone, haunted, not only by his senseless folly in casting away such a precious treasure, but by his ingratitude, his presumption, and his own unworthiness? A dozen times he started towards her house, only to turn back again. She *hadn't* been fair. They *couldn't* be happy that way. If he gave in now, he would have to do it all the rest of his life, and she would despise him for it. As the time which he had stipulated went by, and no message came, he suffered more and more intensely--hoped, savagely, that she was suffering, too, and decided that she could not be, or that he would have heard from her; but resolved, more and more decidedly, with every hour that passed, that he would fight this battle out to the bitter end.

It was even later than usual when he came in on the night of the ball, and when he entered, every one in the house was hurrying about in the inevitable confusion which precedes a "great occasion." Edith, the only one who seemed to be ready, was standing in the middle of the living-room, fresh and glowing as a yellow rose in her bright dress, Peter beside her buttoning her gloves. She glanced at her grimy brother with a feeble interest.

"Mercy, Austin, you'd better hurry! We're going to leave in five minutes."

"Well, *I'm* not going to leave in five minutes! I've got to get out of these clothes and have a bath and it's hardly necessary to tell me all that--one glance at you is sufficient," said Edith flippantly.

"Well, I can come on later alone, I suppose. Where's mother?"

"Still dressing. Why?"

"Do you happen to know whether--Sylvia's been over here this afternoon--or sent a telephone message or a note?"

"I'm perfectly sure she hasn't. Why?"

"Nothing," said Austin grimly, and left the room.

Like most people who try to dress in a hurry when they are angry, Austin found that everything went wrong. There was no hot water left, and he had to heat some himself for shaving while he took a cold bath; his mother usually got his clothes ready for him when she knew he was detained, but this time she had apparently been too rushed herself. He couldn't find his evening shoes; he couldn't get his studs into his stiff shirt until he had had a struggle that raised his temperature several degrees higher than it was already; the big, jolly teamful departed while he was rummaging through his top drawer for fresh handkerchiefs; and he was vainly trying to adjust his white tie satisfactorily, when a knock at the door informed him that he was not alone in the house after all; he said "come in" crossly, and without turning, and went on with his futile attempts.

"Has every one else gone? I didn't know I was so late--but I've been all through the house downstairs calling, and couldn't get any answer. Let me do that for you--let's take a fresh one--"

He wheeled sharply around, and found Sylvia standing beside him--Sylvia, dressed in shell-pink, shimmering satin and foamy lace, with pearls in her dark hair and golden slippers on her feet, her neck and arms white and bare and gleaming. With a little sound that was half a sob, and half a cry of joy, she flung her arms around his neck and drew his face down to hers.

"Austin--I'm--I'm sorry--I do--beg your forgiveness from the bottom of my heart. I promise--and I'll keep my promise--to be reasonable--and kind--and fair--to stop making you miserable. It's been all my fault that we've quarrelled, every bit--and we never will again. I've come to tell you--not just that I'll go to the party with you, gladly, if you're still willing to take me, but that there's nothing that matters to me in the whole world--except you--"

The first touch of Sylvia's arms set Austin's brain seething; after the hungry misery of the past few days, it acted like wine offered to a starving man, suddenly snatched and drunk. Her words, her tears, her utter self-abandonment of voice and manner, annihilated in one instant the restraint in which he had held himself for months. He caught the delicate little creature to him with all his strength, burying his face in the white fragrance of her neck. He forgot everything in the world except that she was in his arms--alone with him--that nothing was to come between them again as long as they lived. He could feel her heart beating against his under the soft lace on her breast, her cool cheeks and mouth growing warm under the kisses that he rained on them until his own lips stung. At first she returned his embrace with an ardor that equalled his own; then, as if conscious that she was being carried away by the might of a power which she could neither measure nor control, she tried to turn her face away and strove to free herself.

"Don't," she panted; "let me go! You--you-hurt me, Austin."

"I can't help it--I shan't let you go! I'm going to kiss you this time until I get ready to stop."

For a moment she struggled vainly. Austin's arms tightened about her like bands of steel. She gave a little sigh, and lifted her face again.

"I can't seem to--kiss back any more," she whispered, "but if this is what you want--if it will make up to you for these last weeks--it doesn't matter whether you hurt or not."

Every particle of resistance had left her. Austin had wished for an unconditional surrender, and he had certainly attained it. There could never again be any question of which should rule. She had come and laid her sweet, proud, rebellious spirit at his very feet, begging his forgiveness that it had not sooner recognized its master. A wonderful surge of triumph at his victory swept over him--and then, suddenly--he was sick and cold with shame and contrition. He released her, so abruptly that she staggered, catching hold of a chair to steady herself, and raising one small clenched hand to her lips, as if to press away their smarting. As she did so, he saw a deep red mark on her bare white arm. He winced, as if he had been struck, at the gesture and what it disclosed, but it needed neither to show him that she was bruised and hurt from the violence of his embrace; and dreadful as he instantly realized this to be, it seemed to matter very little if he could only learn that she was not hurt beyond all healing by divining the desire and intention which for one sacrilegious moment had almost mastered him.

A gauzy scarf which she had carried when she entered the room had fallen to the floor. He stooped and picked it up, and stood looking at it, running it through his hands, his head bent. It was white and sheer, a mere gossamer--he must have stepped on it, for in one place it was torn, in another slightly soiled. Sylvia, watching him, holding her breath, could see the muscles of his white face growing tenser and tenser around his set mouth, and still he did not glance at her or speak to her. At last he unfolded it to its full size, and wrapped it about her, his eyes giving her the smile which his lips could not.

"Nothing matters to me in the whole world either--except you," he said brokenly. "I think these last few--dreadful days--have shown us both how much we need each other, and that the memory of them will keep us closer together all our lives. If there's any question of forgiveness between us, it's all on my side now, not yours, and I don't think I can--talk about it now. But I'll never forget how you came to me to-night, and, please God, some day I'll be more worthy of--of your love and--and your *trust* than I've shown myself now. Until I am--" He stopped, and, lifting her arm, kissed the bruise which his own roughness had made there. "What can I do--to make that better?" he managed to say.

"It didn't hurt--much--before--and it's all healed--now," she said, smiling up at him; "didn't your mother ever 'kiss the place to make it well' when you were a little boy, and didn't it always work like a charm? It won't show at all, either, under my glove."

"Your glove?" he asked stupidly; and then, suddenly remembering what he had entirely forgotten--"Oh--we were going to a ball together. You came to tell me you would, after all. But surely you won't want to now--"

"Why not? We can take the motor--we won't be so very late--the others went in the carryall, you know."

He drew a long breath, and looked away from her. "All right," he said at last. "Go downstairs and get your cloak, if you left it there. I'll be with you in a minute."

She obeyed, without a word, but waited so long that she grew alarmed, and finally, unable to endure her anxiety any longer, she went back upstairs. Austin's door was open into the hall, but it was dark in his room, and, genuinely frightened, she groped her way towards the electric switch. In doing so she stumbled against the bed, and her hand fell on Austin's shoulder. He was kneeling there, his whole body shaking, his head buried in his arms. Instantly she was on her knees beside him.

"My darling boy, what is it? Austin, *don't*! You'll break my heart."

"The marvel is--if I haven't--just now. I told your uncle that I was afraid I would some time--that I knew I hadn't any right to you. But I didn't think--that even I was bad enough--to fail you--like *this*--"

"You *haven't* failed me--you *have* a right to me--I never loved you so much in all my life--" she hurried on, almost incoherently, searching for words of comfort. "Dearest--will it make you feel any better--if I say I'll marry you--right away?"

"What do you mean? When?"

"To-night, if you like. Oh, Austin, I love you so that it doesn't matter a bit--

whether I'm afraid or not. The only thing that really counts--is to have you happy! And since I've realized that--I find that I'm not afraid of anything in the whole world--and that I want to belong to you as much--and as soon--as you can possibly want to have me!"

*   *   *   *   *

It was many months before Hamstead stopped talking about the "Graduation Ball of that year." It surpassed, to an almost extraordinary degree, any that had ever been held there. But the event upon which the village best loved to dwell was the entrance of Sylvia Cary, the loveliest vision it had ever beheld, on Austin Gray's arm, when all the other guests were already there, and everyone had despaired of their coming. Following the unwritten law in country places, which decrees that all persons engaged, married, or "keeping company," must have their "first dance" together, she gave that to Austin. Then Thomas and James, Frank and Fred, Peter, and even Mr. Gray and Mr. Elliott, all claimed their turn, and by that time Austin was waiting impatiently again. But country parties are long, and before the night was over, all the men and boys, who had been watching her in church, and bowing when they met her in the road, and seizing every possible chance to speak to her when they went to the Homestead on errands--or excuses for errands--had demanded and been given a dance. She was lighter than thistledown--indeed, there were moments when she seemed scarcely a woman at all, but a mere essence of fragile beauty and sweetness and graciousness. It had been generally conceded beforehand that the honors of the ball would all go to Edith, but even Edith herself admitted that she took a second place, and that she was glad to take it.

Dawn was turning the quiet valley and distant mountains into a riotous rosy glory, when, as they drove slowly up to her house, Austin gently raised the gossamer scarf which had blown over Sylvia's face, half-hiding it from him. She looked up with a smile to answer his.

"Are you very tired, dear?"

"Not at all--just too happy to talk much, that's all."

"Sylvia--"

"Yes, darling--"

"You know I have planned to start West with Peter three days after Sally's wedding--"

"Yes--"

"Would you rather I didn't go?"

"No; I'm glad you're going--I mean, I'm glad you have decided to keep to your plan."

"What makes you think I have?"

"Because, being you, you couldn't do otherwise."

"But when I come back--"

Her fingers tightened in his.

"I want two months all alone with you in this little house," he whispered. "Send the servants away--it won't be very hard to do the work--for just us two--I'll help. That's--that's-- *marriage* --a big wedding and a public honeymoon--and--all that go with them--are just a cheap imitation--of the real thing. Then, later on, if you like, this first winter, we'll go away together--to Spain or Italy or the South of France--or wherever you wish--but first--we'll begin together here. Will you marry me--the first of September, Sylvia?"

Austin drove home in the broad daylight of four o'clock on a June morning. Then, after the motor was put away, he took his working clothes over his arm, went to the river, and plunged in. When he came back, with damp hair, cool skin, and a heart singing with peace and joy, he found Peter, whistling, starting towards the barn with his milk-pail over his arm. It was the beginning of a new day.

CHAPTER XVII

I, Sarah, take thee, Frederick, to my wedded husband, to have and to hold from this day forward, for better for worse, for richer for poorer, in sickness and in health, to love, cherish, and to obey, till death us do part, according to God's holy ordinance. And thereto I give thee my troth."

The old clock in the corner was ticking very distinctly; the scent of roses in the crowded room made the air heavy with sweetness; the candles on the mantelpiece flickered in the breeze from the open window; outside a whip-poor-will was singing in the lilac bushes.

"With this ring I thee wed, and with all my worldly goods I thee endow: In the name of the Father, and of the Son, and of the Holy Ghost. Amen."

An involuntary tear rolled down Mrs. Gray's cheek, to be hastily concealed and wiped away with her new lace handkerchief; her husband was looking straight ahead of him, very hard, at nothing; Ruth adjusted the big white bow on little Elsie's curls; Sylvia felt for Austin's hand behind the folds of her dress, and found it groping for hers.

Then suddenly the spell was broken. The minister was shaking hands with the bride and groom, Sally was taking her bouquet from Molly, every one was laughing and talking at once, crowding up to offer congratulations, handling, admiring, and discussing the wedding presents, half-falling over each other with haste and excitement. Delicious smells began to issue from the kitchen, and the long dining-table was quickly laden down. Sylvia took her place at one end, behind the coffee-urn, Molly at the other end, behind the strawberries and ice-cream. Katherine, Edith, and the boys flew around passing plates, cakes of all kinds, great sugared doughnuts and fat cookies. Sally was borne into the room triumphant on a "chair" made of her brothers' arms to cut and distribute the "bride's cake." Then, when every one had eaten as much as was humanly possible, the piano was moved out to the great new barn, with its fine concrete floors swept and scoured as only Peter could do it, and its every stall festooned with white crepe paper by Sylvia, and the dancing began--for this time the crowd was too great to permit it in the house, in spite of the spacious rooms. Molly and Sylvia took turns in playing, and each found several eager partners waiting for her, every time the "shift" occurred. Finally, about midnight, the bride went upstairs to change her dress, and the girls gathered around the banisters to be ready to catch the bouquet when she came down, laughing and teasing each other while they waited. Great shouts arose, and much joking began, when Edith--and not Sylvia as every one had privately hoped--caught the huge bunch of flowers and ribbon, and ran with it in her arms out on the wide piazza, all the others behind her, to be ready to pelt Sally and Fred with rice when they appeared. Thomas was to drive them to the station, and Sylvia's motor was bedecked with white garlands and bows, slippers and bells, from one end of it to the other. At last the rush came; and the happy victims, showered and dishevelled, waving their handkerchiefs and shouting good-bye, were whisked up the hill, and out of sight.

Sylvia insisted on staying, to begin "straightening out the worst of the mess" as soon as the last guest had gone, and on remaining overnight, sleeping in Sally's old room with Molly, to be on hand and go on with the good work the first thing in the morning. Sadie and James had to leave on the afternoon train, as James had stretched his leave of absence from business to the very last degree already; so by evening the house was painfully tidy again, and so quiet that Mrs. Gray declared it "gave her the blues just to listen to it."

The next night was to be Austin's last one at home, and he had promised Sylvia to go and take supper with her, but just before six o'clock the telephone rang, and she knew that something had happened to disappoint her.

"Is that you, Sylvia?"

"Yes, dear."

"Mr. Carter--the President of the Wallacetown Bank, you know--has just called me up. There's going to be a meeting of the bank officers just after the fourth, as they've decided to enlarge their board of directors, and add at least one 'rising young farmer' as he put it--And oh, Sylvia, he asked if I would allow my name to be proposed! Just think--after all the years when we couldn't get a *cent* from them at any rate of interest, to have that come! It's every bit due to you!"

"It isn't either--it's due to the splendid work you've done this last year."

"Well, we won't stop to discuss that now. He wants me to drive up and see him about it right away. Do you mind if I take the motor? I can make so much better time, and get back to you so much more quickly--but I can't come to supper--you must forgive me if I go."

"I never should forgive you if you didn't--that's wonderful news! Don't hurry--I'll be glad to see you whatever time you get back."

She hung up the receiver, and sat motionless beside the instrument, too thrilled for the moment to move. What a man he was proving himself--her farmer! And yet--how each new responsibility, well fulfilled, was going to take him more and more from her! She sighed involuntarily, and was about to rise, when the bell sounded again.

"Hullo," she said courteously, but tonelessly. The bottom of the evening had dropped out for her. It mattered very little how she spent it now until Austin arrived.

"Land, Sylvia, you sound as if there'd ben a death in the family! Do perk up a little! Yes, this is Mrs. Elliott--Maybe if some of the folks on this line that's taken their receivers down so's they'll know who I'm talkin' to an' what I'm sayin' will hang up you can hear me a little more plain." (This timely remark resulted in several little clicks.) "There, that's better. I see Austin tearin' past like mad in your otter, and I says to Joe, 'That means Sylvia's all alone again, same as usual; I'm goin' to call her up an' visit with her a spell!' Hot, ain't it? Yes, I always suffer considerable with the heat. I sez this mornin' to Joe, 'Joe, it's goin' to be a hot day,' and he sez, 'Yes, Eliza, I'm afraid it is,' an' I sez, 'Well, we've got to stand it,' an' he--"

"I hope you have," interrupted Sylvia politely.

"Yes, as well as could be expected--you know I ain't over an' above strong this season. My old trouble. But then, I don't complain any--only as I said to Joe, it is awful tryin'. Have you heard how the new minister's wife is doin'? She ain't ben to evenin' meetin' at all regular sence she got here, an' she made an angel cake, just for her own family, last Wednesday. She puts her washin' out, too. I got it straight from Mrs. Jones, next door to her. I went there the other evenin' to get a night-gown pattern she thought was real tasty. I don't know as I shall like it, though.

It's supposed to have a yoke made out of crochet or tattin' at the top, an' I ain't got anything of the kind on hand just now, an' no time to make any. Besides, I've never thought these new-fangled garments was just the thing for a respectable woman-- there ain't enough to 'em. When I was young they was made of good thick cotton, long-sleeved an' high-necked, trimmed with Hamburg edgin' an' buttoned down the front. Speakin' of nightgowns, how are you gettin' on with your trousseau? Have you decided what you're goin' to wear for a weddin' dress? I was readin' in the paper the other day about some widow that got married down in Boston, an' she wore a pink chif*fon* dress. I was real shocked. If she'd ben a divorced person, I should have expected some such thing, but there warn't anything of the kind in this case--she was a decent young woman, an' real pretty, judgin' from her picture. But I should have thought she'd have wore gray or lavender, wouldn't you? There oughtn't to be anything gay about a second weddin'! Well, as I was sayin' to Joe about the minister's wife--What's that? You think they're both real nice, an' you're glad he's got *some* sort of a wife? Now, Sylvia, I always did think you was a little mite hard on Mr. Jessup. I says to Joe, 'Joe, Sylvia's a nice girl, but she's a flirt, sure as you're settin' there,' an' Joe says--"

"Have you heard from Fred and Sally yet?"

"Yes, they've sent us three picture post-cards. Real pretty. There ain't much space for news on 'em, though--they just show a bridge, an' a park, an' a railroad station. Still, of course, we was glad to get 'em, an' they seem to be havin' a fine time. I heard to-day that Ruth's baby was sick again. Delicate, ain't it? I shouldn't be a mite surprised if Ruth couldn't raise her. 'Blue around the eyes,' I says to Joe the first time I ever clapped eyes on her. An' then Ruth ain't got no get-up-and-get to her. Shiftless, same's Howard is, though she's just as well-meanin'. I hear she's thinkin' of keepin' a hired girl all summer. Frank's business don't warrant it. He has a real hard time gettin' along. He's too easy-goin' with his customers. Gives long credit when they're hard up, an' all that. Of course it's nice to be charitable if you can afford it, but--"

"Frank isn't going to pay the hired girl."

"There you go again, Sylvia! You kinder remind me of the widow's cruse, nev- er failin'. 'Tain't many families gets hold of anything like you. Well, I must be sayin' good-night--there seems to be several people tryin' to butt in an' use this line, though probably they don't want it for anything important at all. I've got no patience with folks that uses the telephone as a means of gossip, an' interfere with those that really needs it. Besides, though I'd be glad to talk with you a little longer, I'm plum tuckered out with the heat, as I said before. I ben makin' currant jelly, too. It come out fine--a little too hard, if anything. But, as I says to Joe, 'Druv as I am, I'm a-goin' to call up that poor lonely girl, an' help her pass the evenin'.' Come over an' bring your sewin' an' set with me some day soon, won't you, Sylvia? You know I'm always real pleased to see you. Good-night."

"Good-night." Sylvia leaned back, laughing.

Mrs. Elliott, who infuriated Thomas, and exasperated Austin, was a never-failing source of enjoyment to her. She went back to the porch to wait for Austin, still chuckling.

After the conversation she had had with him, she was greatly surprised, when, a little after eight o'clock, the garden gate clicked. She ran down the steps hurriedly with his name on her lips. But the figure coming towards her through the dusk was much smaller than Austin's and a voice answered her, in broken English, "It ain't Mr. Gray, missus. It's me."

"Why, Peter!" she said in amazement; "is anything the matter at the farm?"

"No, missus; not vat you'd called *vrong*."

"What is it, then? Will you come up and sit down?"

He stood fumbling at his hat for a minute, and then settled himself awkwardly on the steps at her feet. His yellow hair was sleekly brushed, his face shone with soap and water, and he had on his best clothes. It was quiet evident that he had come with the distinct purpose of making a call.

"Can dose domestics hear vat ve say?" he asked at length, turning his wide blue eyes upon her, after some minutes of heavy silence.

"Not a word."

"Vell den--you know Mr. Gray and I goin' avay to-morrow."

"Yes, Peter."

"To be gone much as a mont', Mr. Gray say."

"I believe so."

"Mrs. Cary, dear missus,--vill you look after Edit' vile I'm gone?"

"Why, yes, Peter," she said warmly, "I always see a good deal of Edith--we're great friends, you know."

"Yes, missus, that's vone reason vy I come--Edit' t'ink no vone like you--ever vas, ever shall be. But den--I'm vorried 'bout Edit'."

"Worried? Why, Peter? She's well and strong."

"Oh, yes, she's vell--ver' vell. But Edit' love to have a good time--'vun' she say. If I go mit, she come mit me--ven not, mit some vone else."

"I see--you're jealous, Peter."

"No, no, missus, not jealous, only vorried, ver' vorried. Edit' she's young, but not baby, like Mr. and Missus Gray t'ink. I don't like Mr. Yon Veston, missus, nod ad all--and Edit' go out mit him, ev'y chance she get. An' Mr. Hugh Elliott, cousin to Miss Sally's husband, dey say he liked Miss Sally vonce--he's back here now, he looks hard at Edit' ev'y time he see her. He's that kind of man, missus, vat does look ver' hard."

Sylvia could not help being touched. "I'll do my best, Peter, but I can't promise anything. Edith is the kind of girl, as you say, that likes to have 'fun' and I have no real authority over her."

As if the object of his visit was entirely accomplished, Peter rose to leave. "I t'ank you ver' much, missus," he said politely. "It's a ver' varm evening, not? Good-night."

For a few minutes after Peter left, Sylvia sat thinking over what he had said, and her own face grew "vorried" too. Then the garden gate clicked again, and for the next two hours she was too happy for trouble of any kind to touch her. Austin's interview with Mr. Carter had proved a great success, and after that had been thoroughly discussed, they found a great deal to say about their own plans for September. For the moment, she quite forgot all that Peter had said.

It came back to her, vividly enough, a few nights later. She had sat up very late, writing to Austin, and was still lying awake, long after midnight, when she heard the whirr of a motor near by, and a moment later a soft voice calling under her window. She threw a negligee about her, and ran to the front door; as she unlatched it, Edith slipped in, her finger on her lips.

"Hush! Don't let the servants hear! Oh, Sylvia, I've had such a lark--will you keep me overnight!"

"I would gladly, but your mother would be worried to death."

"No, she won't. You see, I found, two hours ago, that it would be a long time before I got back, and I telephoned her saying I was going to spend the night with you. Don't you understand? She thought I was here then."

"Edith--you didn't lie to your mother!"

"Now, Sylvia, don't begin to scold at this hour, when I'm tired and sleepy as I can be! It wasn't my fault we burst two tires, was it? But mother's prejudiced against Hugh, just because Sally, who's a perfect prude, didn't happen to like him. Lend me one of your delicious night-dresses, do, and let me cuddle down beside you--the bed's so big, you'll never know I'm there."

Sylvia mechanically opened a drawer and handed her the garment she requested.

"Gracious, Sylvia, it's like a cobweb--perhaps if I marry a rich man, I can have things like this! What an angel you look in yours! Austin will certainly think he's struck heaven when he sees you like that! I never could understand what a little thing like you wanted this huge bed for, but, of course, you knew when you bought it--"

"Edith," interrupted Sylvia sharply, "be quiet! In the morning I want to talk with you a little."

But as she lay awake long after the young girl had fallen into a deep, quiet sleep, she felt sadly puzzled to know what she could, with wisdom and helpfulness, say. It was so usual in the country for young girls to ride about alone at night with their admirers, so much the accepted custom, of which no harm seemed to come, that however much she might personally disapprove of such a course, she could not reasonably find fault with it. It was probably her own sense of outraged delicacy, she tried to think, after Edith's careless speech, that made her feel that the child lacked the innate good-breeding and quiet attractiveness, which her sisters, all less pretty than she, possessed to such a marked extent, in spite of their lack of polish. She tried to think that it was only to-night she had noticed how red and full Edith's pouting lips were growing, how careless she was about the depth of her V-cut blouses, how unusually lacking in shyness and restraint for one so young. In the morning, she said nothing and Edith was secretly much relieved; but she went and asked Mrs. Gray if she could not spare her youngest daughter for a visit while Austin was away, "to ward off loneliness." She found the good lady out in the garden, weeding her petunias, and bent over to help her as she made her request.

"There, dearie, don't you bother--you'll get your pretty dress all grass-stain, and it looks to me like another new one! I wouldn't have thought baby-blue would be so becomin' to you, Sylvia. I always fancied it for a blonde, mostly, but there! you've got such lovely skin, anything looks well on you. Do you like petunias? Scarcely anyone has them, an' cinnamon pinks, an' johnnie-jump-ups any more-- it's all sweet-peas, an' nasturtiums, an' such! But to me there ain't any flower any handsomer than a big purple petunia."

"I like them too--and it doesn't matter if my dress does get dirty--it'll wash. Now about Edith--"

"Why, Sylvia, you know how I hate to deny you anything, but I don't see how I can spare her! Here it is hayin'-time, the busiest time of the year, an' Austin an' Peter both gone. I haven't a word to say against them young fellows that Thomas has fetched home from college to help while our boys are gone, they're well-spoken, obligin' chaps as I ever see, but the work don't go the same as it do when your own folks is doin' it, just the same. Besides, Sally's not here to help like she's always been before, summers, an' it makes a pile of difference, I can tell you. Molly can play the piano somethin' wonderful, an' Katherine can spout poetry to beat anything I ever heard, but Edith can get out a whole week's washin' while either one of 'em is a-wonderin' where she's goin' to get the hot water to do it with, an' she's a real good cook! I never see a girl of her years more capable, if I do say so, an' she always looks as neat an' pretty as a new pin, whatever she's doin', too. Why don't you come over to us, if you're lonely? We'd all admire to have you! There, we've got that row cleaned out real good--s'posin' we tackle the candytuft, now, if you feel like it."

Sylvia would gladly have offered to pay for a competent "hired girl," but she did not dare to, for fear of displeasing Austin. So she wrote to Uncle Mat to postpone his prospective visit, to the great disappointment of them both, and filled her tiny house with young friends instead, urging Edith to spend as much time helping her "amuse" them as she could, to the latter's great delight. Unfortunately the girl and one of the boys whom she had invited were already so much interested in each other that they had eyes for no one else, and the other fellow was a quiet, studious chap, who vastly preferred reading aloud to Sylvia to canoeing with Edith. The girl was somewhat piqued by this lack of appreciation, and quickly deserted Sylvia's guests for the more lively charms of Hugh Elliott's red motor and Jack Weston's spruce runabout. Mr. and Mrs. Gray saw no harm in their pet's escapades, but, on the contrary, secretly rejoiced that the humble Peter was at least temporarily removed and other and richer suitors occupying the foreground. They were far from being worldly people, but two of their daughters having already married poor men, they, having had more than their own fair share of drudgery, could not help hoping that this pretty butterfly might be spared the coarser labors of life.

Sylvia longed to write Austin all about it, but she could not bring herself to spoil his trip by speaking slightingly, and perhaps unjustly, of his favorite sister's conduct. As she had rather feared, the short trip originally planned proved so instructive and delightful that it was lengthened, first by a few days and then by a fortnight, so that one week in August was already gone before he returned. He came back in holiday spirits, bubbling over with enthusiasm about his trip, full of new plans and arrangements. His enthusiasm was contagious, and he would talk of nothing and allow her to talk of nothing except themselves.

"My, but it's good to be back! I don't see how I ever stayed away so long."

"You didn't seem to have much difficulty--every time you wrote it was to say you'd be gone a little longer. I suppose some of those New York farmers have pretty daughters?"

"You'd better be careful, or I'll box your ears! What mischief have *you* been up to? I've heard rumors about some bookish chap, who read Keats's sonnets, and sighed at the moon. You see I'm informed. I'll take care how I leave you again."

"You had better. I won't promise to wait for you so patiently next time."

"Don't talk to me about patient waiting! Sylvia, is it really, honestly true I've only got three more weeks of it?"

"It's really, honestly true. Good-night, darling, you *must* go home."

"And *you've* only got three weeks more of being able to say that! I suppose I must obey--but remember, *you'll* have to promise to obey pretty soon."

"I'll be glad to. Austin--"

"Yes, dear--Sylvia, I think your cheeks are softer than ever--

"I don't think Edith looks very well, do you?"

"Why, I thought she never was so pretty! But now you speak of it she *does* seem a little fagged--not fresh, the way you always are! Too much gadding, I'm afraid.”

“I’m afraid so. Couldn’t you--?”

“My dear girl, leave all that to Peter--I’ve got *my* hands full, keeping *you* in order. Sylvia, there’s one thing this trip has convinced me we’ve got to have, right away, and that’s more motors. We’ve got the land, we’ve got the buildings, and we’ve got the stock, but we simply must stop wasting time and grain on so many horses--it’s terribly out of date, to say nothing else against it. We need a touring-car for the family, and a runabout for you and me,--do sell that great ark of yours, and get something you can learn to run yourself, and that won’t use half the gasoline,-- and a tractor to plough with, and a truck to take the cream to the creamery.”

“Well, I suppose you’ll let me give these various things for Christmas presents, won’t you? You’re so awfully afraid that I’ll contribute the least little bit to the success of the farm that I hardly dare ask. But I could bestow the tractor on Thomas, the truck on your father, and the touring-car on the girls, and certainly we’ll need the runabout for all-day trips on Sundays--after the first of September.”

“All right. I’ll concede the motors as your share. Now, what will you give me for a reward for being so docile?”

She watched him down the path with a heart overflowing with happiness. Twice he turned back to wave his hand to her, then disappeared, whistling into the darkness. She knelt beside her bed for a long time that night, and finally fell into a deep, quiet sleep, her hand clasping the little star that hung about her throat.

Three hours later she was abruptly awakened, and sat up, confused and startled, to find Austin leaning over her, shaking her gently, and calling her name in a low, troubled voice.

“What is it? What has happened?” she murmured drowsily, reaching instinctively for the dressing-gown which lay at the foot of the bed. Austin had already begun to wrap it around her.

“Forgive me, sweetheart, for disturbing you--and for coming in like this. I tried the telephone, and called you over and over again outside your window--you must have been awfully sound asleep. I was at my wits’ end, and couldn’t think of anything to do but this--are you very angry with me?”

“No, no--why did you need me?”

“Oh, Sylvia, it’s Edith! She’s terribly sick, and she keeps begging for you so that

I just *had* to come and get you! She was all right at supper-time--it's so sudden and violent that--"

Sylvia had slipped out of bed as if hardly conscious that he was beside her. "Go out on the porch and wait for me," she commanded breathlessly; "you've got the motor, haven't you? I won't be but a minute."

She was, indeed, scarcely longer than that. They were almost instantly speeding down the road together, while she asked, "Have you sent for the doctor?"

"Yes, but there isn't any there yet. Dr. Wells was off on a confinement case, and we've had to telephone to Wallacetown--she was perfectly determined not to have one, anyway. Oh, Sylvia, what can it be? And why should she want you so?"

"I don't know yet, dear."

"Do you suppose she's going to die?"

"No, I'm afraid--I mean I don't think she is. Why didn't I take better care of her? Austin, can't you drive any faster?"

As they reached the house, she broke away from him, and ran swiftly up the stairs. Mr. and Mrs. Gray were both standing, white and helpless with terror, beside their daughter's bed. She was lying quite still when Sylvia entered, but suddenly a violent spasm of pain shook her like a leaf, and she flung her hands above her head, groaning between her clenched teeth. Sylvia bent over her and took her in her arms.

"My dear little sister," she said.

CHAPTER XVIII

When the long, hideous night was over, and Edith lay, very white and still, her wide, frightened eyes never leaving Sylvia's face, the doctor, gathering up his belongings, touched the latter lightly on the arm.

"She'll have to have constant care for several days, perfect quiet for two weeks at least. But if I send for a nurse--"

"I know. I'm sure I can do everything necessary for her. I've had some experience with sickness before."

The doctor nodded, a look of relief and satisfaction passing over his face. "I see that you have. Get her to drink this. She must have some sleep at once."

But when Sylvia, left alone with her, held the glass to Edith's lips, she shrank back in terror.

"No, no, no! I don't want to go to sleep--I mustn't--I shall dream!"

"Dear child, you won't--and if you do, I shall be right here beside you, holding your hand like this, and you can feel it, and know that, after all, dreams are slight things."

"You promise me?"

"Indeed I do."

"Oh, Sylvia, you're so brave--you told the doctor you'd taken care of some one that was sick before--who was it?"

It was Sylvia's turn to shudder, but she controlled it quickly, and spoke very quietly.

"I was married for two years to a man who finally died of delirium tremens. No paid nurse--would have stayed with him--through certain times. I can't tell you about it, dear, and I'm trying hard to forget it--you won't ask me about it again, will you?"

"Oh, *Sylvia*! Please forgive me! I--I didn't guess--I'll drink the medicine--or do anything else you say!"

So Edith fell asleep, and when she woke again, the sun was setting, and Sylvia still sat beside her, their fingers intertwined. Sylvia looked down, smiling.

"The doctor has been here to see you, but you didn't wake, and we both felt it was better not to disturb you. He thinks that all is going well with you. Will you drink some milk, and let me bathe your face and hands?"

"No--not--not yet. Have you really been here--all these hours?"

"Yes, dear."

"With no rest--nothing to eat or drink?"

"Oh, yes, Austin brought me my dinner, but I ate it sitting beside you, and wouldn't let him stay--he's so big, he can't help making a noise."

"Does he know?"

"Not yet."

"And father and mother?"

Sylvia was silent.

"Oh, Sylvia, I'm a wicked, wicked girl, but I'm not what you must think! I'm not a--a murderess! Peter came up behind me on the stairs in the dark last night, and spoke to me suddenly. It startled me--everything seems to have startled me lately--and I slipped, and fell, and hurt myself--I didn't do it on purpose."

"You poor child--you don't need to tell me that--I never would have believed it of you for a single instant." Then she added, in the strained voice which she could not help using on the very rare occasions when she forced herself to speak of something that had occurred during her marriage, but still as if she felt that no word which might give comfort should be left unsaid, "Perhaps your mother has told you that the little baby who died when it was two weeks old wasn't the first that I--expected. A fall or--or a blow--or any shock of--fear or grief--often ends--in a disaster like this."

"Will the others believe me, too?"

"Of course they will. Don't talk, dear, it's going to be all right."

"I must talk. I've got to tell--I've got to tell *you*. And you can explain--to the family. You always understand everything--and you never blame anybody. I often wonder why it is--you're so good yourself--and yet you never say a word against any living creature, or let anybody else do it when you're around; but lots of girls, who've--done just what I have--and didn't happen to get found out--are the ones who speak most bitterly and cruelly--I know two or three who will be just *glad* if they know--"

"They're not going to know."

"Then you will listen, and--and believe me--and *help*?"

"Yes, Edith."

"I thought it happened only in books, or when girls had no one to take care of them--not to girls with fathers and mothers and good homes--didn't you, Sylvia?"

"No, dear. I knew it happened sometimes--oh, more often than *sometimes*--to girls--just like you."

"And what happens afterwards?"

Sylvia shuddered, but it was too dark in the carefully shuttered room for Edith to see her. She said quite quietly:

"That depends. In many cases--nothing dreadful."

"Ever anything good?"

"Yes, yes, *good* things can happen. They can be *made* to."

"Will you make good things happen to me?"

"I will, indeed I will."

"And not hate me?"

"Never that."

"May I tell you now?"

"If you believe that it will make you feel better; and if you will promise, after you have told me, to let me give you the treatment you need."

"I promise--Do you remember that in the spring Hugh Elliott came to spend a couple of months with Fred?"

Sylvia's fingers twitched, but all she said was, "Yes, Edith."

"He used to be in love with Sally; but he got all over that. He said he was in love with me. I thought he was--he certainly acted that way. Saying--fresh things, and--and always trying to touch me--and--that's the way men usually do when they begin to fall in love, isn't it, Sylvia?"

"No, darling, not *usually*--not--some kinds of men." And Sylvia's thoughts flew back, for one happy instant, to the man who had knelt at her feet on Christmas night. "But--I know what you mean--"

"And--I liked it. I mean, I thought the talk was fun to listen to, and that the--rest was--oh, Sylvia, do you understand--"

"Yes, dear, I understand."

"And he was awfully jolly, and gave me such a good time. I felt flattered to think he didn't treat me like a child, that he paid me more attention than the older girls."

"Yes, Edith."

"And I thought what fun it would be to marry him, instead of some slow, poky farmer, and have a beautiful house, and servants, and lovely clothes. I kept thinking, every night, he would ask me to; but he didn't. And finally, one time, just before we got home after a dance, he said--he was going away in the morning."

"Yes, Edith."

"Oh, I was so disappointed, and sore, and--angry! That was it, just plain angry. I had been going with Jack all along when Hugh didn't come for me, and Jack came the very night after Hugh went away, and took me for a long ride. He told me how terribly jealous he had been, and how thankful he was that Hugh was out of the way at last, and that Peter was going, too. So I laughed, and said that Peter didn't count at all, and that I hated Hugh--of course neither of those things was true, but I was so hurt, I felt *I'd* like to hurt somebody, too. And finally, I blurted out how mean Hugh had been, to make me think he cared for me, when he was just--having a good time. Then Jack said, 'Well, *I* care about you--I'm just crazy over you.' 'I don't believe you,' I said; 'I'll never believe any man again.' Just to tease him--that was all.' I'll show you whether I love you,' he said, and began to kiss me. I think he had been drinking--he does, you know. Of course, I ought to have stopped him, but I--had let Hugh--it meant a lot to me, too--the first time. But after I found it didn't mean anything to him--it didn't seem to matter--if some one else *did*--kiss me--I was flattered--and pleased--and--comforted. You mustn't think that what--happened afterwards--was all Jack's fault. I think I could have stopped it even then--if he'd been sober, anyway. But I didn't guess--I never dreamed--how far you could--get carried away--and how quickly. Oh, Sylvia, why didn't somebody tell me? At home--in the sunshine--with people all around you--it's like another world--you're like another person--than when there's nothing but stillness and darkness every-where, and a man who loves you, pleading, with his arms around you--

"And afterwards I thought no one would ever know. Jack thought so, too. Be-sides, you see, he is crazy to marry me--he'd give anything to. But I wouldn't mar-ry him for anything in the world--whatever happened--the great ignorant, dirty drunkard! Only he isn't unkind--or cowardly--don't think that--or let the others think so! He's willing to take his share of the blame--he's *sorry*--

"Then, just a little while ago--I began to be afraid of--what had happened. But I didn't know much about that, either. I thought, some way, I might be mistaken--I hoped so, anyhow. I wanted to come--and tell you all about it--but I didn't dare. I never saw you kiss Austin but once--you're so quiet when you're with him, Sylvia, and other people are around--and it was--it was just like--*a prayer*. After seeing that, I *couldn't* come to you--with my story--unless *I had* to--I felt as if it would be just like throwing mud on a flower.

"Then, yesterday, after the work was done, Peter asked me to go to walk with him. It was so late, when he and Austin got home, that I had scarcely seen him. I was going upstairs, in the dark, and I didn't know that he was anywhere near--it frightened me when he called. So--so I slipped--and fell--all the way down. I knew, right away, that I was hurt; but, of course, I didn't guess how much. I went to walk with him just the same, because it seemed as if it--would feel good to be with Peter--he's always been so--well, I can't explain--*so square*. And while we were out, I began to feel sick--and now, of course, he'll never be willing--to take me to walk--to be seen anywhere with me again! I can't bear it! I mind--not having been square to him--more than anything else--more than half-killing mother, even! Oh, Sylvia, tell them, please, *quickly*! and have it over with--tell them, too, that it was my own fault--don't forget that part! And then take me away with you, where I won't see them--or any one else I know--and teach me to be good--even if you can't help me to forget!"

*   *   *   *   *

Two hours later, when Edith was sleeping again, Mrs. Gray came into the room with a mute, haggard expression on her kind, homely face which Sylvia never forgot, and put her arms around the younger woman.

"Austin's askin' for you, dearie. It's been a hard day for him, too--I think you ought to go to him. I'll sit here until you come back."

Sylvia nodded, and stole silently out of the room. Austin was waiting for her at the foot of the stairs, his smile of welcome changing to an expression of stern solicitude as he looked at her.

"Have you been seeing ghosts? You're whiter than chalk--no wonder, shut up in that hot, dark room all day, without any rest and almost without any food! No matter if Edith does want you most, you'll have to take turns with mother after this. Come out with me where it's cool for a little while--and then you must have some supper, and a bath, and Sally's room to sleep in--if you won't go home, which is really the best place for you."

She allowed him to lead her, without saying a word, to the sheltered slope of the river, and sat down under a great elm, while he flung himself down beside her, laying his head in her lap.

"Sylvia--just think--less than three weeks now! It's been running through my head all day--I've almost got it down to hours, minutes, and seconds--What's the matter with Edith, anyway? Father and mother are as dumb as posts."

"The matter is--oh, my darling boy--I might as well tell you at once--we can't--I've got to go away with Edith. Austin, you must wait for me--another year--" And her courage giving out completely, she threw herself into his arms, and sobbed out the tragic story.

CHAPTER XIX

Sylvia, I won't give you up-- ***I can't!***"

"Darling, it isn't giving me up--it's only waiting a little longer for me."

"Don't you think I've waited long enough already?"

"Yes, Austin, but--Perhaps I won't have to stay away a whole year--perhaps by spring--or we might be married now, just as we planned, and take Edith with us."

"No, no!" he cried; "you know I wouldn't do that--I want you all to myself!" Then, still more passionately, "You're only twenty-two yourself--you shan't darken your own youth with--this--this horrible thing. You've seen sorrow and sin enough--far, far too much! You've a right to be happy now, to live your own life--and so have I."

"And hasn't Edith any right?"

"No--she's forfeited hers."

"Do you really think so? Do you believe that a young, innocent, sheltered girl, so pretty and so magnetic that she attracts immediate attention wherever she goes, who has starved for pretty things and a good time, and suddenly finds them within her reach, whose parents wilfully shut their eyes to the fact that she's growing up, and boast that 'they've kept everything from her'--and then let her go wherever she chooses, with that pitiful lack of armor, doesn't deserve another chance? And I think if you had stayed with her through last night--and seen the change that suffering--and shame--and hopelessness have wrought in that little gay, lovely, thoughtless creature, you'd feel that she had paid a pitifully large forfeit already-- and realize that no matter how much we help her, she'll have to go on paying it as long as she lives."

Austin was silent for a moment; then he muttered:

"Well, why doesn't she marry Jack Weston? She admits that it was half her fault--and that he really does care for her."

"*Marry* him!" Sylvia cried,--" *after that*! He cares for her as much as it is in him to care for anybody--but you know perfectly well what he is! Do you want her to tie herself forever to an ignorant, intemperate, sensual man? Put herself where the nightmare of her folly would stare her perpetually in the face! Where he'd throw it in her teeth every time he was angry with her, that he married her out of charity--and probably tell the whole countryside the same thing the first time he went to Wallacetown on a Saturday evening and began to 'celebrate'? How much chance for hope and salvation would be left for her then? Have you forgotten something you said to me once--something which wiped away in one instant all the bitterness and agony of three years, and sent me--straight into your arms? 'The best part of a decent man's love is not passion, but reverence; his greatest desire, not possession, but protection; his ultimate aim, not gratification, but sacrifice.'"

"I didn't guess then what a beautiful and wonderful thing passion could be--I'd only seen the other side of it."

Sylvia winced, but she only said, very gently: "Then can you, with that knowledge, wish Edith to keep on seeing it all her life? It's--it's pretty dreadful, I think--remember I've seen it too."

"Good God, Sylvia, do stop talking as if the cases were synonymous! *You were married*! It's revolting to me to hear you keep saying that you 'understand.' There's no more likeness between you and Edith than there is between a lily growing in a queen's garden and a sweet-brier rose springing up on a dusty highroad."

"I know how you feel, dear; but remember, the sweet-brier rose isn't a *weed*! They're both flowers--and fragrant--and--and fragile, aren't they?" Then, very softly: "Besides, the lily growing in the queen's garden, even though the wicked king may own it for a time, is usually picked in the end--by the fairy prince--to adorn his palace; while the little sweet-brier rose any tramp may pluck and stick in his hat--and fling away when it is faded. And if it was really the property of an honest woodman and his wife, and the highroad ran very close to the border of a sheltered wood, where their cottage was--wouldn't they feel very badly when they found their rose was gone?"

"You plead very well," said Austin almost roughly, "and you're pleading for every one *but me*--for Edith and father and mother, who've all done wrong--and now you want to take the burden of their wrongdoing on your own innocent shoulders, and make me help you--no matter how *I* suffer! *I've* tried to do *right*--never so hard in all my life--and mostly--I 've succeeded. You've helped--I never could have done it without you--but a lot of it has been pulling myself up by my own bootstraps. Now I've reached the end of my rope--and I suppose, instead of thinking of that --the next thing you do will be to make excuses for Jack Weston."

"Yes," said Sylvia, very gently, "that's just what I'm going to do. I know how hard you've tried--I know how well you've succeeded. I know there aren't many men like you--*as good as you*--in the whole world. I'm not saying that because I'm in love with you--I'm not saying it to encourage you--I'm saying it because it's true. You've conquered--all along the line. It's so wonderful--and so glorious--that sometimes it almost takes my breath away. Darling--you know I've never reproached you--even in my own mind--for anything that may have happened before you knew me--and *I* know, that much as you wish now it never had happened--still you can comfort yourself with the old platitudes of 'the double standard.' 'All men do this some time--or nearly all men. I haven't been any worse than lots of others--and I've always respected *good* women'--oh, I've heard it all, hundreds of times! Some day I hope you'll feel differently about that, too--that you won't teach *your* son to argue that way--not only because it's wrong, but because it's dangerous--and very much out of date, besides. This isn't the time to go into all that--but I wonder if you would be willing to tell me everything that went through your mind for five minutes--when I came to you the night of the Graduation Ball, and you took me in your arms?"

"*Sylvia!*" The cry came from the hidden depths of Austin's soul, wrung with grief and shame. "I thought you never guessed---Since you did--how could you go on loving me so--how can you say what you just have--about my--*goodness*?"

"Darling, *don't*! I never would have let you know that I guessed--if everything else I said hadn't failed! That wasn't a reproach! 'Go on loving you'--how could I help loving you a thousand times more than ever--when you won the greatest fight of all? It's no sin to be tempted--I'm glad you're strong enough--and human enough--for that. And I'm thankful from the bottom of my heart--that you're strong enough--and *divine* enough--to resist temptation. But you know--even a man like you--what a sorceress plain human nature can be. What chance has a weakling like Jack Weston against her, when she leads him in the same path?"

For all answer, he buried his face in the folds of her dress, and lay with it hidden, while she stroked his hair with soft and soothing fingers; she knew that she had wounded him to the quick, knew that this battle was the hardest of all, knew most surely that it was his last one, and that he would win it. Meanwhile there was nothing for her to do but to wait, unable to help him, and forced to bear alone the burden of weariness and sacrifice which was nearly crushing her. Should Austin sense, even dimly, how the sight of Edith's suffering through the long, sleepless night had brought back her own, by its reawakened memories of agony which he had taught her to forget; should divine that she, too, had counted the days to their marriage, and rejoiced that the long waiting was over, she knew that Edith's cause would be lost. She counted on the strength of the belief that most men hold--they never guess how mistakenly--that fatigue and pain are matters of slight importance among the really big things of life, and that women do not feel as strongly as they do, that there is less passion in the giving than in the taking, that mother-love is the greatest thing they ever know. Some day, she would convince him that he was wrong; but now--At last he looked up, with an expression in his eyes, dimly seen in the starlight, which brought fresh tears to hers, but new courage to her tired heart.

"If you do love me, and I know you do," he said brokenly, "never speak to me about that again. You've forgiven it--you forgive everything--but I never shall forgive myself, or feel that I can atone, for what I meant--for that one moment--to do, as long as I live. On Christmas night, when there was no evil in my heart, you thought you saw it there, because your trust had been betrayed before; I vowed then that I would teach you at least that I was worthy of your confidence, and that most men were; and when I had taught you, not only to trust me, but to love me, so that you saw no evil even when it existed--I very nearly betrayed you. It wasn't my strength that saved us *both*--it was your wonderful love and faith. There's no desire in the world that would profane such an altar of holiness as you unveiled before me that night." He lifted her soft dress, and kissed the hem of her skirt. "I haven't forgiven myself about--what happened before I knew you, either," he whispered; "you're wrong there. I used those arguments, once, myself, but I can't any more.

We'll teach-- **our son**--better, won't we, so that he'll have a cleaner heritage to offer his wife than I've got for mine--but he won't love her any more. Now, darling, go back to the house, and get some rest, if you can, but before you go to sleep, pray for me--that when Edith doesn't need you any more--I may have you for my own. And now, please, leave me--I've got to be alone--"

"Dat," said a voice out of the darkness, "is just vat she must nod do."

Austin sprang to his feet. It was too dark to see more than a few feet. But there could be no doubt that the speaker was very near, and the accent was unmistakable. Austin's voice was heavy with anger.

"*Eavesdropping, Peter*?"

"No--pardon, missus; pardon, Mr. Gray. Frieda is sick. I been lookin' ev'ywhere for Mr. Gray to tell him. At last I hear him speak out here, I come to find. Then I overhear--I cannot help it. I try--vat you say--interrupt--it vas my vish. Beliefe me, please. But somet'ing hold me--here." He put his hand to his throat. "I could not. I ver' sorry. But as it is so I haf heard--I haf also some few words to speak.

"Dere vas vonce a grade lady," he said, coming up closer to them, "who vas so good, and so lofly, and so sveet, that no vone who saw her could help lofing her; and she vas glad to help ev'y vone, and gif to ev'y vone, and she vas so rich and vise dat she could help and gif a great deal.

"And dere vas a poor boy who vas stupid and homely and poor, and he did nodings for any vone. But it happened vone time dat dis boy t'ought dat he and the grade lady could help the same person. So he vent to her and say--but ve'r respectful, like he alvays felt to her, 'Dis is my turn. Please, missus, let me haf it.'"

"What do you mean, Peter?" asked Sylvia gently.

He came closer still. It was not too dark, as he did so, to see the furrows which fresh tears had made on his grimy face, to be conscious of his soiled and stained working clothes, and his clumsiness of manner and carriage; but the earnest voice went on, more doggedly than sadly:

"Vat I heard 'bout Edit' to-night, I guessed dis long time ago. Missus--if you hear that Mr. Gray done som ver' vrong t'ing--even **dis** ver' vrong t'ing--"

"I know," said Sylvia quickly; "it wouldn't make any difference now--I care too much. I'd want him--if he still wanted me--just the same. I'd be hurt--oh, dreadfully hurt--but I wouldn't feel angry--or revengeful--that's what you mean, isn't it,

Peter?"

"Ya-as," said Peter gratefully, "dats yust it, missus, only, of course I couldn't say it like dat. I t'ank you, missus. Vell, den, I lof Edit' ever since I come here last fall, ver' much, yust like you lof Mr. Gray--only, of course, you can't believe dat, missus."

"Yes, I can," said Sylvia.

"So I say," went on Peter, looking only at Sylvia now, "Edit' need you, but Mr. Gray, he need you, too. No vone in t'e vorld need me but Edit'. You shall say, 'Peter's fat'er haf sent for him, Peter go back to Holland ver' quick'--vat you say, suddenly. 'Let Edit' marry Peter and go mit.' Ve stay all vinter mit my fat'er and moder--"

"You'll travel," interrupted Sylvia. "Edith will have the same dowry from me that Sally had for a wedding present. She won't be poor. You can take her every-where--oh, Peter, you can--*give her a good time*!"

Peter bowed his head. There was a humble grace about the gesture which Sylvia never forgot.

"You ver' yust lady, missus," he said simply; "dat must be for you to say. Vell, den, after my fat'er and moder haf welcomed her, ve shall travel. Dem in de spring if you need me for de cows--Mr. Gray--if you don't t'ink shame to haf boy like me for your broder--ve come back. If nod, ve'll stay in Holland. You need no fear to haf--I vill make Edit' happy--"

Some way, Austin found Peter's hand. He was beyond speech. But Sylvia asked one more question.

"Edith thinks you can't possibly love her any more," she said--"that you won't even be willing to see her again. If she thought you were marrying her out of char-ity, she'd die before she'd let you. How are you going to convince her that you want to marry her because you love her?"

"Vill you gif me one chance to try?" replied Peter, looking straight into her eyes.

CHAPTER XX

W ell, I declare it's so sudden like, I should think your breath would be took away."

Mrs. Gray smiled at Mrs. Elliott, and went on with her sewing, rocking back and forth placidly in her favorite chair. If the latter had been a woman who talked less and observed more, she would have noticed how drawn and furrowed her old friend's rosy, peaceful face had grown, how much repression there was about the lips which smiled so bravely. But these details escaped her.

"'Course it does look that way to an outsider," said Mrs. Gray, slowly, as if rehearsing a part which had been carefully taught her, "but when you come to know the facts, it ain't so strange, after all."

"Would you feel to tell them?" asked Mrs. Elliott eagerly.

"Why, sure. Edith an' Peter's been sort of engaged this long time back, but they was so young we urged 'em to wait. Then Peter's father wrote sayin' he was so poorly, he wished Peter could fix it so's to come home, through the cold weather, an' Edith took on terrible at bein' separated from him, an' Peter declared he wouldn't leave without her; an' then--well, Sylvia sided with 'em, an' that settled it."

Mrs. Elliott nodded. "You'd never think that little soft-lookin' creature could be so set an' determined, now, would you?" she asked. "I never see any one to beat her. An' mum! She shuts her mouth tighter'n a steel trap!"

"If any family ever had a livin' blessin' showered on 'em right out of heaven," said Mrs. Gray, "we did, the day Sylvia come here. Funny, Austin's the only one of us can see's she's got a single fault. He says she's got lots of 'em, just like any other woman--but I bet he'd cut the tongue out of any one else who said so. Seems as if I couldn't wait for the third of September to come so's she'll really be my daughter, though I haven't got one that seems any dearer to me, even now."

"Speakin' of weddin's," said Mrs. Elliott, "why didn't you have a regular one for Edith, same as for Sally?"

"Land! I can't spend my whole time workin' up weddin's! Seems like they was some kind of contagious disease in this family. James was married only last December, an' even if we wasn't to that, we got all het up over it just the same. An' now we've hardly got our breath since Sally's, an' Austin's is starin' us in the face! I couldn't see my way clear to house-cleanin' this whole great ark in dog-days for nobody, an' Edith an' Peter's got to leave the very day after Sylvia 'n Austin get married. Peter was hangin' round outside Edith's door the whole blessed time, after her fall--"

"Strange she should be so sick, just from a fall, ain't it?"

"Yes, 't is, but the doctor says they're often more serious than you'd think for. Well, as I was sayin', Sylvia come out of Edith's room an' found Peter settin' on the top of the stairs for the third time that day, an' she flared right up, an' says, 'For Heaven's sake, why don't you get married right off--now--to-day--then you can go in an' out as you like!' And before we half knew what she was up to she had telephoned the new minister. Austin said he wished she'd shown more of that haste about gettin' married herself, an' she answered him right back, if she'd been lucky enough to get as good a feller as Peter, maybe she might have. It's real fun to hear 'em tease each other. Sylvia likes the new minister. She says the best thing about the Methodist Church that she knows of is the way it shifts its pastors around--nothin' like variety, she says--an' a new one once in three years keeps things hummin'. She says as long as so many Methodists don't believe in cards an' dancin' an' such, they deserve to have a little fun some way, an'--"

"You was talkin' about Edith," interrupted Mrs. Elliott, rather tartly, "you've got kinder switched off."

"Excuse me, Eliza--so I have. Well, Sylvia got Edith up onto the couch (the doctor had said she might get up for a little while that day, anyhow) an' give her one of her prettiest wrappers--"

"What color? White?"

"No, Sylvia thought she was too pale. It was a lovely yellow, like the dress she wore to the Graduation Ball. We all scurried 'round an' changed our clothes-

-Austin's the most stunnin'-lookin' thing in that white flannel suit of his, Sylvia wants he should wear it to his own weddin', 'stead of a dress-suit--an' I wore my gray--Well, it was all over before you could say 'Jack Robinson' an' I never sweat a drop gettin' ready for it, either! I shall miss Edith somethin' terrible this winter, but she'll have an elegant trip, same as she's always wanted to, an' Peter says he knows his parents'll be tickled to death to have such a pretty daughter-in-law!"

"Don't you feel disappointed any," Mrs. Elliott could not help asking, "to have a feller like Peter in the family?"

Mrs. Gray bit her thread. "I don't know what you got against Peter," she said; "I look to like him the best of my son-in-laws, so far."

But that evening, as she sat with her husband beside the old reading-lamp which all the electricity that Sylvia had installed had not caused them to give up, her courage deserted her. Howard, sensing that something was wrong, looked up from "Hoard's Dairyman," which he was eagerly devouring, to see that the **Wallacetown Bugle** had slipped to her knees, and that she sat staring straight ahead of her, the tears rolling down her cheeks.

"Why, Mary," he said in amazement--"Mary--"

The old-fashioned New Englander is as unemotional as he is undemonstrative. For a moment Howard, always slow of speech and action, was too nonplussed to know what to do, deeply sorry as he felt for his wife. Then he leaned over and patted her hand--the hand that was scarcely less rough and scarred than his own--with his big calloused one.

"You must stop grieving over Edith," he said gently, "and blaming yourself for what's happened. You've been a wonderful mother--there aren't many like you in the world. Think how well the other seven children are coming along, instead of how the eighth slipped up. Think how blessed we've been never to lose a single one of them by death. Think--"

"I do think, Howard." Mrs. Gray pressed his hand in return, smiling bravely through her tears. "I'm an old fool to give way like this, an' a worse one to let you catch me at it. But it ain't wholly Edith I'm cryin' about. Land, every time I start to curse the devil for Jack Weston, I get interrupted because I have to stop an' thank the Lord for Peter. An' all the angels in heaven together singin' Halleluia led by Gabriel for choir-master, couldn't half express my feelin's for Sylvia! I guess 'twould always be that way if we'd stop to think. Our blessin's is so much thicker than our troubles, that the troubles don't show up no more than a little yellow mustard growin' up in a fine piece of oats--unless we're bound to look at the mustard instead of the oats. As it happens, I wasn't thinkin' of Edith at all at that moment, or really grievin' either. It was just--"

"Yes?" asked Howard.

"This room," said Mrs. Gray, gulping a little, "is about the only one in the house that ain't changed a mite. The others are improved somethin' wonderful, but I'm kinder glad we've kept this just as it was. There's the braided rugs on the floor that I made when you was courtin' me, Howard, an' we used to set out on the doorstep together. An' the fringed tidies over the chairs an' sofa that Eliza give me for a weddin' present--they're faded considerable, but that good red wool never wears out. There's the crayon portraits we had done when we was on our honeymoon, an' the ones of James an' Sally when they was babies. Do you remember how I took it to heart because we couldn't scrape together the money no way to get one of Austin when he come along? He was the prettiest baby we ever had, too, except--except Edith, of course. An' after Austin we didn't even bring up the subject again--we was pretty well occupied wonderin' how we was goin' to feed an' clothe 'em all, let alone havin' pictures of 'em. Then there's the wax flowers on the mantelpiece. I always trembled for fear one of the youngsters would knock 'em off an' break the glass shade to smithereens, but they never did. An' there's your Grandfather Gray's clock. I was a little disappointed at first because it had a brass face, 'stead o' bein' white with scenes on it, like they usually was--an' then it was such a chore, with everything else there was to do, to keep it shinin' like it ought to. But now I think I like it better than the other kind, an' it's tickin' away, same as it has this last hundred years an' more. Do you remember when we began to wind it up, Saturday nights, 'together?--All this is the same, praise be, but--"

"Yes?" asked Howard Gray again.

"For years, evenin's," went on Mrs. Gray, "this room was full of kids. There was generally a baby sleepin'--or refusin', rather loud, to sleep!--in the cradle over in the corner. The older ones was settin' around doin' sums on their slates, or playin' checkers an' cat's-cradle. They quarrelled considerable, an' they was pretty shabby, an' I never had a chance to set down an' read the *Bugle* quiet-like, after supper, because the mendin'-basket was always waitin' for me, piled right up to the brim. Saturday nights, what a job it was all winter to get enough water het to fill the hat-tub over an' over again, an' fetch in front of the air-tight. Often I was tempted to wash two or three of 'em in the same water, but, as you know, I never done it. Thank goodness, we'd never heard of such a thing as takin' a bath every day then! I don't deny it's a comfort, with all the elegant plumbin' we've got now, not to feel you've got to wait for a certain day to come 'round to take a good soak when you're hot or dirty, but it would have been an awful strain on my conscience an' my back both in them days. I used to think sometimes, 'Oh, how glad I shall be when this pack of unruly youngsters is grown up an' out of the way, an' Howard an' I can have a little peace.' An' now that time's come, an' I set here feelin' lonely, an' thinkin' the old room **ain't** the same, in spite of the fact, as I said before, that it ain't changed a mite, because we haven't got the whole eight tumblin' 'round under our heels. I know they're doin' well--they're doin' most **too** well. I'm scared the time's comin' when they'll look down on us, Howard, me especially. Not that they'll mean to-- but they're all gettin' so--so different. You had a good education, an' talk right, but I can't even do that. I found an old grammar the other day, an' set down an' tried to learn somethin' out of it, but it warn't no use--I couldn't make head or tail of it. An' then they're all away--an' they're goin' to keep on bein' away. James is South, an' Thomas is at college, an' Molly's studyin' music in Boston, an' before we know it Katherine'll be at college too, an' Edith an' Austin in Europe. That leaves just Ruth an' Sally near us, an' they're both married. I don't begrudge it to 'em one bit. I'm glad an' thankful they're all havin' a better chance than we did. If I could just feel that some day they'd all come back to the Homestead, an' to us--an' come because they **wanted** to--"

Howard put his arm around his wife, and drew her down beside him on the old horsehair sofa. One of the precious red wool tidies slipped to the floor, and lay there unnoticed. Slowly, while Mrs. Gray had been talking, the full depth of her trouble became clear to him, and the words to comfort her rose to his lips.

"They will, Mary," he said; "they will; you wait and see. How could you think for one moment that our children could look down on their mother? It's mighty seldom, let me tell you, that any boy or girl does that, and only with pretty good reason then--never when they've been blessed with one like you. I haven't been able to do what I wanted for ours, but at least I gave them the best thing they possibly could have--a good mother--and with that I don't think the hardships have hurt them much! Have you forgotten--you mustn't think I'm sacrilegious, dear--that the greatest mother we know anything about was just a poor carpenter's wife--and how much her Great Son loved her? Her name was Mary, too--I'm glad we gave Molly that name--she's a good girl--somehow it seems to me it always carries a halo of sacredness with it, even now!--Then, besides--Thomas and Austin are both going to be farmers, and live right here on the old place. Austin's so smart, he may do other things besides, but this will always be his home and Sylvia's. Peter and Edith'll be here, too, and Sally and Ruth aren't more than a stone's-throw off, as you might say. That makes four out of the eight--more than most parents get. The others will come back, fast enough, to visit, with us and them here! And think of the grandchildren coming along! Why, in the next generation, there'll be more kids piling in and out of this living-room than you could lug water and mend socks for if you never turned your hand to another thing! And, thank God, you won't have to do that now--you can just sit back and take solid comfort with them. You had to work so hard when our own children were babies, Mary, that you never could do that. But with Ruth's and Austin's and Sally's--"

He paused, smiling, as he looked into the future. Then he kissed her, almost as shyly as he had first done more than thirty years before.

"Besides," he said, "I'm disappointed if you're lonely here with me, just for a little while, because I'm enjoying it a whole lot. Haven't you ever noticed that when two people that love each other first get married, there's a kind of *glow* to their happiness, like the glow of a sunrise? It's mighty beautiful and splendid. Then the burden and heat of the day, as the Bible says, comes along. It doesn't mean that they don't care for each other any more. But they're so tired and so pressed and so worried that they don't say much about their feelings, and sometimes they even avoid talking to each other, or quarrel. But when the hard hours are over, and the sun's gone down--not so bright as it was in the morning, maybe, but softer, and spreading its color over the whole sky--the stars come out--and they know the best part of the day's ahead of them still. They can take time then to sit down, and take each other's hands, and thank God for all his blessings, but most of all for the life of a man and a woman together. Austin and Sylvia think they're going to have the best part now, in the little brick cottage. But they're not. They'll be having it thirty years from now, just as you and I are, in the Old Gray Homestead."

Mary Gray wiped her eyes. "Why, Howard," she said, "you used to say you wanted to be a poet, but I never knew till now that you *was* one! I'd rather you'd ha' said all that to me than--than to have been married to Shakespeare!" she ended with a happy sob, and put her white head down on his shoulder.

CHAPTER XXI

Uncle Mat, whose long-postponed visit was at last taking place, sat talking in front of the fire in Sylvia's living-room with the "new minister." The room was bright with many candles, and early fall flowers from her own garden stood about in clear glass vases. In the dining-room beyond, they could see the two servants moving around the table, laid for supper. A man's voice, whistling, and the sound of rapidly approaching footsteps, came up the footpath from the Homestead. And at the same moment, the door of Sylvia's own room opened and shut and there was the rustle of silk and the scent of roses in the hall.

A moment later she came in, her arm on Austin's. Her neck and arms were bare, as he loved to see them, and her white silk dress, brocaded in tiny pink rosebuds, swept soft and full about her. A single string of great pearls fell over the lace on her breast, and almost down to her waist, and there was a high, jewelled comb in her low-dressed hair. She leaned over her uncle's chair.

"Austin says the others are on their way. Am I all right, do you think, Uncle Mat?"

"You look to me as if you had stepped out of an old French painting," he said, pinching her rosy cheek; "I'm satisfied with you. But the question arises, is Austin? He's so fussy."

Austin laughed, straightening his tie. "I can't fuss about this dress," he said, "for I chose it myself. But I'm not half the tyrant you all make me out--I'm wearing white flannel to please her. Is there plenty of supper, Sylvia? I'm almost starved."

"I know enough to expect a man to be hungry, even if he's going to be hanged--or married," she retorted, "but I'll run out to the kitchen once more, just to make sure that everything is all right."

The third of September had come at last. There was no question, this time, of a wedding in St. Bartholomew's Church, with twelve bridesmaids and a breakfast at Sherry's; no wonderful jewels, no press notices, almost no trousseau. Austin's family, Uncle Mat, and a few close friends came to Sylvia's own little house, and when the small circle was complete, she took her uncle's arm and stood by Austin's side, while the "new minister" married them. Thomas was best man; Molly, for the second time that summer, maid-of-honor. Sadie and James were missing, but as "a wedding present" came a telegram, announcing the safe arrival of a nine-pound baby-girl. Edith was not there, either, and the date of sailing for Holland had been postponed. She had gained less rapidly than they had hoped, and still lay, very pale and quiet, on the sofa between the big windows in her room. But she was not left alone when the rest of the family departed for Sylvia's house; for Peter sat beside her in the twilight, his big rough fingers clasping her thin white ones.

There proved to be "plenty of supper," and soon after it was finished the guests began to leave, Uncle Mat with many imprecations at Sylvia's "lack of hospitality in turning them out, such a cold night." Even the two capable servants, having removed all traces of the feast, came to her with many expressions of good-will, and the assurance of "comin' back next season if they was wanted," and departed to take the night train from Wallacetown for New York. By ten o'clock the white-panelled front door with its brass knocker had opened and shut for the last time, and Austin bolted it, and turned to Sylvia, smiling.

"Well, **Mrs. Gray**," he said, "you're locked in now--far from all the sights and sounds that made your youth happy--shop-windows, and hotel dining-rooms, the slamming of limousine doors, and the clinking of ice in cocktail-shakers. Your last chance of escape is gone--you've signed and sealed your own death-warrant."

"Austin! don't joke--to-night!"

"My dear," he asked, lifting her face in his hands, "did you never joke because you were afraid--to show how much you really felt?"

"Yes," she replied, "very often. But there's nothing in the whole world for me to be afraid of now."

"So you're really ready for me at last?" he whispered.

*   *   *   *   *

Whatever she answered--or even if she did not answer at all--to all appearances, Austin was satisfied. His mother, seeing him for the first time three days
later, was almost startled at the radiance in his face. It was, perhaps, a strange honeymoon. But those who thought so had felt, and rightly, that it was a strange marriage. After the first few days, Austin spent every day at the farm, as usual, walking
back to the little brick cottage for his noonday dinner, and leaving after the milking
was done at night; and Sylvia, dressed in blue gingham, cooked and cleaned and
sewed, and put her garden in shape for the winter. In spite of her year's training at
Mrs. Gray's capable hands, she made mistakes; she burnt the grape jelly, and forgot
to put the brown sugar into the sweet pickle, and took the varnish off the dining-
room table by polishing it with raw linseed oil, and boiled the color out of her
sheerest chiffon blouse; and they laughed together over her blunders. Then, when
evening came, she was all in white again, and there was the simple supper served by
candle-light in the little dining-room, and the quiet hours in front of the glowing
fire afterwards, and the long, still nights with the soft stars shining in, and the cool
air blowing through the open windows of their room.

Then, when the Old Gray Homestead had settled down to the blessed peace-
fulness and security which, the harvest safely in, the snows still a long way off,
comes to every New England farm in the late fall, they closed their white-panelled
front door behind them, and sailed away together, as Austin had wished to do.
There were a few gay weeks in London and Paris, The Hague and Rome--"enough,"
wrote Sylvia, "so that we won't forget there *is* any one else in the world, and use
the wrong fork when we go out to dine." There was a fortnight at the little Dutch
house where by this time Peter and Edith were spending the winter with Peter's
parents--"where our bed," wrote Sylvia, "was a great big box built into the wall, but,
oh! so soft and comfortable; with another box for the very best cow just around the
corner from it, and the music of Peter's mother's scrubbing-brush for our morning
hymn." And then there were several months of wandering--"without undue haste,
but otherwise just like any other tourists," wrote Sylvia. They went leisurely from

place to place, as the weather dictated and their own inclinations advised. Part of the time Edith and Peter were with them, but even then they were nearly always alone, for Edith was not strong enough to keep up, even with their moderate pace. They revisited places dear to both of them, they sought out many new ones; early spring found them in Paris; and it was here that there finally came an evening when Austin put his arms around his wife's shoulders--they had made a longer day of sight-seeing than usual, and she looked pale and tired, as having finished dressing earlier than he she sat in the window, looking down at the brilliant street beneath them, waiting for him to take her down to dinner--and spoke in the unmistakably firm tone that he so seldom used.

"It's time you were at home, Sylvia--we're overstaying our holiday. I'll make sailing arrangements to-morrow."

So, by the end of May, they were back in the little brick cottage again, and the two capable servants were there, too, for there must be no danger, now, of Sylvia's getting over-tired. Those were days when Austin seldom left his wife for long if he could help it; found it hard, indeed, not to watch her constantly, and to keep the expression of anxiety and dread from his eyes. He had not proved to be among those men, who, as some French cynic, more clever than wise, has expressed it, find "the chase the best part of the game." His engagement had been a period containing much joy, it is true, but also, much doubt, much self-adjusting and repression--his marriage had not held one imperfect hour. Sylvia, as his wife, with all the petty barriers which social inequality and money and restraint had reared between them broken down by the very weight of their love, was a being even much more desired and hallowed than the pale, black-robed, unattainable lady of his first worship had been; that Sylvia should suffer, because of him, was horrible; that he might possibly lose her altogether was a fear which grew as the days went on. It fell to her to dispel that, as she had so many others.

"Why do you look at me so?" she asked, very quietly, as, according to their old custom, they sat by the riverbank watching the sun go down.

"I don't mean to. But sometimes it seems as if I couldn't bear all this that's coming. Nothing on earth can be worth it."

"You don't know," said Sylvia softly. "You won't feel that way--after you've seen him. You'll know then--that whatever price we pay--our life wouldn't have been complete without this."

"I can't understand why men should have all the pleasure--and women all the pain."

"My darling boy, they don't! That's only an old false theory, that exploded years ago, along with the one about everlasting damnation, and several other abominable ones of like ilk. Do you honestly believe--if you will think sanely for a moment-- that you have had more joy than I? Or that you are not suffering twice as much as I am, or ever shall?"

"You say all that to comfort me, because you're twice as brave as I am."

"I say it to make you realize the truth, because I'm honest."

Molly and Katherine were busy at the Homestead in those days, Sally and Ruth in their own little houses; but Edith was at the brick cottage a great deal. In spite of all Peter's loving care, and the treatment of a great doctor whom Sylvia had insisted she should see in London, she was not very strong, and found that she must still let the long days slip by quietly, while the white hands, that had once been so plump and brown, grew steadily whiter and slimmer. She came upon Sylvia one sultry afternoon, folding and sorting little clothes, arranging them in neat, tiny piles in the scented, silk-lined drawers of a new bureau, and after she had helped her put them all in order, with hardly a word, she leaned her head against Sylvia's and whispered:

"I do wish there were some for me."

"I know, dear; but you're very young yet. Many wives are glad when this doesn't happen right away. Sally is."

"I know. But, you see, I feel that perhaps there never will be any for me--and that seems really only fair--doesn't it?"

Sylvia was silent. Her sympathy would not allow her to tell all the London doctor had said to her about her young sister-in-law; neither would it allow her to be untruthful. But certain phrases he had used came back to her with tragic intensity.

"Many a woman who can recuperate almost miraculously from organic disease fails to rally from shock--we've been overlooking that too long."--"Every sleepless night undoes the good that the sunshine during the daytime has wrought, and after many sleepless nights the days become simply horrible preludes to more terrors."-- "I can't drug a child like that to a long life of uselessness--make her as happy as you can, but let her have it over with as quickly as Nature will allow it--or take her to some other man--I can't in charity to her tell you anything else."

So Sylvia and Peter made her "as happy as they could," and that they hoped at times was very happy, indeed; but the look of dread never left her eyes for long, and the tired smile which had replaced her ringing laugh came less and less often to her pale lips.

There was another faithful visitor at the brick cottage that summer, for after the end of June, Thomas, who came home from college at that time, seemed to be on hand a good deal. He, as well as Austin, had proved false to Uncle Mat's prophecy; for far from falling in love with another girl within a year, he showed not the slightest indication of doing so, but seemed to find perfect satisfaction in the society of his own family, especially that portion of it in which Sylvia was, for the moment, to be found. Austin at first marvelled at the ease with which he had accepted her for a sister; but the boy's perfect transparency of behavior made it impossible to feel that the new and totally different affection which he now felt for her was a pose. Gradually he grew to depend on Thomas to "look after Sylvia" when, for one reason or another, he was called away. His interests at the bank took him more and more frequently to Wallacetown; there were cattle auctions, too important to neglect, a day's journey from home; there was even a tiny opening beginning to loom up on the political horizon. Austin was too bound by every tie of blood and affection to the Homestead ever to build his hearth-fire permanently elsewhere; but he was also rapidly growing too big to be confined by it to the exclusion of the new opportunities which seemed to be offering themselves to him in such rapid succession in every direction.

Coming in very late one evening in August after one of these necessary absences, he found Sylvia already in bed, their room dark. She had never failed to wait up for him before. He felt a sudden pang of anxiety and contrition.

"Are you ill, darling? I didn't mean to be so late."

"No, not ill--just a little more tired than usual." She drew his head down to her breast, and for some minutes they held each other so, silently, their hearts beating together. "But I think it would be better if we sent for the doctor now--I didn't want to until you came home."

She slipped out of bed, and walked over to the open window, his arm still around her. The river shone like a ribbon of silver in the moonlight; the green meadows lay in soft shadows for miles around it; in the distance the Homestead stood silhouetted against the starlit sky.

"What a year it's been!" she whispered, "for you and me alone together! And how many years there are before us--and our children--and the Homestead--and all that we stand for--as long as the New England farms and the Great Glorious Spirit which watches over them shall endure!"

A cloud passed over the moon dimming its brightness. It brought them to the realization that the long, hard hours of the night were before them both, to be faced and conquered. The New York doctor, whom Sylvia had once before refused to send for, and the fresh-faced, rosy nurse, who had both been staying at the brick cottage for the last few days, were called, the servants roused to activity. There came a time when Austin, impotent to serve Sylvia, marvelling at her bravery, wrung by her suffering, felt that such agony was beyond endurance, beyond hope, beyond anything in life worth gaining. But when the breathless, horrible night had dragged its interminable black length up to the skirts of the radiant dawn, the mist rose slowly from the quiet river and still more quiet mountains, the first singing of the birds broke the heavy stillness, and Austin and Sylvia kissed each other and their first-born son in the glory of the golden morning.

The Codes Of Hammurabi And Moses
W. W. Davies

QTY

The discovery of the Hammurabi Code is one of the greatest achievements of archaeology, and is of paramount interest, not only to the student of the Bible, but also to all those interested in ancient history...

Religion   **ISBN:** *1-59462-338-4*   **Pages:132**

MSRP $12.95

The Theory of Moral Sentiments
Adam Smith

QTY

This work from 1749. contains original theories of conscience amd moral judgment and it is the foundation for systemof morals.

Philosophy   **ISBN:** *1-59462-777-0*   **Pages:536**

MSRP $19.95

Jessica's First Prayer
Hesba Stretton

QTY

In a screened and secluded corner of one of the many railway-bridges which span the streets of London there could be seen a few years ago, from five o'clock every morning until half past eight, a tidily set-out coffee-stall, consisting of a trestle and board, upon which stood two large tin cans, with a small fire of charcoal burning under each so as to keep the coffee boiling during the early hours of the morning when the work-people were thronging into the city on their way to their daily toil...

Pages:84

Childrens   **ISBN:** *1-59462-373-2*   *MSRP $9.95*

My Life and Work
Henry Ford

QTY

Henry Ford revolutionized the world with his implementation of mass production for the Model T automobile. Gain valuable business insight into his life and work with his own auto-biography... "We have only started on our development of our country we have not as yet, with all our talk of wonderful progress, done more than scratch the surface. The progress has been wonderful enough but..."

Pages:300

Biographies/   **ISBN:** *1-59462-198-5*   *MSRP $21.95*

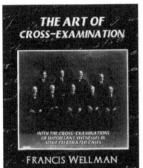

The Art of Cross-Examination
Francis Wellman

QTY

I presume it is the experience of every author, after his first book is published upon an important subject, to be almost overwhelmed with a wealth of ideas and illustrations which could readily have been included in his book, and which to his own mind, at least, seem to make a second edition inevitable. Such certainly was the case with me; and when the first edition had reached its sixth impression in five months, I rejoiced to learn that it seemed to my publishers that the book had met with a sufficiently favorable reception to justify a second and considerably enlarged edition. ..

Reference   ISBN: *1-59462-647-2*

Pages:412

MSRP $19.95

On the Duty of Civil Disobedience
Henry David Thoreau

QTY

Thoreau wrote his famous essay, On the Duty of Civil Disobedience, as a protest against an unjust but popular war and the immoral but popular institution of slave-owning. He did more than write—he declined to pay his taxes, and was hauled off to gaol in consequence. Who can say how much this refusal of his hastened the end of the war and of slavery ?

Law   ISBN: *1-59462-747-9*

Pages:48

MSRP $7.45

Dream Psychology Psychoanalysis for Beginners
Sigmund Freud

QTY

Sigmund Freud, born Sigismund Schlomo Freud (May 6, 1856 - September 23, 1939), was a Jewish-Austrian neurologist and psychiatrist who co-founded the psychoanalytic school of psychology. Freud is best known for his theories of the unconscious mind, especially involving the mechanism of repression; his redefinition of sexual desire as mobile and directed towards a wide variety of objects; and his therapeutic techniques, especially his understanding of transference in the therapeutic relationship and the presumed value of dreams as sources of insight into unconscious desires.

Pages:196

Psychology   ISBN: *1-59462-905-6*

MSRP $15.45

The Miracle of Right Thought
Orison Swett Marden

QTY

Believe with all of your heart that you will do what you were made to do. When the mind has once formed the habit of holding cheerful, happy, prosperous pictures, it will not be easy to form the opposite habit. It does not matter how improbable or how far away this realization may see, or how dark the prospects may be, if we visualize them as best we can, as vividly as possible, hold tenaciously to them and vigorously struggle to attain them, they will gradually become actualized, realized in the life. But a desire, a longing without endeavor, a yearning abandoned or held indifferently will vanish without realization.

Pages:360

Self Help   ISBN: *1-59462-644-8*

MSRP $25.45

QTY

☐ **The Rosicrucian Cosmo-Conception Mystic Christianity** *by Max Heindel*   ISBN: *1-59462-188-8*   **$38.95**
The Rosicrucian Cosmo-conception is not dogmatic, neither does it appeal to any other authority than the reason of the student. It is: not controversial, but is: sent forth in the, hope that it may help to clear..   New Age/Religion Pages 646

☐ **Abandonment To Divine Providence** *by Jean-Pierre de Caussade*   ISBN: *1-59462-228-0*   **$25.95**
"The Rev. Jean Pierre de Caussade was one of the most remarkable spiritual writers of the Society of Jesus in France in the 18th Century. His death took place at Toulouse in 1751. His works have gone through many editions and have been republished...   Inspirational/Religion Pages 400

☐ **Mental Chemistry** *by Charles Haanel*   ISBN: *1-59462-192-6*   **$23.95**
Mental Chemistry allows the change of material conditions by combining and appropriately utilizing the power of the mind. Much like applied chemistry creates something new and unique out of careful combinations of chemicals the mastery of mental chemistry...   New Age Pages 354

☐ **The Letters of Robert Browning and Elizabeth Barret Barrett 1845-1846 vol II**   ISBN: *1-59462-193-4*   **$35.95**
by Robert Browning and Elizabeth Barrett   Biographies Pages 596

☐ **Gleanings In Genesis (volume I)** *by Arthur W. Pink*   ISBN: *1-59462-130-6*   **$27.45**
Appropriately has Genesis been termed "the seed plot of the Bible" for in it we have, in germ form, almost all of the great doctrines which are afterwards fully developed in the books of Scripture which follow...   Religion/Inspirational Pages 420

☐ **The Master Key** *by L. W. de Laurence*   ISBN: *1-59462-001-6*   **$30.95**
In no branch of human knowledge has there been a more lively increase of the spirit of research during the past few years than in the study of Psychology, Concentration and Mental Discipline. The requests for authentic lessons in Thought Control, Mental Discipline and...   New Age/Business Pages 422

☐ **The Lesser Key Of Solomon Goetia** *by L. W. de Laurence*   ISBN: *1-59462-092-X*   **$9.95**
This translation of the first book of the "Lernegton" which is now for the first time made accessible to students of Talismanic Magic was done, after careful collation and edition, from numerous Ancient Manuscripts in Hebrew, Latin, and French...   New Age/Occult Pages 92

☐ **Rubaiyat Of Omar Khayyam** *by Edward Fitzgerald*   ISBN: *1-59462-332-5*   **$13.95**
Edward Fitzgerald, whom the world has already learned, in spite of his own efforts to remain within the shadow of anonymity, to look upon as one of the rarest poets of the century, was born at Bredfield, in Suffolk, on the 31st of March, 1809. He was the third son of John Purcell...   Music Pages 172

☐ **Ancient Law** *by Henry Maine*   ISBN: *1-59462-128-4*   **$29.95**
The chief object of the following pages is to indicate some of the earliest ideas of mankind, as they are reflected in Ancient Law, and to point out the relation of those ideas to modern thought.   Religiom/History Pages 452

☐ **Far-Away Stories** *by William J. Locke*   ISBN: *1-59462-129-2*   **$19.45**
"Good wine needs no bush, but a collection of mixed vintages does. And this book is just such a collection. Some of the stories I do not want to remain buried for ever in the museum files of dead magazine-numbers an author's not unpardonable vanity..."   Fiction Pages 272

☐ **Life of David Crockett** *by David Crockett*   ISBN: *1-59462-250-7*   **$27.45**
"Colonel David Crockett was one of the most remarkable men of the times in which he lived. Born in humble life, but gifted with a strong will, an indomitable courage, and unremitting perseverance...   Biographies/New Age Pages 424

☐ **Lip-Reading** *by Edward Nitchie*   ISBN: *1-59462-206-X*   **$25.95**
Edward B. Nitchie, founder of the New York School for the Hard of Hearing, now the Nitchie School of Lip-Reading, Inc, wrote "LIP-READING Principles and Practice". The development and perfecting of this meritorious work on lip-reading was an undertaking...   How-to Pages 400

☐ **A Handbook of Suggestive Therapeutics, Applied Hypnotism, Psychic Science**   ISBN: *1-59462-214-0*   **$24.95**
by Henry Munro   Health/New Age/Health/Self-help Pages 376

☐ **A Doll's House: and Two Other Plays** *by Henrik Ibsen*   ISBN: *1-59462-112-8*   **$19.95**
Henrik Ibsen created this classic when in revolutionary 1848 Rome. Introducing some striking concepts in playwriting for the realist genre, this play has been studied the world over.   Fiction/Classics/Plays 308

☐ **The Light of Asia** *by sir Edwin Arnold*   ISBN: *1-59462-204-3*   **$13.95**
In this poetic masterpiece, Edwin Arnold describes the life and teachings of Buddha. The man who was to become known as Buddha to the world was born as Prince Gautama of India but he rejected the worldly riches and abandoned the reigns of power when...   Religion/History/Biographies Pages 170

☐ **The Complete Works of Guy de Maupassant** *by Guy de Maupassant*   ISBN: *1-59462-157-8*   **$16.95**
"For days and days, nights and nights, I had dreamed of that first kiss which was to consecrate our engagement, and I knew not on what spot I should put my lips..."   Fiction/Classics Pages 240

☐ **The Art of Cross-Examination** *by Francis L. Wellman*   ISBN: *1-59462-309-0*   **$26.95**
Written by a renowned trial lawyer, Wellman imparts his experience and uses case studies to explain how to use psychology to extract desired information through questioning.   How-to/Science/Reference Pages 408

☐ **Answered or Unanswered?** *by Louisa Vaughan*   ISBN: *1-59462-248-5*   **$10.95**
Miracles of Faith in China   Religion Pages 112

☐ **The Edinburgh Lectures on Mental Science (1909)** *by Thomas*   ISBN: *1-59462-008-3*   **$11.95**
This book contains the substance of a course of lectures recently given by the writer in the Queen Street Hall, Edinburgh. Its purpose is to indicate the Natural Principles governing the relation between Mental Action and Material Conditions...   New Age/Psychology Pages 148

☐ **Ayesha** *by H. Rider Haggard*   ISBN: *1-59462-301-5*   **$24.95**
Verily and indeed it is the unexpected that happens! Probably if there was one person upon the earth from whom the Editor of this, and of a certain previous history, did not expect to hear again...   Classics Pages 380

☐ **Ayala's Angel** *by Anthony Trollope*   ISBN: *1-59462-352-X*   **$29.95**
The two girls were both pretty, but Lucy who was twenty-one who supposed to be simple and comparatively unattractive, whereas Ayala was credited, as her Bombwhat romantic name might show, with poetic charm and a taste for romance. Ayala when her father died was nineteen....   Fiction Pages 484

☐ **The American Commonwealth** *by James Bryce*   ISBN: *1-59462-286-8*   **$34.45**
An interpretation of American democratic political theory. It examines political mechanics and society from the perspective of Scotsman James Bryce   Politics Pages 572

☐ **Stories of the Pilgrims** *by Margaret P. Pumphrey*   ISBN: *1-59462-116-0*   **$17.95**
This book explores pilgrims religious oppression in England as well as their escape to Holland and eventual crossing to America on the Mayflower, and their early days in New England...   History Pages 268

QTY

The Fasting Cure *by Sinclair Upton* ISBN: *1-59462-222-1* **$13.95**
In the Cosmopolitan Magazine for May, 1910, and in the Contemporary Review (London) for April, 1910, I published an article dealing with my experiences in fasting. I have written a great many magazine articles, but never one which attracted so much attention... New Age/Self Help/Health Pages 164

Hebrew Astrology *by Sepharial* ISBN: *1-59462-308-2* **$13.45**
In these days of advanced thinking it is a matter of common observation that we have left many of the old landmarks behind and that we are now pressing forward to greater heights and to a wider horizon than that which represented the mind-content of our progenitors... Astrology Pages 144

Thought Vibration or The Law of Attraction in the Thought World ISBN: *1-59462-127-6* **$12.95**
by William Walker Atkinson Psychology/Religion Pages 144

Optimism *by Helen Keller* ISBN: *1-59462-108-X* **$15.95**
Helen Keller was blind, deaf, and mute since 19 months old, yet famously learned how to overcome these handicaps, communicate with the world, and spread her lectures promoting optimism. An inspiring read for everyone... Biographies/Inspirational Pages 84

Sara Crewe *by Frances Burnett* ISBN: *1-59462-360-0* **$9.45**
In the first place, Miss Minchin lived in London. Her home was a large, dull, tall one, in a large, dull square, where all the houses were alike, and all the sparrows were alike, and where all the door-knockers made the same heavy sound... Childrens/Classic Pages 88

The Autobiography of Benjamin Franklin *by Benjamin Franklin* ISBN: *1-59462-135-7* **$24.95**
The Autobiography of Benjamin Franklin has probably been more extensively read than any other American historical work, and no other book of its kind has had such ups and downs of fortune. Franklin lived for many years in England, where he was agent... Biographies/History Pages 332

Name	
Email	
Telephone	
Address	
City, State ZIP	

☐ **Credit Card**   ☐ **Check / Money Order**

Credit Card Number	
Expiration Date	
Signature	

Please Mail to: Book Jungle
PO Box 2226
Champaign, IL 61825
or Fax to: 630-214-0564

ORDERING INFORMATION

web: *www.bookjungle.com*
email: *sales@bookjungle.com*
fax: *630-214-0564*
mail: *Book Jungle PO Box 2226 Champaign, IL 61825*
or PayPal *to sales@bookjungle.com*

Please contact us for bulk discounts

DIRECT-ORDER TERMS

**20% Discount if You Order
Two or More Books**
Free Domestic Shipping!
Accepted: Master Card, Visa,
Discover, American Express

CPSIA information can be obtained at www.ICGtesting.com
Printed in the USA
LVOW03s1104120914

403799LV00005B/52/P